Isabella Michelle
Mr. Complicated
Love or Lust

Isabella Michelle was born and bred in Toronto, Canada- she possessed a love for the sexually open city and enjoyed pushing her writing limits. Growing up in an over-populated big city allowed her to create many diverse characters. She is best known for her love of writing Mainstream Erotica, BDSM, Ménage, Gay, Lesbian, Bi-sexual, and Romantic Suspense. She finally decided it was time to bring her trilogy 'A Twist of Complicated Events,' to many readers who love the saucy side of complicated leaving the mind twisted when it comes to the bedroom.

BOOKS BY ISABELLA MICHELLE

Mr. Complicated Love or Lust
A Touch of Past Unwanted
A Final Twist Too Complicated

MR. COMPLICATED

LOVE or LUST

A Twist of Complicated Events
Trilogy

Isabella Michelle

W & B Publishers Colfax, NC, USA

Mr. Complicated Love or Lust © 2015 All rights reserved by Michelle Trempe

W & B Book Publishers

For information
W & B Publishers
Post Office Box 193
Colfax, NC 27235
www.a-argusbooks.com

ISBN: 978-1-9429810-2-2
ISBN: 1-942981023

Book Cover designed by Dubuya
Book Edited by Sarah Toews

For More Information on Isabella Michelle
www.isabellamichelleauthor.com

For the hardest love to read; comes the best love once he became open.
For my Jim

Acknowledgements

I would like to first start out by 'Thanking' my amazing fiancé Jeremy for taking the time to read my story, and falling in love with all the characters as much as I am in love with him. I especially want to 'Thank' him for coming into my life during a time when most I needed a best-friend and someone to love me.

I also owe a huge 'Gratitude' to both my 'Parents,' Art and Nancy, for cheering me on while I have made my long time passion a dream come true.

I have a few additional 'Friends' I would like to 'Thank' for not only being 'True' friends, for me when I needed them, but also supporting my goals and dreams over many wonderful years of continued friendship. A special 'Thanks' to my best-friend Meg-you have been my shoulder to cry on, and always been my family and support when I have needed someone so far away from home. I would also like to 'Thank' my friend Pearlie who has kept in touch with me, no matter the distance we will always be friends.

Lastly, I would like to 'Thank' Sarah for editing my final draft of Mr. Complicated Love or Lust- without your help I would not have figured this all out.

From: Little Ms. Twisted

My heart lingered alone at twenty-six, and decided to drop a few years to find twenty-four. Age is only a number; sometimes the best number is not older but younger. Because even younger can know more than one who thinks they have seen everything. This is the story of how I met Mr. Complicated.

Contents

Interview Mr. Complicated
Meet Little Ms. Twisted

Mr. Complicated in Love or Lust, between Estelle and Publisher

Mr. Complicated-Book One- Love or Lust; A Twist of Complicated Events Trilogy Continued

INTERVIEW WITH MR. COMPLICATED

Have you ever been on the quest to meet a one-night stand, or maybe that guy you could randomly fuck on every other occasion after the one-night stand, but have no emotional attachment? Well if you answered yes to the following question, you are not alone.

Four Months from Now
Interviewer: Estella Ella Whiteside (Little Ms. Twisted)
Interviewee: Zacharie Gagne (Mr. Complicated)

It's January 18th, 2015 and I hand him the letter I wrote two months ago. "Zacharie, I want you to read this before our interview," I smile and hand him the crumpled up letter, address to 'Mr. Complicated.'

Dear Zacharie,

I am appalled by your blatant disregard for the opposite sex, and my emotional attachment to all men who decide to bed me.

If you have not already noticed, I am broken-hearted and a mess; I was not looking for a fucked-up relationship to make things worse.

The deal was, there was to be no flowers, strings of broken promises, and bullshit lines of 'I love you'. This was to be an arranged bedtime greeting, with a 'see you only for sex' goodbye meeting.

I did not want to be cuddled, or kissed passionately by a 'man' who would do these things without showing any emotional attachment, or justify that he does not feel a thing for me and actually mean it.

By the way you fuck me, sex is strictly for your gratification only; when it comes to pleasing me, it just doesn't happen unless you're in a giving mood.

I mean the first time you ever had sex with me nicely, was when you woke up in the morning out of the blue and didn't put your cap on.

Maybe it was not bright enough for you that morning? You still have me wondering.

That morning really fucked me up, because it felt like we made love for the first time, and sex was such a climax for me. The further you pushed inside, the more pleasure I felt, and 'cuming' finally occurred; I was now yours. Your head really roped me in, and this is where I now must figure you out, Mr. Complicated.

Can 'Complicated' actually love the 'Twisted?' Because maybe I might just be that all sorts of fucked-up you're looking for?

Only our time together will tell.

Cheers to all the great sex we will have going forward, Mr. Complicated.

From
Yours Truly,
Little Ms. Twisted

Zacharie finishes reading the crumpled-up letter, and licks his lips slightly, and then directs a dark glare of excitement towards my direction.

I bite down on my upper-lip gently, and look cautiously in his direction. "Mr. Complicated, were you aware the entire time we have been seeing each other, that you were simply a plot for me to end up Fucking?" I asked, whisking my head back so that my long, dirty, dark hair would fall evenly down my back.

"Ms. Twisted, I am aware of your blatant disrespect for the opposite sex," Zacharie replied, keeping his dark brown eyes focused on my posture while he pressed his soft lips into a straight line. *I could not help but notice, and my throat suddenly became desperate to produce saliva so my tongue could wet my dry lips that I was dying for him to brush his against.*

"Mr. Complicated, you are aware that this entire scenario occurred because of your lack of respect for the women you bed, correct?" I asked, while I gently bit down on my lip, and then opened my mouth slightly to run my wet tongue across the dry cracks. *I was hoping he wanted to fuck me in the front closet after we finished making a 'trailer of sex': a saucy epilogue for my book 'Mr. Complicated.'*

"Ms. Twisted, if the women I bed should develop an emotional attachment simply after I have only fucked them, how can I be to blame for this?" He said in a smart-ass tone, while taking his left hand and brushing it against my naked kneecap.

I could feel myself start getting a little excited by his touch, and we had only finished fucking moments before starting the interview: *I needed to contain myself.*

"Well, Mr. Complicated, if you don't mind me pointing out: you did not advertise you were looking for a one-night stand," I replied, pressing my lips into a firm line, and then taking my tongue I licked my wet lips again, and again, hoping he would notice I was being a little naughty.

"Please Ms. Twisted, call me Zacharie. And by the way, you did not publicize you were not looking for a one-night stand. If I do recall, your journal entries were very forthcoming; you were looking for a 'see you only for sex bedtime greeting," he teased, lingering his exquisite fingertips up my skirt.

I immediately closed my legs, and bit down on my bottom lip. *He was making it extremely difficult for me to concentrate on the interview.*

"Actually, if I can remember my choice of writing correctly, this was a meeting," I whispered, trying to catch my breath.

"Ms. Twisted, I was exactly everything you asked me to be," Zacharie said while looking me in the eye with his serious look.

I could only defensively bat my eyelashes at him, hoping he would receive my invite to fuck on the edge of the fold out just aside from where we fucked (taping the whole thing, for his pleasure and my twisted).

"Please, Zacharie, I would like you to elaborate." I begged.

"I never gave you my heart, and did not come with flowers, and when push came to shove, I was the selfish mother-fucker you were looking for." He replied, firmly squeezing the inside of my leg towards my pussy, making me flinch.

"So, why did you finally open up to me, Zacharie?" I asked hesitantly.

"Because after reading your journal entries I realized just how bad I really did treat you," Zacharie replied, un-gripping his hold on my leg and starting to pat my vagina gently.

"So, because you read my journal, this suddenly gave you a change of heart about Little Ms. Twisted?" I asked.

"Yes, Ms. Twisted, it did," he said again looking me directly in the eyes, and I couldn't take mine away from his. *The dirty on-set look he gave me was direct, and to the fucking point.*

"Please call me Estelle," I said softly.

"Ok then, Estelle," he replied, taking his nose and sniffing my hair.

"I love the way that sounds coming from you," I replied, tilting my head further towards his nose. *I was hoping he would take his tongue and start running it down my neck, the way he did in bed when we made love.*

"I love the way my name sounds when you scream it out loud while I fuck you," Zacharie moaned, pressing his lips to my forehead.

"How did you feel the first time you fucked me?" I asked pressing my lips to the bottom of his chin, while I looked him deep in his dark eyes.

"Well Estelle, I felt like I just fucked you," Zacharie said, moving his head a little more than half an inch from my lips.

"So it did not mean anything to you?" I whispered slowly.

"No," he said painfully.

"When did sex with me start to feel like 'something' to you?" I asked.

"The first time I fucked you without a cap," Zacharie answered softly.

"Why?" I asked, taking the tips of my fingers and twirling them through his medium length, dark brown hair.

"Because I fucked you that morning out of the blue, and it was strange for me to ever want to make the opposite sex feel good." Zacharie answered, and I knew he was being honest.

"Did you love me that morning, Zacharie?"

"Yes."

"Then why couldn't you show it?" I asked, trailing my fingertip up and down his strong jaw, while we stared directly at one another.

"I did not want to get close to you, because I was so afraid of getting hurt again."

"And then when you found my journal, this did not prove your theory?" I said, changing the tone of my voice to mock him.

"I knew you would not publish the book, Estelle," he said in a lowered tone.

"How could you be so sure?"

"Because you would not have the guts to exploit your own sexual life and let others read about you, for the sake of making money."

"But what would make you think anyone would know this book is about me, Zacharie?"

"When your friends from back home would walk into their local bookstore in Chicago and buy a copy of Mr. Complicated, they would all know who the book refers to."

"I think you are sadly mistaken. My friends do not know me as well as you think," I replied in a manipulative tone.

"The ones who know about your fucked past do. People in big cities talk; all it takes is one person to open his or her mouth, and then the truth is out about Estelle Ella Whiteside."

"You do not think I have already aired my dirty laundry for the entire world to see and cast their judgment on?" I accused.

"Estelle, this is our sexual life you are talking about here. I do not think you would have the guts to do such a thing," he replied with a jerked smile.

"You would be more afraid about me exploiting myself, than the world finding out about Mr. Complicated?" I replied, surprised.

"Mr. Complicated is just a character," Zacharie snorted.

"No, Zacharie, Mr. Complicated is you," I laughed.

"Yes, Estelle, even utterly so, the world would still know the story is referring to you, and would have no idea who the hell I am. So are you not happy with the decision you made to be in love with me and say "fuck you" to your publisher?"

"Well, now that you think I have fucked my publisher over, you do realize that in less than three weeks the entire world will know all about 'Mr. Complicated' and 'Little Ms. Twisted,' right?" I replied, looking directly into Zacharie's eyes, as the tone suddenly changed from loving to serious.

"What are you talking about, Estelle? I thought you told me you didn't submit the Book?" He replied in an angry tone.

"Zacharie, I am Little Ms. Twisted, I lied of course."

"Do you realize what you have done?" He shouted, and moved completely away from me.

MEET LITTLE MS. TWISTED

September 3rd, 2014

Journal Entry; By Estelle Ella Whiteside

The life of an Author is never an easy career choice, I must say moving so far away from my family for the love of pen to paper, or fingertips to keyboard, is not something I imagined leaving home for. My career has dragged me to a small town called Medicine Hat, in the Canadian province of Alberta, when I have lived in the big city of Chicago for the last twenty-five years of my life.

The sunrays catch the corner of my eye, momentarily blinding my vision and distracting my thoughts from my most recent daily journal entry. I place my pencil down on the desk. I close my journal for a moment, and raise my right fingertip towards my lips; they feel chapped.

Careful not to disposition neither my journal, nor pencil, from their perfect position, I get up out of my chair and head towards the washroom.

Closing my eyes, I know exactly where to reach, and run my hand along the sharp edges of the medicine-cabinet. I grab the familiar bottle and pop it open. Taking one pill and placing it gently on my tongue, with my eyes still closed, I swallow deeply.

Swallowing, I like to swallow, right?

My eyes flutter open, trying not to re-visit the past, but remaining in the present. I look directly into the mirror.

Hazel eyes, so warm they invite anyone to join me for a lonely swim on a warm September day. With dark mocha hair, curled and pinned perfectly up and out of my oval shaped face, I raise my chin, then turn around to walk away.

I make my way back to the wooden desk, situated in my living-room, possibly where there would be a television, if this apartment belonged to a normal person.

I pick up my pencil, and continue my journal entry for today.

At twenty-six, I must say my life is not everything I imagined it would be. In less than two months from today, I was supposed to go to New York, and start my first Book tour out of Jersey City, heading west towards Washington. Instead, I am now trying to deal with an overbearing workload that my Publisher has assigned. I also had to break the news to my Father back home in Chicago, Illinois, that the tour will need to be placed on hold, until next August.

It's rather embarrassing, especially from a newly Published Author's perception, when you tell everyone back home that your Publisher & Agent think you really have a 'golden' piece of work, yet they halt all the plans that took months to coordinate, and re-route your professional career path.

An entire year of my life not wasted, but lived in Medicine Hat, Alberta with no one to love me, and my life so not together.

My life before moving to Medicine Hat was simple and uncomplicated, until my fabulous Publisher launched my first book, 'Loved by No Other.'

The book was launched one month too early, and it really took off in the United States of America. Almost two months later my book saw the same chain of events take place within Canada. Everyone wanted to know: who is 'Estelle Ella Whiteside?'

"Who am I?" I stop to re-think my entry just for a moment, and continue writing.

> My Publisher decided to fly me out to New York last Christmas, and tell me it would be best-suited if I would relocate to a much smaller town, with little-to-no population. It would give me the chance to expand my writing talent, instead of leading me down the road map to writer's block, which is where I was headed if I stayed in Chicago. Especially after a recent nympho breakdown I had at my previous place of employment.
> Taking my Publisher only one week to decide the next year of my life would be spent in Medicine Hat, Alberta, I was shortly packing whatever belongings I could fit into my suitcases, and saying goodbye to my friends, and preparing for a goodbye to my family.

'Oh no, I am thinking about it!' And I begin to rationalize where my mind is drifting off to, and I pray the anti-depressant kicks in, before my mind can think too much.

It was July 28th, 2011, and work was about to close-up tabs for the Boozer's at the Wet-Bar, and the Sober party on the strip platform, where 'Butter-Scotch' was greasing her tits against the wooden end of the stage. A cup was plugged into her asshole catching some quarters, and a blissful audience was applauding her.

I was not shocked by the way 'Butter-Scotch' chose to make a living; I was only jealous that I was too scared to put myself out there like she did, for the entire pornographic-alcoholics non-anonymous strip club Chicago-on.

Keeping a discreet sexual curtain over my private parts was more my forte; so when it came time to *make my money, the janitors closet was always open for washing away my dirty sin's. And I was open to many well-paying Customers who met my 'clean' criteria.*

Mr. Hopkins was a regular of mine: thirty-nine years old, tall, tanned, with straight, blonde hair. I must say, he kept himself very well groomed. Married to the upscale Mrs. Hopkins, who is a big Realtor in Chicago and makes a ton of money, Mr. Hopkins enjoys dropping hundred dollar bills in my private dirty black pantie and on occasion, sliding them between my combusting sized D-38 tits.

It was past closing time, and I had a 'Submission' due in the morning to my Publisher; however, my Customer Mr. Hopkins was not very submissive tonight. Instead, he was being a little dominating, holding me down firmly with my back against the cold floor in the janitor's closet, and then gently parting my legs while patting my privates.

He lifted my legs and slowly my body lifted off the ground, and his tongue unwound my panty. He started molesting my vagina; the more he swirled, the wetter I became. The voices in the background outside the door hiding my shame became more and more distant.

Mr. Hopkins was paying me two thousand dollars for him to pleasure the fuck out of me, and I only needed to enjoy myself; how fucking twisted is that? This thinking process occurred over, and over in my head. Finally I busted my climax in his open-to-receive mouth, and he buried his head into my vagina as far as it could go.

He inserted his tongue up inside my pussy, and I flinched because it was the most un-welcome feeling

after being pleasured. Now he was just hurting me. I
began to shiver from the memories of my abusive ex.
Now I was in the grip of Mr. Hopkins, who did not give
a fuck about my feelings, and showed no mercy on the
grip he held on my legs.

He grabbed me harder, as I tried to shudder
away from him.

"Donald, where is my Husband? He asked me to
pick him up over twenty minutes ago, and still he is
nowhere to be found. Do you have a phone I can use to
call him?" The worried women asked.

"Sure thing Mrs. Hopkins," the young boy's
voice replied, sincere to her concern.

Oh shit...

And his phone started to ring, I tried to reach for
it, but my reflexes while on my back were not as quick
as those of Mrs. Hopkins were in grabbing the door
handle and swinging it open.

"What the fuck, Gregory?" She screamed, and I
was humiliated.

Of course the entire strip club was roaring
about my private little business I had going on the
side, and I was dismissed on the spot by the cleaning
staff. Then the next morning I was fired by the owner,
Geraldine, after she had just finished dealing with an
angry mob of Realtors associated with Mrs. Hopkins,
and then with the News Press and all the community
questions related to running a Burlesque House, out of
a strip club.

My mind welcomed the return to reality after
the pill kicked in. I continued my journal entry.

*My parents and I talked, but never argued about the move I
would make, which I ultimately knew would end the life we shared so*

close together and for so long. Associated with my little scandal, but after everything that happened, they thought it would be best for the time being.

I never kept any secrets from my Father or Mother growing up, and with my twin Sister just getting married a couple of years prior to me launching my career as an Author, what was there really to keep me in Chicago anyway?

I had no one who loved me in Chicago, except family and friends. Fans claimed to love me, but I knew they only loved my talent of storytelling, not the 'girl' I was inside.

No one ever thought I was a decent enough girl to date, because my past was too twisted for them. I mean my track record for sexual ways to exploit myself was all over the internet; it might as well be broadcasted on a billboard for the entire 'World' to see my shame. Since I decided to publish my first book, the amount of criticism surrounding my sexual intellect can sometimes become overbearing.

I can remember back to most of my childhood, which I spent rebelling against my parents by doing drugs, or partaking in any illegal event where I could get a free ride home in the back of a cop cruiser.

I wanted to be everything the opposite of my twin sister Adeline, who was so perfect her entire life.

On days I was not over-dosing on Alcohol, I was drowning myself in writing my daily diaries; something I have done ever since I could first remember being able to hold a pen.

Some of my best works of writing are derived from such truth, or jarred memory of an abusive past, or fucked-up scenario I was role-playing with a random oral sex partner that I found on the internet. I have continued to advertise my body over the years, since I found that trying to hold a steady relationship with an un-abusive guy, just wasn't in the cards for me.

I placed my pencil down on the paper, *and started to the think carefully.* The first guy I was ever serious with ended up finding out about my little wet t-shirt belittlement at one of the local Bars in my hometown:

August 23rd, 2008 was a dizzy summer night. I blacked out very quickly after drinking several blue alcoholic beverages, and hitting the bar with two of my closest friends.

From what I can remember, my boyfriend was at the pool hall and decided it wasn't a good idea to invite me out that night, because we should learn to spend some time apart from one another.

I was horny as fuck and needed to get off some-how: whether it was with a random guy, or even someone I knew. I didn't care, once the alcohol hit my blood-stream I became 'Estelle the Invincible.' I didn't care who I hurt, only when and how I could get fucked.

I grabbed a t-shirt, and created a catastrophic dirty shirt that was sure to please the crowd, once my partner-in-crime came up on stage to join. Cline was always the life of a party with his bad-ass Angel Es-telle, so why not get wet or go home, and then 'Your Dirty Little Girl' came on and the show had to begin.

While provocative eyes glared at me from a crowd of drunks, I remember swinging my hips and bending down, until my tits were so wet that my nip-ples just wanted to bust through my wet t-shirt, all while my skirt was pressed so tight against my ass. I ripped my shirt off, and the crowd hollered for more, as cameras started to snap randomly, and then ag-gressively, as I removed my skirt, and then my panties.

I walked over to the pole, and screamed out loud: "how wet do you want little 'Ms. Twisted' to get?"

"We want to see you wet," the crowd shouted and applauded.

I danced like a little ripper, and got all of my anger and frustrations out. I mean I wasn't on my anti-depressants, and I didn't need to be; I was getting all the attention I needed to feed my twisted subconscious at the time.

As I finished putting on the show, my best-friend Trisha was hanging out at the Bar telling some guy that I do this regularly, all while my other best-friend, Cline, was fucking a girl randomly in the Women's bathroom.

I was then approached by one of the owners of The Old Chicago Rippers Club, and offered a spot in their upcoming PJ Bunny Party the following Saturday. Of course I accepted, and let the owner painfully finger my pussy while I sat on the Bar. I remember the next morning how bad my vagina was throbbing, but I enjoyed it.

I bring my attention back to my journal entry. I pick up the pencil and continue writing:

I have always wondered, if I had never decided to take my shirt off that night, would the two of us still be together; but being that I am so fucking twisted, I wished I would have done that at a concert. Honestly in the state of mind I was in, I would have sexually exploited myself for attention any way at that time.

Not much has changed from the girl I once was, to the woman I am not today.

My Publisher and Agent suggested I not get involved with anyone in Medicine Hat, because I would not be staying long; after one year of living here, I would be leaving for my tour, re-united with my Father who would join me, as my Mother would still working full-time.

During the first year I spent living in Medicine Hat, away from my family, I worked vicariously on my writing. I wrote several books that I could not finish because my mind was going in so many different, uncertain directions.

I attempted to concentrate on other matters, like my fan-blogging site, or answering fan e-mail, but it was not enough to keep my mind from lingering to other areas ready to become a disaster.

I felt so alone and so scared to fall in love. When my Publisher broke the news to me that I would not be going on tour until next August, creating some free time for myself, I decided to fill the void.

I started to plot a sadistic storyline, and thought how sick and twisted it would actually be if I made my characters come to life in the real world. I mean most of the stories I wrote were about fantasy, erotica, and romantic suspense. But what if I created a female character; a character just as 'Twisted' as I am?

Could I actually find a random guy to fall in love with me? Why not put this 'Twisted' character out in Medicine Hat, for the sole purpose of fucking different guys, and twisting the nice one which could fall in love with her? Would it be possible, could I actually find a true love this way, since I can never find it normally because I lived so uncomplicated, and in a manner everyone expected?

Surely I would be the first writer to develop my own self into a role-playing character, but living in the realistic world of reality. The one where you pay bills, actually have a job aside from a writing career, and deal with all the hardships life has to offer. I could mold myself into a normal girl, but mentally still be that all sorts of 'Twisted' everyone knows back home.

Until my character is sought out and planned.

Yours truly,

Little Ms. Twisted

Mr. Complicated
Part One of Two
Love or Lust

MEET & GREET

Since I was not going to be leaving to go on tour for my book in November, it gave me just the right amount of time to focus on launching my new character: the one who would relate to my inner 'Twisted' on all levels of my fucked-up. Being the first week of September, this was the perfect time to put my project into motion. I decided to put everything else my Publisher wanted my attention focused toward right now on the backburner.

I have no one out here. I thought I should put myself out there in the real world, and fuck multiple guys in Medicine Hat, sort of like how an escort promotes her services. Except I need to be doing so in a classier sort of manner, one that would not get me into trouble, but would still be discreet and yet tasteful.

I would need to do what anyone else in the real world would do, outside my usual science-fiction writings. I really needed to step things up and think like I wanted my dirty twisted character to think, *but how did I want to play her in reality?* This thinking process really had my mind working.

Why not do what anyone else in my situation would do: find someone who only wanted something physical like I did. No strings attached, and maybe even complicated, because uncomplicated never seemed to work for me; therefore, it would not work for the character I am going to play either.

I really want to relate to the character I am launching in every manner possible, on all the levels of my fucked-up-ness. The plot should be twisted, and the guy should be complicated. Being that today is Friday, I should have no problem finding a target for this weekend.

***

Later that evening, I decided to go and have a coffee with my friend Christina, who lived in the same apartment complex in the Harwood Heights area that I did. After sitting and talking to Christina for the first half an hour during my visit, I told her just how sexually frustrated I was.

Christina told me about a site that local singles in the Medicine Hat area were using to meet locals and have a fling, or have ongoing sexual encounters with the same guy. I was interested in a one-night stand, but nothing serious until I was ready to find my 'Complicated' victim, and see if 'Twisted' could actually manipulate his inner-self to fall in love with the character I was role-playing.

"Why should you let your Publisher leave you alone in Medicine Hat, and fuck you over? And then have the nerve to tell you not to find true love. I know you feel as though you are not allowed to screw them over, Estelle." Christina said while rolling her eyes in disbelief. *I wondered how I was getting her to take my lines of bullshit so seriously.*

"I don't know what to say to my Publisher, Christina. If I do not do what Art asks me to, I will be out of a job, and he will have me packing up my shit in Medicine Hat, catching the next flight back to Chicago. Do you have any idea what my life would be like if I went back home?" I replied, forming a fake tear in the ducts of my eyes.

I was always so good at acting; sometimes I wish I would have taken up a career in it, instead of writing.

"If you ask me, your publisher, Art is an asshole. Does he have a wife?" Christina asked.

"Now that I really think about it, I think he is divorced," I smiled back a reply.

"I just think you should take my advice, Estelle. You need to get fucking laid, so putting up an ad on a local dating site will not do you any harm."

"Christina, really, you expect me to put an ad on a random dating site, and do what?" I replied in a childish tone, *knowing full well, I was really getting into my character.*

"As I said before, and I will say it again: it's called meeting a random guy, and getting fucked, Estelle." *Wow, we both had the same idea but I cannot let her know about my 'Twisted' plans of playing a character for a new book that I have in the works.* Everything is working out nicely, and maybe at the end of all of this role-playing I will offer Christina a role of her own in my book, for implying such great ideas that I will now take advantage of.

"I do not do random," I snorted, *while trying to contain myself from laughing hysterically.*

"Well obviously you did 'commitment' to your Publisher and look where you are now?" Christina replied, *mocking my twisted.*

"Ok, so maybe you're right, but what would I put on this random dating site about myself?" I asked, while folding my arms, and wondering *what the fuck would I put on there?*

"The truth," she replied, smiling.

"So you would like me to put an ad up on a dating site telling the entire world that I am a successful and well known Author, whose lavished tour just got bumped to next August. And I am now stuck in this shit hole?" *Maybe deep down inside of my broken fucked-up heart I didn't really want to play a role; I wanted to find something real, because maybe having someone to love me would not be such a bad thing. Right now though, the best thing for me to do is concentrate on this new role-playing for my book. I need to forget all about the tour, and the bullshit. I needed to just let things happen.*

"Well Estelle, you don't need to be so blunt, but why not just put an ad up, and see what kind of guys respond," Christina replied, looking me directly in the eyes.

I never stopped to admire Christina's eyes before: light green with a hint of mocha brown. *I wish I had nice eyes like hers.*

"Christina, they are all pigs," I replied in a huff.

"Estelle, they are 'lays,' don't put yourself up high on a pedestal. You are looking for one thing and one thing only: and that's to find a guy who wants the same thing you need right now; sex and nothing more."

"What if it means more to him?" I asked her, pressing my lips in a firm line. *I started to wonder to myself: what would I do if it actually meant more to a random guy I wanted just for fucking, and to trick into falling in love with me? Just so I could exploit how to make a guy randomly fall in love with a girl he fucks?*

"Estelle, they are guys on a dating site and not your star crossed lover; simply a fish you want to lay and then let him swim away," she replied, and walked over to the fridge to pour herself a drink of apple juice.

I started to wonder if maybe Christina was as twisted as I am. She was politically correct; could I really put myself out there, fuck another guy, not care and keep doing it? I didn't tell her, but I tend to get emotionally attached to anyone I sleep with, but I needed to play the role of 'Little Ms. Twisted' and be uncomplicated.

I mean I can remember back to the first guy I ever slept with, Tyson. When I was fifteen, I decided going to a rave with a bunch of guys who picked me and my wagon of hoes off the side of W Randolph Street, and it was a party night to be remembered. I marked my territory with a random guy by fucking on the first night. I thought I would spend the rest of my life with him, just based off of our physical communication in bed. Does that even make any sense? So I moved to Michigan City and dropped out of school. My friends thought I lost my fucking marbles, and now to think back, so do I. Who the hell in their right mind does that? I guess I do.

"Ok, Christina, I am going to do it," I said to her in an assertive tone.

I went and sat in front of her computer that was positioned on top of a moving crate, and sat down on the carpet that smelled as though it was soiled in urine from her dog, Duke. He didn't exactly pee on the spot I was sitting on, but he did pee on the drapes. The smell didn't really faze me, since my old dog Becker would pee all over my parents house back home too.

Slowly I typed: www.medicinehatrelationship-finder .com in and was directed to a site full of sexually starving men and conniving women who wanted to get pregnant by a man who had one of those high paying jobs in Medicine Hat. The difference between me and those women was, I was looking for a clean guy to have sex with, and I didn't want multiple partners. I was looking for just one clean guy who wouldn't care how 'twisted' my life was at this moment. The man I wanted to pursue would want one thing, and that was the same thing I wanted: to fuck with absolutely no-strings-attached.

I needed to create the perfect ad about myself, so I came up with something simple: *The perfect lie.*

About me: *Enjoy sitting down writing a Book, depending on my mood. I also like meeting new people (first lie), and know how to be the life of the party (how should have been replaced with 'how to drink'). I like the outdoors (another lie, I hate anything cold, or too hot). I am not picky (another famous Estelle lie. Of course I am picky, but I just don't want to come off as too needy).*

If you are looking for a one-night stand, or someone to be bed friends with 'I' am not for you (another lie, oh yes I am). I am looking for a nice guy, who knows how to treat a girl (this is yet another infamous Estelle bullshit line; I am looking for an asshole because assholes don't leave, and the nice guys do).

Looks don't make the cut for me, so if you are a vain person who is all about looks, please don't send me a message (ok so this part was the most honest).

"Good job, Estelle, now post some hot pictures of when you were a little younger and one picture that is recent," Christina nagged.

"Christina, I cannot do that, I need to post photos of what I look like now. If I post old ones, I will get people wanting to meet me yes, but they will be disappointed when they meet someone who is not what they were initially expecting."

"Really, Estelle, after what you have been through, you really give a shit about being honest with some lame guy you're going to fuck, and not care whether or not you see again?"

Well, Christina had a point again. I mean for the last year, I have sexually been starving to get fucked.

"Well, I guess you're right," I replied, trying not to feel guilty. I pulled two pictures off my cellphone and uploaded them onto the site.

I decided going to bed was the next best move for me that night, and that when I wake up in the morning, maybe the whole 'tour on hold phase' with my Publisher would blow over, and the tour would be back on in no time. Then I would be out of this shit hole for good.

September 6th, 2014 'You've got Mail,' and showed not just one message, but twenty-four. I found it a little overwhelming how many guys were actually interested in me. I checked my cell-phone and there were no missed calls from my Publisher, Art, at Exelby Publishing, so I decided to follow through with my original plan. I started structuring the beginning of my new life story as 'Little Ms. Twisted,' and maybe read through a couple of the messages I got.

By the time I got out of the shower, I had thirty-one messages in my inbox, and I didn't know which one to start reading first. I decided to start from twenty-four and work my way down to one; then from thirty-one down to twenty-five. It just seemed that complicated and uncomplicated were not appealing to my senses anymore as 'Little Ms. Twisted.'

MESSAGE TWENTY-SIX: FROM FRENCHIE_ZACH
Hello, my name is Zacharie. I read your profile, and I just wanted to say, you have really nice dark eyes.

I decided to check out this FRENCHIE_ZACH's profile, because he was the first guy who wrote to me, and the fact he didn't ask about my bust size, or ask how I liked to fuck was sort of interesting. Especially with the shit I have heard about these sites.

I clicked on FRENCHIE_ZACH's profile, and read he was not looking for a relationship, and was also not looking for anything serious. *This has some lovely promise, because I was looking for the exact same thing.*

He also came with a job, and his own vehicle. This was more than I could say that I was expecting, *but assets are good.*

MESSAGE FROM SANEWRITER TO FRENCHIE_ ZACH - Him Zacharie, my name is Estelle, I moved up here from Chicago approximately one year ago. I don't know anyone in the city, and I pretty much keep a low profile, being that I am a writer. I am looking to meet some new friends so why don't you text me and we can hang out sometime. (587) 555-5555.

I hope I do not seem too desperate, I thought to myself for the brief moment. I decided to skip reading the other messages and get on with my day of plotting.

Later that afternoon, I got a text from FRENCHIE_ZACH.

Zacharie to Estelle

Zacharie – Hi, Estelle, this is Zacharie aka FRENCHIE_ZACH.

Estelle- Hi, Zacharie, thanks for texting me. It is very nice to hear from you. Might I ask how your day is going?

Zacharie- My day is perfect, and you?

Estelle- It could be better, but at least today is Saturday, and not a Monday. ☺

Zacharie - What would make your day better?

Estelle- Having someone to hang out with sure would be nice. ⍰

Zacharie - Would you like to hang out?

Estelle- Sure would.

Zacharie - Where would you feel safe meeting?

Wait a second, this guy wants me to meet up with him. Whatever happened to guys offering to pick up a girl on an arranged first date? Am I missing something?

Estelle- Does the Coffee on North Harlen Avenue work for you?

Zacharie - Yes.

Estelle- What time?

Zacharie - 7:00pm.

Estelle- Ok, I will be the girl in the pink sweater, with a hood.

Zacharie - Ok I will see you then.

It's five minutes after 7:00pm on September 6th, 2014, and my phone dings with a message.

Zacharie to Estelle

Zacharie - I'm here where are you?

Estelle- I am just walking through the parking lot, I will be right there.

Zacharie - Ok, I don't like sitting alone in here, all these guys might jump me in here.

I stopped for a moment while walking, *is this guy for real?* I wondered.

As I opened the door to the Coffee shop, there was not much of a line-up. Hopefully he waited to order with me. *I disliked going into a place like this and ordering for myself when someone is already sitting down.*

I took a quick glance around, and in the back corner saw Zacharie wearing a baseball cap, sitting down with a cup already.

He had dark hair, a thin, but still muscular build, with tanned skin, and dark eyes. *I must say his eyes were not very inviting, and I felt almost intimidated about this whole plot. Maybe I should head for the nearest exit.*

Damn it, the thought just crossed my mind as I passed Zacharie's dark glare. I am stuck ordering myself, of course. I rolled my eyes and walked towards him.

"You must be Zacharie?"

"And you must be Estelle?" He replied with a smile.

"Yes, you guessed right. Who would have thought I would be anyone else?" I replied, unamused.

"Are you going to join me?" He asked, while twitching his smile.

"Yeah I will in a moment, I am going to run up to the cashier and get a tea. I will be right back," I replied giving a friendly wink, to hopefully soften his hard-ass up a bit.

I took my jacket off, and hung it over the chair directly in front of where he was sitting, and hurried up to the counter to place my order with the cashier.

After I got my tea, I walked back and saw Zacharie examining what felt like my every move; *he was 'kind of a little creepy' I must say.* Usually the guys I meet look around to see what everyone else is doing in the room, not just me.

As Zacharie kept his dark eyes on my lighter hazel colored eyes, I thought I would start a conversation. "So where are you from, Zacharie?" I asked, while taking a sip of my hot tea.

He gazed at me from the corner of his eye, I was sure he did not want to answer my off-the-bat prying into his life question. "I am from Boucherville, Quebec," he replied with a rather cute French accent.

"Oh, that's different," I replied.

"Where are you from, Estelle?" He asked curiously.

"I am from Chicago, Illinois. That's in the United States of America."

"I am aware of where Chicago is located, but thanks for pointing that out," Zacharie replied rudely.

"Oh, I'm sorry, I did not know if you knew where it was. Most people working out this way do not have any clue where Chicago is," I laughed.

"Well I am sure if they paid attention in Geography class, they would have a good idea, like any smart person would."

Arrogance, I like that.

"Well maybe some people are not as geographically inclined as yourself, Zacharie. I mean, I would have no idea where Boucherville is, unless you told me."

"Again, any smart person who took Geography would associate a French city with Quebec. It's the only fluent French speaking province in all of Canada."

I rolled my eyes at him again in annoyance. "So tell me something about yourself, Zacharie. How long have you been in Medicine Hat?"

"Four years, and three months," he replied, while taking a swig of his drink.

"That's interesting. What is that you are drinking?" I asked curiously.

"What do most people drink at a coffee shop?" He replied.

"Coffee, I guess."

"Well, then I guess that answers your question, now doesn't it."

Why the fuck is he being so rude?

"Well, I am drinking tea," I replied with a smile.

"Did I ask what you were drinking?"

"No," I frowned.

"Then, thanks for letting me know."

"I just want to start off by saying this is totally out of my normal routine, Zacharie. I have never met someone on the internet before." *This was the biggest line of bullshit, if it were not coming out of my mouth, one would think it would be released as a bowel movement from my ass.*

"That's ok," he replied, in a tone nicer than the ones he previously used with me.

Huh, maybe that softened him up a little.

"I am assuming this is a regular routine for yourself," I said softly, while taking a sip of my tea. I mean this guy is not ugly, so why the fuck would he have any problem meeting a normal nice girl, if he did not only want a girl for sex.

"I'm sorry, a regular thing for me?" He replied, furrowing his right eyebrow.

Uh-oh, I think I hit a nerve with him...

"Oh, my apologies, I mean you must meet several random girls all the time on the dating site, right?" I replied, trying not to sound too accusing.

"No, actually you are the first girl I have met off of there in six months. The last girl I met off of there really wasn't for me," he laughed, while picking up his coffee to take a quick swig.

Finally, he is laughing.

"Why is that?" I asked curiously.

"Because we went out a few times, and she ended up fucking some guy I work with while we were still getting to know one another. Just knowing she slept with that guy turned me right off of her," he said with a serious tone.

"Wow, that's different, most guys would enjoy that," I laughed, trying not to be too modest, *but honestly, what guy would not enjoy hearing from a co-worker how good a chick is in bed that he can potentially fuck next?*

"I don't," he answered, in a more serious tone than the one he used before, *but I believed him.*

"You must have had someone burn you in the past, I am guessing," I replied while I picked up my tea, and took a sip of it.

"Yes, I have, but I don't want to talk about it," he replied, looking at his hands, while he was intertwining his fingers, like most guys do when they are nervous.

"It's all good Zacharie, I mean I am twenty-six years old, and I know all about being burned. I mean fuck, I have had the shittiest of relationships, so I decided in my adolescent years that staying single was being smart," I smiled, *knowing the single life was awesome, especially for having random one-night stands, like I was planning with Zacharie.*

'I won't compare situations," he replied, while taking another drink from his coffee.

"Yes, maybe we shouldn't. So let me ask you an honest question: am I everything you thought I would be on my profile?" I bluntly requested to know. **I wonder, will he answer me honestly? I mean I did post a picture on the website from several years ago,** I thought to myself, while a smile stretched across my face.

"You're the same person that I saw, except younger in one of the pictures," he replied, looking straight at me.

Good answer, and honest I guess...

"Yeah, I will be honest, my friend Christina told me to post a picture of when I was younger and one from how I look now. I picked the best two I had, and just wanted to make sure I didn't disappoint you. I find guys older than me sometimes like to look at a girl they are meeting from two perspectives: a younger, and then a more mature outlook."

"Older?" He said in a serious tone again, while taking a drink from his coffee. *Was he nervous or something?*

"Yeah, you are older than me," I replied, trying to hold in my laughter.

"Did you not read my profile?" He asked confused.

"Yes," I replied giggling.

"I am twenty-four."

My eyes locked on him for a moment, and my jaw was ready to drop, but the chemical imbalance in my brain was working hard to keep my mind focused on keeping myself together. A younger guy interested in me? *Why? Did he think I would school him in bed? This poor boy was in for the shocker of a lifetime. Maybe I would just give it to him straight.*

"Zacharie, how many girls have you fucked?"

"Don't you think that's a direct question, considering it's our first time meeting and we are just getting to know each other?"

"Well you don't need to tell me, but I am just going to be honest with you. I have only fucked one guy in my entire life, so I don't know if that is a problem for you." *I thought it was funny, because lying made my track-record for fucking more than forty-five different random guys seem like a fabrication of truth, but this was my story and I was going with it.*

"Why would that be a problem for me? It's not like we are going to leave the Coffee shop and go to your place or mine to fuck."

Really...I was hoping we were.

"You are very much right, I am a hard girl to bed."

Actually that is also another 'Estelle' bullshit line; I will fuck anything on two legs, with a middle that is hot. What time are you going to take me to bed?

"Really," he replied, almost shocked.

"Yes, I most certainly am," I replied with a smile. "What is wrong, Zacharie, you look sort of shocked?" I smiled wickedly.

"I see," he replied, twitching his lower lip.

"So Zacharie, are your parents still married?" I asked him in a flirting tone.

"Yes," he replied. *I thought it was nice that he comes from a traditional family background.*

"I thought they might be," I replied, trying to hide the sarcasm in my voice.

"Why is that?" He asked.

"Because French families are usually very committed," I answered.

"And how would you know that?"

"Because my parents have been married for over twenty-five years," I smiled, warmed to his tone.

"Well thank you for that special glimpse into your life," he replied sarcastically.

"Do you play any sports?" I asked, while reaching for my cup. I then opened the lid and placed it inside the cup, and then to the right of myself.

"Hockey," he smiled.

"Really, that's awesome; I play goalie." *If only I could find a guy that plays the same position as myself in net. I wonder if he would be into 'shutouts' in the bedroom.* I cocked my head to one side, trying to picture Zacharie attempting to score tonight in bed with me, and then I finally got my mind out of the net, and back into the conversation.

"So do I," he replied. *Shit, another Goalie; so he does not play Centre, or Defense. Two Goalies in the bedroom can be a tricky combination, but I must say he is cute, so I am willing to play.*

"Yeah, right," I smiled politely, and looked down at my empty cup.

"No, really I do," he replied, taking a sip of his coffee. *How the hell isn't he done drinking that yet?*

"Well I am older, so I have been playing longer," I belted out boldly, hoping he would see how confident I was that I would have more experience in net than him.

"Just because you are older, does not make you better," he grinned.

"That's very true, but my age does make me wiser," I teased back with a flirty smile.

"Oh my god," he snapped.

I guess I must have got under the foreskin between his legs; definitely not snipped downstairs is he?

"What?"

"Stop with the age, you are not old," he demanded.

"Thanks for the compliment, but I most certainly am," I replied again in a teasing tone. *I wanted to get under that foreskin.*

"You are only as old as you feel, Estelle, and to be honest I would have thought you were not any older than twenty-five," he replied, taking a napkin from the holder to wipe his mouth.

I looked directly at his lips, and wondered what they could do for my vagina later tonight. Shit! I really need to stop thinking about sex, and start trying to pretend like I want to get to know this guy.

"I am so sure, Zacharie."

"What time is it?" He asked.

"It is almost 9:00pm."

"It's getting late, did you want to go back to your place for a bit?" He asked kindly.

Finally, maybe we are going to have sex now.

"Yes, that sounds like a great idea."

"I see," he smiled.

I grabbed my purse off the table, and slowly started to get up. I took my jacket that was draped over the back of my chair, and put it on.

"You do realize it is not that cold out," he said in a mocking tone.

"Well maybe to girls, September is cold, Zacharie," I replied with a wink.

"Are you ready to go yet, Estelle?" he asked in a disapproving tone.

"Yes, I don't have anything else I brought to cover myself up in," I teased him again.

Zacharie rolled his eyes at me, and then started walking towards the exit of the coffee shop "Ok, well I will get my truck and follow you then."

"Uh sure but I walked here, so you will need to drive really slowly," I replied with a sheepish grin.

I wonder if he will think I am like most girls, who don't drive, and am on the prowl for that special man to take care of me for the rest of my life? Fuck will he be in dire shock.

"Why would you walk here, that's not very safe," he said sternly.

"Because I live four streets over, and generally don't tend to care about how safe anything really is."

"I will drive us then," he replied.

What the hell is his problem? I think it's stupid to drive some place that is only a short walking distance from where I live; I will fix him.

"I'm not getting in a truck with you," I replied, pretending to sound scared.

"And why not?" Zacharie asked.

"Because you could be some crazy serial killer, who could try to rape me," I teased.

"Yet you want me to come to your house," Zacharie replied in an un-amused tone.

"Number one, it's not a house; and number two, I have a really big goalie stick," I replied smiling.

"I see," he said in an annoyed tone.

"Ok, I will go with you, as long as you promise not to hurt me," I looked at him and batted my eyelashes.

"Sure," he replied, not even noticing my mocking him.

We walked outside into the parking lot, and I examined the area around: there was no truck I saw out here, and then as we walked further towards the restaurant across the Coffee shop, there was a muddy work truck. Wow, he brought his work truck, sexy.

He walked around to the driver side of the truck and unlocked the vehicle. *Wow a guy that does not open the door for me; I like him already, I thought.*

I got in his truck; it was messy, but it was a work truck, so what did I really expect. I mean at least his truck was cleaner than the one I owned.

He turned and looked at me, "where do you live?"

"Just over in the apartment complex North of Harlen Avenue."

He started the truck, and I jumped a little; it was louder than the one I drove too.

We started driving out of the parking lot, "turn right here," I said nicely.

"Estelle, I know where I am going."

"Oh, I am sorry then," I replied, a little embarrassed.

I sat quietly, and there were a few moments of silence between the two of us. Does he even listen to Music?

"You can turn left into the apartment complex here," I shouted out.

Zacharie gave me a dark stare again, and I looked away. "Is there even visitor parking here?" He asked in an angry tone.

"No, but you can park on the street out front. Just drop me at the doors here, and I will wait inside for you."

"Won't my truck get towed?" He asked.

"No one else's ever has," I replied.

That night we sat in, spending a few hours to get to know one another a little more: our likes and some of our dislikes.

For example, he was not into girls that do drugs or that smoked. It was a big turn off for him. I am sure if I told him the truth about my past, he would not like the person I was back then, because I was all of those things he found a turn off.

He was more or less not my type, because I liked the guys who were into the drugs that smoked, and drank; it gave me an excuse to do the same when I felt like bending the halo on my inner angel, and twisting it into a thorn that matched my inner devil. But I would leave that for Zacharie to realize; I am anything but perfect.

CHINESE

The next morning, I was in shock when I got a text at 7:03 am from Zacharie.

Zacharie to Estelle
Zacharie- Good morning, Estelle, how are you today?
Estelle- Good morning, Zacharie, I am fine, thank you for asking.
Zacharie- How is your day going?
Estelle- My day has not started yet, I am just rolling out of bed. How is your day going?
Zacharie- Mine is going, I guess you could say. With it being really slow at work, it's kind of dull. Hopefully my work will have some more contracts in the near future that will keep me much busier.
Estelle- I really wish I could say the same, my job is never busy. I create my own work and set my own schedule.
Zacharie- What do you do?
Estelle- Plot, act and not much writing lately.
Zacharie- I see. I forgot you are a writer.
Estelle- I told you I was a writer yesterday when we were having coffee.
Zachary- I was having coffee, and you were having tea.
Estelle- Whichever way you would like to put it, I told you.
Zacharie- How many books have you published?
Estelle- Only one book so far.

Zacharie- Why only one?

Estelle- Because I only became a published author last year, so having more than one book within the first year of being published is uncommon.

Zacharie- What is the name of the book you published?

Estelle- 'Loved by No Other.'

Zacharie- What's the book about?

Estelle- You have never heard of my book?

Zacharie- No! Was I supposed too?

What the fuck is wrong with this guy? Has he never been to a local bookstore in Medicine Hat? My book is all over.

Estelle- Well if I told you what my book was about, it would ruin it for you. Why don't I just send you the Preface?

Zacharie- What is a preface?

Estelle- Can your cell-phone receive files?

Zacharie- Obviously.

Estelle- Would you like me to send you the Preface?

Zacharie- I guess so.

Estelle- Well do you want to know what the book is about or not?

Zacharie- Go ahead and send it to me.

Estelle- Do you promise to read it as soon as you get the file?

Zacharie- Maybe.

Estelle- I will only send it to you if you promise to read it as soon as you download the file to your cell-phone.

Zacharie- Whatever! Upload the file and send it to me already.

I closed my conversation with Zacharie, and scrolled through the files on my cell phone, until I reached the prologue for 'Loved by No Other.' I immediately attached the file to our conversation and hit send, and waited patiently for Zacharie to read it.

Loved by No Other- By: Estelle Ella Whiteside
Preface

As two 'human men' assist in directing my weak body, I stagger towards the Darga cliff's among Garzabov, where an audience awaits to pass their judgement. These two weak fools cannot help but breathe in my sweet, delicate, yet forbiddingly delicious scent; their 'wives' look on with scrutiny. I show no fear, only watch all the 'women' whose 'husbands' souls I will forever hold claim over, because he was naïve enough to submit to the Oman.

"Witch, you have been brought before the 'wives' and 'women' of Garzabov, where you have chosen to live outside of 'Coven', and men come bidding their body and soul for promise of ever-lasting love, acquainted with unspeakable sexual favors. You have claimed these innocent 'men' and turned them into a hideous beasts, sworn to forever love only 'one;' but not the 'wife they married, but a 'Witch.' You cast these 'beasts' to a forbidden enchanted forest to live out the remainder of their days alone, to be forever loved by no other. You are hereby charged with committing unspeakable crimes against those who simply cannot help themselves, and are sentenced to death by slice, and hanging. Plead yourself party to guilty, and may the Gods have mercy upon your hideous soul."

Glancing down towards the ropes that bind my hands, and the chains that shackle my bare feet, I wonder of the chance this Priest is thinking I will submit to defeat, and simply die. As long as the eye of the beloved Beast who submitted to such an Oman remains alive, the World will be plagued with my Soul, and I will be awaken in the body of mine, dead under Earths dirt, reborn into the World on a cold morning.

"I will submit to no such crime, and contest that all "human men' are simply tainted by those forbidden to be understood by those less fortunate to our uniqueness."

"So be that as it may Witch, you will be stripped of your blood," the Priest directs the two 'men' to slit my ankles; they do so eagerly to be rid of my scent, but as they cut deep beneath my flesh, the scent becomes overwhelming. "You must be quick cut her wrists" the Priest demands.

One of the 'men' can barely contain himself, as the drool pools outwards and spills onto the dirt. I look him directly in the eyes, his eyes; are now fixated on my hazel eyes, "I promise you ever lasting love, and sex beyond your wildest dreams. You only must speak the Oman, and you will belong to me."

"What is the Oman?" The 'human men' begs.

"Don't listen to her, you fool," the Priest screams, and immediately pushes the 'human man' out of the way, grabbing the knife. "I will finish this; you cast the rope around the witch's legs. She must hang for seven days before she is cast beneath Earths water and cleansed of her sins." The other 'human man' quickly slices deep into my right wrist; the odor of my blood becomes intoxicating. As the Priest ties the rope binding my legs once more over, I give a wicked smile, and throw myself over the Darga Cliffs to die, and rise again in eleven days.

Ten minutes passed, and I figured maybe Zacharie was giving himself a hand-job because it was taking him so long to reply back to me. I cannot imagine it should take someone that long to read my Preface, but coming from someone who had no idea about my book, or has not even heard of it, I figured Zacharie was very sheltered. *Poor guy!*

And then my phone dinged...

Zacharie to Estelle

Zacharie- I must say, your preface was very interesting.

Estelle- Really! You liked it?

Zacharie- It was different for sure.

Estelle- I made a lot of money writing the book, so it really paid off.

Zacharie- Well as long as writing makes you happy, that is what matters most.

Estelle- Well do not kid yourself, my happiness never lasts long.

Zacharie- Really and why is that?

Estelle- Because something bad always happens, the cards are never dealt kindly in my favor.

Zacharie- I have learned from my past experiences; life is only what you make it, Estelle.

Estelle- Yes, well my life has never really been a bowl of cherries.

Zacharie- Then I guess you do not like cherries?

Estelle- Why would you assume that?

Zacharie- Because you said your life has never really been a bowl of cherries.

Estelle- It's a phrase.

Zacharie- I see.

Estelle- Is that your favorite phrase to say, or what?

Zacharie- Maybe.

Estelle- I see.

Zacharie never texted me back after my smart ass remark, so I decided to roll out of bed and start my day.

I walked into the kitchen, opened the fridge, and poured myself a glass of orange juice. I broke two eggs and emptied them into a separate cup. While plugging my nose, I gulped them down quickly to avoid concentrating on the slimy taste.

I went over to my computer, deciding to send my publisher an email, and let him know what I was working on today.

From: Estelle
Subject: Today's Forecast
Date: September 7th, 2014 07:56 am
To: Art Campbelle
Good morning Mr. Campbelle, the 'man' who pays my bills. I just wanted to send you a quick email this morning to let you know, I am working on a new book. I am at this moment in time, in the brainstorming stage. I do not have any further information to provide you with right now. But please know once I have my plot clear, I will forward you a quick Query, and you can run it past the board of directors and let me know what you think. If you are interested in the storyline, I will then send you the Synopsis with a breakdown of my story.
Have a great day <3
Estelle Ella Whiteside ☺
Author of 'Loved by No Other.'

I grabbed onto my phone, furious as to why I had to be the one to continue 'our' conversation. Zacharie had such a closed-off interesting side to him that I was curious to figure out.

Estelle to Zacharie
Estelle- So I was interested to ask what your plans are for tonight?

Zacharie- Think I am going to go home after work, to watch a movie.

Estelle- I just remembered today is Sunday and if I am not mistaken, normal people are off today. You even said yourself earlier that your work is really slow. Why are you working today?

Zacharie- I work every day that ends with a 'y'.

Estelle- You did not work yesterday.

Zacharie- How can you be sure of that?

Estelle- Because you never mentioned anything about working to me, when we were at the coffee shop.

Zacharie- You never asked.

Estelle- You never shared. ☺

Zacharie- Well, you mentioned earlier that your day has not started yet, so I am assuming that you must be working today on something as well. Why are you working on a Sunday?

Smart ass!

Estelle- Being that I am a writer, whenever I feel creative I write.

Zacharie- Do you use a notepad, or do you prefer to do all of your writing using a computer?

Estelle- Depends on how I am feeling.

Zacharie- Well can you tell me something then?

Estelle- What would you like to know?

Zacharie- How does the rest of your night look, after writing?

Estelle- Well my Publisher isn't hounding me for anything much today. So I am thinking my night is looking wide open.

Zacharie- Would you want to come and watch a movie at my place tonight?

Estelle- Are you asking me out on a date on the second day we have known each other?

Zacharie- No, I am asking 'someone' I just met yesterday, to come over to my place and watch a movie.

Estelle- How do you know I would not drive you crazy? You might want to throw me out of your house.

Zacharie- Well you have not driven me crazy up to this point, because I am still texting with you. So I think we should be fine.

Estelle- Are you going to be nice to me if I come over tonight?

The thought of a guy being the least bit mean to me in anyway really turned me on; it was kind of sick, but if I could get Zacharie to be mean to me, I would be in sexual heaven. I could get off at any moment by just thinking about any one mean thing he has done to me. Twisted.

Zacharie- Maybe.

Estelle- Ok, as long as you are undecided about whether or not you may be mean to me, then I will come over. What time would you like me there?

Zacharie- I will come by and pick you up after I am done work.

Estelle- Ok.

Zacharie- See you tonight.

As I sat at my desk at home, and read across the last text message from Zacharie, I tried to collect my thoughts and focus on my writing. I noticed I had a message in my inbox.

From: Art Campbelle
Subject: Today's Forecast

Date: September 7th, 2014 9:24 am
To: Estelle

Good morning Estelle, I want to 'thank you' for sending an email this morning to let me know that you have a project in the works. You know I like to hear what is going on with my star Author.

I am really sorry that we had to put your book tour on hold until next August, but we are doing what is best at this time for you. Next year will be a busy one, as I am hoping to have you launch the sequel to 'Loved by No Other.'

I am looking forward to reviewing your sequel, so do not keep me waiting too long.

Let me know what you come up with darling.

Art
Managing Director at Exelby Publishing

Is he fucking serious? He wants the sequel already to 'Loved by No Other.' *Whatever.* Art will merely have to accept whatever the fuck I draft up for him. I am not even done brainstorming anything for the continuation of my 'Bare-back' Series.

I could feel my blood boiling, as I opened my drawer and grabbed out my black journal. *Surely an entry would make me feel better.*

September 7th, 2014

I am so angry right now with Art, my Publisher, with Exelby Publishing. I was trying to tell him about a new book I have in the works, but he is too focused on continuing my last big seller: 'Loved by No Other.'

When do I get to call the shots? It seems as though everyone else makes my life decisions for me.

One year ago, I was happy living in Chicago. I had my family, and could go out with my friends whenever I wanted. Everyone knew who 'Estelle Ella White side' was.

Since I have moved to Medicine Hat, Alberta, no one recognizes me out in public, or points a finger and says 'look there she is.' Instead, I walk down the street on a sidewalk, because the red carpet has been pulled out from under my feet by my goddamn publisher.

I have millions, but feel so poor at heart, because I have no one to share my fame and fortune with.

The only thing I can spend my time doing is writing stories for other people to turn pages, and fall in love with. Or else I spend my time plotting to meet a guy, to trick him into falling in love with me.

Why would anyone ever want to love Estelle Ella Whiteside? Would they want to love me for money? Fame? How about my Fortune that will continue to roll in from all the works I publish going forward?

Is there no one real in this screwed up World anymore that 'we' all need to just pretend, and read about how great life could or should be?

I guess after my movie night later, I might have something to write about.

At least my journal will always love me, because I can keep writing, and there will always be pages to turn until I am finished.

Love Estelle Ella Whiteside

Xoxo

It was hard, but I managed to get through my stressful day of work and blogging to fans on my site. I could not help but wonder what was going to happen tonight. Would Zacharie try to fuck me? I mean last night he left after we had such a lengthy conversation, and he did not even kiss me.

I sat on my couch, and tried to close my eyes for a few minutes. I just wanted to role-play in my head what my next move would be with Zacharie, and the only thing that came to mind was the different ways I wanted him to tie me up, or maybe even gag me with a huge cock. *Did he even have a huge cock?*

Bang, Bang, Bang

I was immediately startled out of my thoughts, and brought back into the reality this afternoon had to offer me.

I got up off my couch, and walked over towards the door to see who it was.

"Who is it?"

"It's Christina," she answered in a soft-spoken tone.

I opened the door, and she stepped inside.

"How are you?" I asked her.

"I am doing alright," she replied.

"Oh, is everything ok?" I said hesitantly, as the sweat was dripping down the side of her face.

"No Estelle, today I found out my boyfriend does not want to be together anymore," Christina sobbed, wiping the sweat from her forehead.

"Wait, you have a boyfriend?" I asked in confusion.

"Yes, Perry."

"I never knew that you had a boyfriend. I thought you were fucking guys off that dating site too?" I asked.

"No, I was never fucking guys off that dating site; I only suggested it to you, because you were desperate to get fucked. I have been dating Perry for just over six months now."

I guess with being so self-absorbed in my own life, I never stopped to notice what was going on in anyone else's.

"So tell me what happened?" I asked, pretending to give a shit.

"Well, we were having sex last night, and I faked my orgasm like usual, but I guess he caught on to it, because I did not notice he stopped fucking me, and I just continued moaning."

"I cannot imagine how he could have caught on to your faking orgasms so easily Christina? You sure would have me fooled," I replied, in a smart ass tone.

"Could you at least try to sound fucking sympathetic, Estelle," she whined.

"Well if I really gave a shit, I could definitely write you a poem that is sympathetic, or else a script, Christina, but right now I have my own drama show going on."

"Estelle, why do you always need to make everything about you? Can you not just listen to how I feel and stop worrying about your own problems for once?"

Maybe Christina is right, I mean I am her friend. Right?

"That is exactly it, Christina. I do think about myself way too much, instead of the needs of others. What exactly would you like me to do for you?"

"Well you could..."

I stopped her while she was speaking. "Why don't you just give me Perry's phone number, and I will invite him over to your place tonight. I will tell him that you are going to make him a really nice dinner, and then you will have sex and actually pretend to orgasm while he fucks you, but this time you will pay better attention to any signs of him stopping. Does that sound like a good idea?"

"Estelle, what the fuck is your problem?" Christina asked.

"I have plans tonight, and you come down to my apartment with your bullshit drama-show. I do not have the fucking time for it right now, I have plans with Zacharie," I shouted.

"Well if you are too busy to talk to your friend, then why do you not just say so, and I will leave and come back another time, when you can talk to me about it," she snorted in frustration.

"Come back tomorrow and we can talk about it Christina. I am really sorry; I am just pinched for time right now. I need to get ready, I will talk to you tomorrow," I replied, while escorting her to the door of my apartment.

"Estelle, why are your plans so important again?" She asked nosily.

"I need to get ready to fuck the random guy I met off the dating site, who I will not commit to having a relationship with. Now if you would excuse me, we can talk about this tomorrow. Have a good night." I said nicely, while pushing her ass out the door.

As she left, I went back and sat on my couch, wondering what the fuck am I doing?

***

As I jumped in the shower and started washing my hair, I thought I heard my phone ring.

After I finished washing myself, I got out of the shower, and wiped the steam off the mirror. I wondered what the hell Zacharie saw in me, but maybe it was the same thing I saw: an opportunity to get my sexual frustrations out, and maybe just let loose for the first time in my life. I mean it's not like Zacharie was my boyfriend, so I could date and fuck multiple guys.

I grabbed my cell-phone to check and see who called; oddly enough it was a Milwaukee phone number. One I did not recognize.

I called and listened to my voicemail: *Hey Estelle, it's me Nathan, I was thinking of taking a road trip up to Medicine Hat next month. I have never been out that way, and I am really interested in seeing the West Coast of Canada. There has not been much work out my way, so I thought I may relocate, however I am still undecided. It would be really nice to catch up with you, if you are available. Give me a call back when you get a chance and we can discuss your schedule.*

Wow, Nathan's is planning a road-trip to the West Coast, and he wants to make plans to get together, maybe he would want to fuck too. I mean it would not be such a bad thing, to save myself for a guy I fucked when I was nineteen at a house warming party for his sister.

Ping...

I was startled by the sound of my phone going off in my hand, while I was in thought.

Zacharie to Estelle

Zacharie- I will be there in twenty minutes.

Estelle- Ok.

Shit, I better hurry. I quickly blow dried my hair, and then straightened it.

Ping...

Zacharie to Estelle

Zacharie- I am here

Holy shit! He got here fast.

Estelle- Ok can you give me five minutes?

Zacharie- Do you want me to come in?

There is no way I am letting Zacharie see me without makeup.

Estelle- No it's quite alright, I may take longer if I let you come in. Just give me five minutes and I will be right out.

Zacharie- Ok.

I quickly put myself together, grabbed my purse, and ran out the door. It was a little cold out, and I forgot my jacket, but I already kept Zacharie waiting long enough. I didn't want to make him mad, by asking him to wait while I go grab my jacket because I am not prepared.

"Hey," he said with a smile.

"I am really sorry Zacharie; I tried to get ready as quick as I could. Had an unexpected meeting with a friend who stopped in, and our visit went a little longer than usual," I replied, almost out of breath.

"It's ok," he replied, as he turned his truck back on me.

"Thanks, most guys would be annoyed, but I guess the younger you are, the more patience you have," I replied smiling.

"I see," he replied.

As we started driving, I realized that I never thought to ask where and who he lived with. It never really occurred to me that I didn't know where I was going, but then I thought: *I would text Christina when I got to Zacharie's place with the address.*

I looked at Zacharie as he made a left to go down towards the main roadway.

It occurred to me that we were heading towards the new housing development, which just started construction during the month of July.

"Where exactly do you live?" I asked him.

"In Medicine Hat," he nicely replied in a joking sort of tone.

"I know you live in Medicine Hat, so do I," I replied with a smile. I glanced out towards the window, and then asked: "do you have roommates?"

"No."

"Oh," I replied, a little startled.

It would just be Zacharie and I at his place! This could prove to be entertaining.

"Does that bother you?" Zacharie asked, as he turned his head to glare at me darkly while we stopped at a red light.

"No," I replied.

"Are you cold?" He asked.

I guess I never stopped to notice both my arms wrapped around my bare shoulders; with my hair pinned up, it left my neck wide open to receive any cold breeze.

"Kind of," I replied, wondering why he would even be concerned.

He turned the heat on full blast; *it's September, who does that?*

It kind of threw me for a loop, I mean I thought only a guy that cared would bear through anything for a girl they either 'loved' or really 'cared' about. I just started seeing Zacharie randomly for hopes of having a sexual relationship. *What the fuck is wrong with him? Is he normal?*

I wondered: is *that how guys in Medicine Hat get girls to sleep with them?*

I mean the fact that he had a French accent was cute. I really liked it, but I was not driven crazy over it. It might drive any other girl wild, but because I can speak three different languages fluently, the accent did not win over my sexual needs.

"Is everything ok?" Zacharie asked.

"Yes, I am fine thanks."

"Ok, good," he replied.

My stomach started to growl.

"Are you hungry?" Zacharie asked.

"Kind of," I replied, a little embarrassed that my stomach gave my hunger away.

"There is a Chinese food place in the plaza across from where my house is. Do you like Chinese?"

Considering that in the last three days I really didn't eat anything and lost approximately ten pounds because I was too busy plotting, maybe liking Chinese was a good indicator.

"Sure," I replied with a mused smile.

"Ok," he replied, pulling into the Chinese food place.

We ordered some different, interesting dishes; his were more interesting than mine, and I didn't even really eat my food, just picked at it. I am sure he was wondering whether or not I had a phobia of eating in front of a complete stranger.

"Is everything ok?" Zacharie asked.

"Yes. Why does it seem like there is something wrong with me?"

"Well, you have not touched your food."

"Does that bother you?" I asked.

"Well, if you order food, you should eat it," he said rudely.

I think I am going to stop picking at my fucking food, and just stare at it, to see if it pisses him off more.

"So Zacharie, tell me what do you do for fun in your spare time?"

"What do you mean?"

"Exactly what I asked," I huffed. "You must do something fun, other than meet random girls off a dating site," I smiled, while swirling my beef noodles with my fork.

"I have fun like any normal person does?" He replied, and gulped down a sip of his soda.

"Well, I mean do you have people over for beers every day of the week, or do you go out to the bar? I want to know what you like to do."

"You just met me. Why do you care so much about what I do for fun," he replied rudely, furrowing his brow.

"I am sorry for showing any interest in what you like to do. I will just sit here and play with my food, I guess. Since that seems to be the only way I can get you to express any sort of emotions or interest to get to open up to me about your likes and dislikes."

"I see that," he laughed and put his fork down, grabbing a napkin.

"There really is not anything I like to do in Medicine Hat. The only fun I find is a soft cushy mattress, with four posts, and maybe some rope," I replied with a wink, hoping he would receive my open invite for play.

"You like to sleep a lot," he asked, *oblivious to my entire point. I am guessing a more direct point is needed.*

"No I like to masturbate a lot," I replied bluntly.

"Excuse me?" Zacharie replied in an angered tone.

"Did you not hear what I said?" I asked.

"Yes, I did. But I do not think it's appropriate for you to announce in a public restaurant that you enjoy masturbation on your own bed, with four posts," he snapped.

Maybe he was right, but at least I got a reaction from him.

"I enjoy it on any bed with four posts. Does your bed have four posts?" I asked curiously.

"Are you ready to go and watch that movie?" Zacharie asked, changing the subject.

"It depends what kind of movie we are going to watch?"

"What kind of movies are you into?"

"Porn," I said bluntly, *hoping he would get a fucking clue. I don't want to watch a move, I just want to fuck, and then write about it.*

"Do you want dessert, Estelle?"

"Do they serve Zacharie on the menu?"

The waitress came to the table; "is there anything else I can get for you two today?"

I glanced at her for a moment, admiring her short blonde hair, pale white tone, thin and tiny build. *She could definitely use a set of tits.* I smiled nicely, and looked towards Zacharie.

"No, I will just get the check thank you," Zacharie said, and then started to grab his sweater he took off when we first walked in and sat down.

When it came time to pay for dinner, I was about to, but he did, *this was also very strange to me. I don't like guys paying for me to do anything; why the hell is someone younger than myself paying for dinner anyhow? Surely he should be saving his money, not spending it?*

"Thanks for dinner," I mumbled.

"No problem, are you ready to go and watch that movie?"

"Sure am," I replied, *hoping he had some really good porn.*

BUNGALOW

As we pulled up outside of a cute little bungalow, it sort of reminded me of my parent's summer home back in Ontario, California. My sister and I used to spend every summer there when we were kids, before my parents started renting it out.

It felt weird knowing he lived in a house *all on his own* and that I lived in an apartment. I was the one with millions, not him.

"What do you think?" Zacharie asked.

"I think it's lovely," I replied, smiling trying not to show my slight jealousy.

"Thanks, I did the landscaping myself," he smiled.

"Why would you do the landscaping yourself? Is that not what a landlord is for?" I laughed out loudly, and rolled my eyes at him.

"I am the landlord."

"You own a house?" I replied in utter shock. *A twenty-four year old, owning a house in Medicine Hat, really? Well I guess it could happen, right?*

I mean if I could sign a huge Publishing contract at twenty-five, then maybe a twenty-four year old could buy a two hundred thousand dollar place in Medicine Hat.

"Yes, is there a problem?" Zacharie asked, looking a little irritated at my astounded self. *If anything, you would think he would be flattered that I am this shocked.*

"No, just strange is all," I replied.

"What is strange about it?" He asked, while leaning over the center console towards me, with his dark glare. The one that made me feel uncomfortable the first time we met.

"I have never met a guy who owned a house before; most of the guys I meet are bums," I replied in a lower tone, and immediately looked away towards my hands, because I did not want his eyes to cut into me anymore.

"Well I think that is strange," he huffed, and leaned back only half an inch away from me.

"Well, then cheers to being strange," I said in a lighter tone, hoping to make the air between us both clear for this evening, and not awkward.

I got out of the truck and so did Zacharie. He started walking towards the side of the house.

"Where are you going?" I asked him.

"Inside with you," he smiled.

"Then why are you going towards the side of the house? Why not use the front door?" I asked confused.

"Because the entrance to my part of the house is the side door," he replied.

"Uh-ok," I replied, trying not to choke.

"Just come Estelle, you will see what I am talking about."

"Ok."

As he opened the door attached to the side of the bungalow, there was a set of stairs that led down towards a washer, with a dryer stacked on top, and a fridge, as soon as you landed below ground. *Interesting, my parent's bungalow in California did not have a basement. It was only one floor.*

"Come," Zacharie, requested as he took off his shoes, and started walking down a long hallway.

"This is different," I tried to say nicely.

"You like it? I did this myself, with the help of my builders of course."

"Is this even legal?"

"Yes."

"Really, in Medicine Hat they actually allow people to build like this?"

"What is wrong with it?" Zacharie turned around and cut into me with his cold dark brown eyes again.

"Everything, there isn't two exits, uh – there is a stove and that is not even safe. What if there was a fire down here, and it was in front of the doorway, how would you exit? Drill a hole through the wall in hopes to build a tunnel upwards?"

Zacharie looked at me for a minute. I am sure he was not impressed by my judgment of his living conditions, but I mean shit, I was living in an apartment not by choice. My Publisher's love of keeping me off the radar was working well, *but at least I have two exits and it's legal.*

"Let us just watch the movie."

"Ok, but can I ask you a very simple question without prying into your personal affairs?"

"Sure."

"Why on Earth would you live in this small, confined space, when clearly you have an entire upstairs that is much bigger than this one, with no one living in it?"

"Because I rent the top of the house out to tenants; it just happens that no one is living up there at present, but I will be renting it out next month once I am done the few renovations I need to finish."

Different, a guy who was gifted with a brain, thinks logically, and acts based on his logic; I like that. He must have gone to College.

"Did you go to College?" I asked.

"Yes."

"I see." I replied with a smart tone.

"So now, you would like to watch the movie?"

"Sure."

We walked into the bedroom: to the right was a love-seat, to the left was a bed, and straight ahead was a large TV, and at the foot of the bed was an old wooden trunk that needed to be opened by key.

Zacharie walked over to the love-seat and re-arranged some of the pillows: "we can sit here and watch the movie."

"Sounds good to me," I replied, *wondering how in the hell we are supposed to fuck on a love-seat. Maybe I could sit on him, and fuck him like a dirty stripper using a pole to get off.*

He put a movie in, and oddly enough it was 'Random Night of Countless Sexual Encounters," *weird how that works out.*

I wondered what guy would watch a movie about two random people meeting and falling in love.

I sat for the duration of the movie, and tried not to talk or ask questions, but I tend to be a talker during movies, until you nicely tell me to 'shut up'.

"Zacharie, can I ask you another question?"

"Can you wait until after the movie?" He asked.

"Well, I was really curious."

"Estelle please, I am really into this movie," he scorned.

Why the hell couldn't he just be as interested as fucking me, as I was interested in fucking him. Well that's it, tonight I am going on a 'sex strike.' Teach this inconsiderate asshole a lesson.

After the movie, Zacharie got up off the love-seat: "I am ready for bed?"

"Yeah, I am pretty tired," I replied, *while pretending to fake yawn.* "I am ready whenever you are."

"Ready for what?" Zacharie asked, while he started getting undressed down to his boxers. I felt a little uncomfortable, because I am not used to undressing in front of anyone.

"Well are you not going to drive me home?" I asked, confused.

"Estelle, I am too tired to take you home. If you like, you can call a cab, or I can drive you home in the morning."

Oh- so now he wants me to spend the fucking night, and do what? Well there is no way I am going to have sex with this little prick; I am sticking with my strike.

"I will be right back," I said nicely.

I went into his washroom, turned on the light, and started undressing. I had a t-shirt on with a pair of booty-shorts, and walked back into his room. It was dark, and my inner-self was feeling a little dark and at her meanest right now.

I wanted to see how easy it was to make Zacharie hard, so I immediately reverted back to striking mode.

I sat down on the love-seat during the movie, we didn't do anything, so I thought *why not something now? But not sex.*

I rolled close enough toward him so that my cold skin was against his warmed.

"Do you want to cuddle or something?" He asked in an annoyed tone.

What the fuck kind of a question is that? One would think he would ask 'do you want to fuck?'

"Sure," I said in a naughty tone that I knew all too well.

"Well I am not the cuddling type," he replied, while jerking himself away from me.

Not the cuddling type, then what type is he?

I got up and out of the bed, climbed in front of him, and then moved inwards so my ass was facing his package. I could feel it was not awake yet.

"Estelle, what did I tell you?" He asked in an angry tone.

"You told me that you do not like to cuddle, but you never said you did not like to share body temperature to keep a girl warm," I replied smiling.

"If you are cold I have another blanket that you can wrap yourself in. If you do not mind, I need to get up in the morning, and do not appreciate your cold ass against me."

Huh? Why was he being so mean all of a sudden?

"Zacharie, can I ask you a question?" I said, while trying to move myself inwards towards him, so that his body could warm me up, because I was truly really cold. Using an extra blanket to wrap myself in is sure not keeping me as warm as his body right now.

"Estelle, ask the question? Then can you please move away from me? I am not going to ask you again."

"Zacharie, I am really cold, and I just want you to keep me warm. What is so wrong with having my body against yours? Did I do something to make you angry with me?" I asked.

"Beds are for sleeping or fucking. If we are not fucking, then we are sleeping. Now if you would please move away from me, I have an early day tomorrow."

"Zacharie, do you realize how early it is?"

"It's not early for me Estelle; now if you do not move, I will move myself."

"Why don't you move me?" I said, trying to sound playful.

"You want me to move you?" He asked.

"Zacharie, I want to play a game."

"You want to play a game?" He chuckled.

"Yes."

"Ok Estelle. We can play a game, but I get to choose what type of game we play. Wait right here," he demanded, and got out of the bed. I could hear him jingle his keys out of his pant pocket. *I wondered what the fuck he would need his keys for at this time of night.*

He turned the bedroom light on and I immediately covered my face with the comforter on Zacharie's bed; I was not pleased right now. "Could you please turn the light off," I demanded.

"I will turn it off in a second, I need to see right now," he hissed, and then turned a lock, opening up what appeared to my ears as the trunk at the end of the bed. "Ah- this will work perfectly," he sounded mused.

"What will work perfectly?" I asked confused, but did not peek my head out from under the covers.

"You want to play a game still, correct?"

"Yes, I will play, but can you please turn out the fucking light?"

Zacharie then switched off the light, and I took the comforter and removed it from covering me completely.

"Estelle, as part of the game, you will need to do exactly everything I tell you too."

"Ok, how hard can that be," I laughed.

"I want you to stand up," he directed.

"No way, it's too cold," I whined.

"Estelle, you either do everything I tell you too, or we are going to bed, and the game is over."

"For fuck sakes, fine," I cried, and got up out of the bed.

"I want you to stand up, with your back to the edge of the bed, lifting your arms up."

"Why?"

"You are asking too many questions, so I am going to gag your mouth shut."

"What!" And before I could finish my sentence, Zacharie leaned my face downwards with my hands still in the air, and inserted the end of a rubber, which appeared to be a dildo into my mouth. *I was in shock.* He then took a fold and wrapped it around my head closing the dildo in my mouth, so that I could no longer speak, tying it firmly.

"I am going to undress you now, Estelle, and if you flinch, I am going to tie your fucking hands. I want you to nod if you understand," he directed.

I gently nodded my head up and down; *I did not know if I liked this game too much, but maybe Zacharie has a kinky way of getting off. And I was getting a little wet.*

Zacharie lifted my shirt off, and I could feel a sudden chill. "I told you not to fucking move, Estelle," and before I could even move my body, he let go of my shirt around my neck, bound my hands together and above my head, pulling them down over my front, while my t-shift draped over my shoulders. He then removed my t-shirt completely.

I tried to move my hands, but they were bound tight. *I was praying he was not going to hurt me. I hardly knew him at this point, but this was all about sex. Right?*

He then took his fingertips and pulled my booty-shorts slightly at the front, so that the tip was riding the crease of my ass. *I moaned a little.*

"I told you not to say anything Estelle, so now I am going to bind your legs," he snapped, while binding my legs tightly below the kneecap.

I could feel a tear trickle down the side of my face. I was so cold, *yet this was so fucking hot.* Tomorrow I would have so much to write about.

Zacharie then pushed me backwards on his bed until I was on my back with my knees bent and my pussy wide open, only covered by my booty-shorts that he did not manage to get off, before binding my legs.

He took his face, using the tip of his nose, without even breathing, and started running it up and down the lips of my vagina; *I got overly excited.*

As soon as I could feel myself wet, Zacharie immediately moved his nose, and raised his head. He turned my body to lie straight, and then unbent my knees. "Estelle, you are a bad girl, I did not say you could get wet."

What the fuck? Am I supposed to stay dry?

"Now I am going to punish you, because I am going to keep you like this until tomorrow morning, when I am ready to take you home."

Zacharie crawled into bed, and left my body completely uncovered. *I was hoping he would cover me with the blanket.*

A few minutes passed, and I could hear him snoring; the bastard was out cold.

The next morning was lucky number 8, a day that I remember every year, because for the last twenty-five years, my parents have been happily married. They spent most of their days arguing and then making up by having sex. *I wondered if maybe Zacharie fell from the wrong tree, because he was fucked.*

Really, how could two people who are so wrong for each other stay married for so long? I guess its fate's way of screwing them over.

I looked down towards my feet, only to see that they were still bound shut. My hands were still tied together, and I was still gagged with a dildo in my mouth.

Then the quacking started, and Zacharie reached over for his cell-phone that was placed under his pillow. I was still really cold, and could think of nothing else right now than wanting to go home

He rolled over and looked at my figure, I was sure he could clearly see my nipples hard as a rock. "Are you getting up?" Zacharie moaned.

Is this mother-fucker for real? How the hell am I supposed to get up?

"Here, allow me to ungag you, but remember if you are a bad girl, the dildo is going back in that filthy mouth of yours," he teased. While twitching his lip, he reached over to untie the gag from my mouth, and then I spit the dildo out immediately.

"Of course, your quacking alarm scared the shit out of me; I thought it was a girl choking on cock," I snorted.

"That would be nice," Zacharie said, with a bad boy tone.

"Zacharie, you forget, I don't have a set work schedule, being an Author; I can 'cum' and 'go' as I so please," I teased.

"Is that so?"

I rolled over towards him, with the binds still over my hands and around my legs. I was so cold, I did not give a shit, the bastard was kept warm all night by the blankets. I sniffed his skin, and suddenly Zacharie moved away.

"Is there something wrong?" I asked.

"I don't like that!"

"Don't like what?"

"I don't like it when a girl does that."

"Ok," I said, confused.

"Estelle, tell me something. Do you enjoy sucking dick?" He asked.

"Yeah, I enjoy sucking a real one, rubber is not for me."

"I am going to unbind your hands, because I want you to show me how you like to suck dick."

"What?"

"Estelle, if you do not want to do it, I will gag you with the dildo again."

I pouted, and then nodded in agreement to suck his dick. Zacharie unbound my hands, and I focused on getting his little friend downstairs attention.

I started to take my tongue and lick his neck, and then I started to suck from his bare neck down his six-pack; as my tongue lingered down the happy trail along boxer line, I could feel his penis erecting.

"Do you like that?" I asked.

"Less talking please," he ordered.

I started to wonder, what the fuck was wrong with this guy, everyone likes talking during sex, or oral; well from at least what I could remember anyways.

I decided it was time to fuck him silly with my tormenting tongue.

I unleashed my worse on him and tornado tongued his dick. I made it rain with his pre-cum, but after sucking him off for several minutes, his erection was slipping; there was something wrong.

"What's wrong, you don't want to cum?"

"You're not pleasing me the right way," he moaned.

I immediately stopped, and wondered: *was this complicated asshole for real?*

"Excuse me?"

"Never mind, I am just being grumpy. I hate getting up for work."

"Yes, me too."

Zacharie got up out of bed and flicked his bedroom light on.

I decided to give up on 'Mr. Complicated' for the time being; there is no pleasing a little boy, who doesn't want to cave and be a fucking man. *This was definitely making it into my top ten things to exploit Zacharie with by writing about what happened last night and this morning in my book.*

I rolled over, got up and untied my legs.

"Zacharie, what time do you start work?" I asked.

"I need to be at the office for 8:00am."

"That's great, so I will be home nice and early."

***

I started my morning off with a nice cup of hot chocolate, it was a typical day working and disliking my job. I mean when I was not on calls with my Publisher, I was trying to please everyone, except myself.

I decided to shoot my boss, Art, a quick email to let him know I don't have anything for him just yet, *but bullshitting about a sequel to 'Loved by No Other,' would prove funny since it would be a crock of shit.*

From: Estelle
Subject: My plans
Date: September 8th, 2014 07:39 am
To: Art Campbelle

Hello there 'Fart,' shit I mean 'Art.'

I thought you could use some humor in the morning. I am sure you are probably frowning at this point as there is no attachment to my email, but I want you to know I have started master-mining the next sequel to 'Loved by No Other,' and my friends simply think it's amazing.

***

My phone started singing; it was my new way of knowing I had a text message.

Christina to Estelle

Christina- I dropped by this morning and knocked on your apartment but didn't get an answer.

Estelle- You would not get an answer, because I was not home this morning.

Christina- Are you still with that guy?

Estelle- Obviously I am not, because I am texting you. I just got home.

Christina- Do you mind if I come and see you?

Estelle- I guess I could spare a few minutes of my day for you.

Christina- Whatever, forget that I even asked.

Estelle- Well someone woke up on the wrong side of the bed this morning. If you change your mind, I am only a knock away.

***

Estelle to Zacharie

Estelle- How do you feel about another sleepover tonight?

Zacharie- What did you have in mind?

Estelle- I was thinking we could maybe expand your game from last night.

Zacharie- I see.

Estelle- What's wrong? Did you not like my submission to your dominant side?

Zacharie- No, I liked your slipping tongue this morning, but was disappointed when my erection was deflated.

Estelle- Maybe tonight will be different.

Zacharie- I see.

Estelle- I am guessing that means I will see you tonight.

Zacharie- Maybe.

Estelle- Shut up Zacharie: just say 'yes' or 'no.'

Zacharie- Ok, come to my place around 9:00pm.

Estelle- Wow, why so late?

I waited a few minutes and he never responded. *Maybe his phone died?*

I decided that maybe I should work on starting my book about my relationship so far with Zacharie, and start jotting down about how I was feeling. Keeping a journal and then going back to it would be the best method for me to keep track of what we were doing daily; I almost wished I started it the first day we met at the coffee shop. But wait, I did. My daily journal entry, that was perfect. I will write my book using it.

September 8th, 2014

What makes a good writer a successful Author? For me it was never really about writing about what happened in my life, but writing about fantasy and erotic behavior that I wanted my characters to role-play.

I only dreamed of becoming a famous 'anything' and now here I sit, ten years post that daydream, configuring my career path into a real life scenario. One where I am playing the main character, and I held only one audition. Now here I have a young man, so complicated, yet so appealing to try and understand his complicated sexual methods.

I have never attempted to put an ad on a dating site. Well ok, maybe that's an utter line of spilt bullshit, but so is a lot of things I say.

I find it sexy that Zacharie drove his work truck to the coffee shop to meet me, and does not feel he needs to impress me with expensive accessories, because really, that's all money is to someone like myself who already has everything.

Love and passion; it does not seem like Zacharie is really made for these things, so the two of us might hit it off very well. I am planning on staying with him for a minimum of four months so that my research can be conducted properly. I will make sure to note every detail, from the time we fuck for the first time, to the time I suck his penis and finally get him off.

This morning was the angriest morning I have had in a long time, and also the most degrading.

He didn't say anything rude to me, but the fact that I cannot make him cum, this is a problem for me.

I am the queen of sucking cock; ok, maybe at one point in my life I use to be, but just because I am getting older does not mean I can't suck cock the way I use to.

I almost feel like taking a pole and stripping myself off in front of Zacharie, and see how complicated his penis feels when I give it a lap dance, and take my panties off.

But being allowed to take charge in the bedroom might be a problem with Zacharie. He did some kinky shit last night that I have never been exposed to.

He asked if I wanted to play a game, and then tied my hands and legs, not to mention gagging me with a dildo. What the fuck is up with that?

I hope he did not have a video camera taping the two of us? That would be some fucked-up shit.

Sorry, maybe I am just full of it. Most guys do this to get off or something; I really need to get a grip. I mean why the hell is Zacharie having such an effect on me? We just met for fuck sakes.

Could it be that I have spent too long away from the real world, and fabricated my life plot with science fiction, rather than reality?

If he would have just lifted me up this morning for being naughty, and held me against his bedroom door, and let me fucking have it, I would have been so happy. I want him to make me cum, but how the hell do I get him to bed me? Should I take control? Does he want me to take control?

I am really good at wanting to fuck, but I have never played the lead role. Maybe I should have a few drinks tonight and indulge in my submissive side?

Only tonight will tell....

Until such times

Little Miss Twisted

My pussy would like to be assaulted by Mr. Complicated.

I decided to give my hand a break, because I would need all the strength I had in both tonight, when I would put some hot lube on Zacharie's penis, and give him an erecting wake up call.

I was bound and determined to make his penis mine, and I really didn't care how it happened, but I needed to brainstorm a plot to make his penis come tumbling down into my mouth.

The idea of putting some warmed lubricated oil on his dick was the greatest idea I could come up with, because if my mouth was not wet enough for him, then maybe putting the lube on his dick would help; *I mean what normal guy could resist that?*

I know if he decided to take his tongue and invade my vagina with it, I would more than welcome him with a wet greeting, but I wonder: with him being so fucking complicated, if he would even have the balls to have mastered the art of going down on a woman.

I mean, I really like the way he binds my hands and the way his dildo fit so nicely in my mouth. I almost wish he was shoving one in my mouth right now, the way he did last night. Mr. Complicated is a ten minute drive away, and has this rule about seeing me so fucking late.

I decided to text him, and see if he wanted to see me earlier than 9pm; my pussy was eager and roaring for action at this point.

Estelle to Zacharie

Estelle- Is it ok if I come a little earlier than 9pm, I really don't like driving at night; I have bad eyes.

Zacharie- I would prefer that you come at 10pm actually, I am out at a restaurant with some friends.

Estelle- You went out for dinner?

Zacharie- Yeah, I got off work early, decided to stop in and visit a friend, and he wanted to grab something to eat.

Estelle- Oh then I will not rush you.

I started to think for a moment: it would have been nice if he offered to come and pick me up, that would give us some time alone in his big dirty, I mean, maybe sucking him off while driving would get him off.

Estelle- Do you think that you could pick me up on your way?

Zacharie- I would like it better if you could drive, then I do not have to take you home in the morning.

Estelle- Ok, no problem.

NOT SO GIVING

I arrived at Zacharie's place five minutes after 10pm; I would gather there is nothing sexier or interesting than a late arrival.

Estelle to Zacharie
Estelle- I am outside.
Zacharie- I am in bed.
Estelle- Already?
Is this loser for real...
Zacharie- Yeah I am tired.
Estelle- So do I just let myself in?
Zacharie- Sure.
Estelle- Ok then.

I got out of my truck, and almost thought it was retarded for me to even continue this; it was obvious he was not interested in me at all, or was just fucking around, because who invites a girl over at 10pm for a bedtime date? *What the hell is his last name anyways? Zacharie Complicated? That fits!* I chuckled to myself.

I opened the side door to his basement apartment, and took my shoes off. He didn't even turn a light on so I could see where the hell I was going, *what if I tripped, fell and hurt myself? Would he even get out of bed to help me?*

I walked down the stairs, and could see his television was on in the bedroom, by glancing down the long hallway. It was almost blinding me. As I peeked my head into his room, he was staring at the TV and didn't even say hello.

I put my overnight bag down on the carpet, and looked him directly in the eyes, which were still focused on the TV.

"Hello?"

'Shht'

"Ok, I am going to take it that you would like me to be completely quiet and just undress and get into bed."

He didn't answer.

I got undressed until I was in my bra and panties. Last time I retreated to the washroom to change, but tonight he was so interested in the TV that I didn't need to worry about his eyes finding my tits. *I mean shit, after I dressed myself for bed last night, he undressed me anyways.*

I climbed over top of him and towards the opposite side facing the wall. As I lay there, neither of us said a word. Forty or so minutes passed and the movie on TV was finally over. He reached for the converter and shut it off.

He then rolled his back to me and didn't say a word.

"Are you mad at me or something?" I asked.

"No, why?"

"Uh-because you didn't say one word to me since I got here."

"That's because I was watching a movie."

"Oh," I replied sadly.

A few minutes passed.

"Do you mind if I sleep on that side, Zacharie? I don't like this side of the bed when I am not tied up."

"Sure," he replied.

I only did this so that I could put my ass against his penis again. I liked testing my limits with him, maybe it would prompt him to gag me again, or maybe bind my legs and hands, *leaving my mouth open to receive his cock.*

Zacharie rolled over to the side I was lying on, and I got into bed. He then turned his back to me again; this prevented me from being able to put my ass in front of his dick like yesterday.

I decided maybe I would start humming, and then I began.

"Estelle, do you mind, I am trying to get some sleep?" He moaned.

"Then I guess you will just need to shut me up," I laughed.

"Estelle, if I have to shut you up, I will put my fucking dick in your mouth."

"Really," I said happily.

"It will not be pleasant, I assure you. Now stop with the humming, and sleep like good girls do."

"I am not a good girl, Zacharie," I muttered, and with my last spoken word, he was on top of me, my back sinking into the mattress.

Oh shit, I think I made Mr. Complicated angry.

When I tried to move, he firmly held both my wrists down. "Ouch, you are hurting me," I winced.

"Well Estelle, when you are a bad girl, you get hurt. And when you don't shut you're mouth when you're told, you get a dick shoved in it," he replied. He then immediately shoved his erection firmly into my mouth, so hard I was almost gagging.

We had never even kissed, and yet his dick is in my mouth, his hands on my wrists holding me down. What the hell was wrong with Mr. Complicated? We totally missed first & second base, and flew right to third, and *I sure as hell was not doing the homer without the kissing first.*

I quickly moved my head back, so his penis would slip out of my mouth. "Kiss me," I begged him.

He didn't comply. Instead, he shoved his dick so hard into my mouth, and I started chocking. I then moved my head back further this time, and again begged him to "kiss me," I winced.

As he went to insert his dick into my mouth again, I used all of my force to strain my neck and draw my lips to his mouth, gently started kissing his non-moving lips; it was quite dull. *Must not be much of a kisser.*

He removed his lips from mine, and I could see he was now angry, "I don't want you to ever kiss me again Estelle, unless I kiss you, which will never happen, unless you are kissing my penis."

"Huh," I cried in confusion.

"Now, I am going to shove my dick so far down your throat, and will keep it there until you gag enough times. I want you to choke on it for being a bad girl."

I tried to move my face away from his penis, but he belted it into my mouth, and deeply. I could not breath, and as I tried to stop Zacharie, he pushed further. I felt as though I was going to pass out, so I started to gag like he wanted. Every time I gagged, he would pull out a little so I could breath, and then he would push in harder, *maybe if I listen, that's the sexual point?* I thought.

After gagging on his penis for a little over half an hour, he removed his still pretty hard penis from inside my mouth.

My throat was so sore from deep throating his cock, I just wanted to roll over and cry, because he hurt me so much and didn't even care.

"Estelle, if you don't go to bed now, I am going to fuck you."

"Well I didn't give you permission to fuck me, Zacharie," I muttered.

I took my fingertips, and licked my index finger, running the wet saliva along the cracks of my lips.

"Estelle, I do not need permission to fuck you, because you willingly came over to my house with the knowledge that I would dominate you."

"How the fuck are you dominating me? I do not understand?"

"Estelle, you did not go to bed like I told you too," he scolded.

"I don't need to do anything you tell me to, Zacharie."

"That's it, I am fucking you."

Oh shit! Really, this ought to be kinky.

He positioned himself firmly over top of me, and reached over towards the inside of the pillowcase, reaching into what looked to be an open box of condoms. *Thinking maybe I was not the only girl he brought home so often, I started to get turned off.*

I quickly dried up. As I could hear him remove the foil and slip the condom on his dick, I was about to squirm away, but he firmly sat on me.

He then reached under the pillowcase, and pulled out two sets of handcuffs. He cuffed my right hand to the bedpost, and then my left hand, so that only my legs were free.

"Why do you need to cuff my hands, Zacharie? It hurts," I groaned.

"I want you to hurt, Estelle, that's the entire point."

Really?

He harshly inserted his penis inside of me; I was so dry that having his penis inside of me right now reminded me of my last Physical with Dr. Jonker.

Slowly moving in and out of me for only a moment, Zacharie sat upwards, and started assaulting my breasts with both his free hands.

He squeezed them both firmly, so it was not pleasurable at all.

While fully erected inside of me, he leaned backwards towards the end of the bed, and grabbed something out of the trunk, but I could not lift my head high enough to see what exactly it was that Zacharie was grabbing.

He then leaned forward again, and snapped what sounded like a strap. "Do you know what I have in my hands, Estelle?"

"No?" I replied, confused.

"I have a belt in my hands. And do you know what I am going to do with it?" He asked.

"No?" I replied, again but this time in a nervous tone.

"I am going to spank your tits really hard, while I fuck you, until I cum."

"What?" I snapped, and then the spanking began.

I started to cry; Zacharie was hurting me. *What the hell is wrong with him?*

"Zacharie, please, you are hurting me," I began to cry.

"Good girl Estelle. I want you to cry for me, scream at me for hurting you. Tell me how much it fucking hurts," he demanded.

"Zacharie, please, I..." begged, while trying to speak through all my tears, "You are hurting me, please don't hurt me anymore," I moaned.

As he spanked my breasts a few more times, he started to suck my nipples. *Holy shit,* the sucking was amazing and I started to get wet.

He let one more snap go against my tits gently, "Oh," I shouted, and then I felt him combust his erection inside my glove, yet his closed plastic didn't let an inch of his sperm invade my vagina.

When Zacharie was finished, he went to the washroom, and then came back to bed, leaving both my hands tied to each end of the bedposts.

September 9th, 2014

Mr. Complicated is 'fucked.'

I am really confused? I do not understand why Mr. Complicated needed to keep both my left and right hands cuffed to his bedpost last night?

I mean the fact that he spanked my tits, and then fucked me harshly, until he got off on causing me pain was fucked-up enough. Is it even legal to have sex with someone of the opposite sex in such a manner?

His ad on the dating site never said 'Mr. Complicated seeks submissive,' and this is certainly not what I signed up for.

Yet, my ad did not say 'Little Ms. Twisted seeks Complicated for exploitation,' so as long as both our needs are being satisfied, I guess there really is no harm.

But I do want to highlight the first thing that initially turned me off from wanting Zacharie to fuck me, was the fact that he didn't even kiss me back two nights ago. Not to mention, he had a box of open condoms under his pillowcase, and told me he was going to fuck me. Who tells a girl he is going to fuck her? Just do it, don't talk about it.

Is it normal for a guy to be this fucking difficult? I mean I don't think I have been unreasonable. I mean I let him use his trunk of sexual pain on me, and I will continue to, but when do I get pleasured?

Maybe I am being the difficult one; I mean it was my idea to be the Author who decides she is going to start writing a random book about how to find a guy, and make him fall in love with her, based off sex. But Zacharie makes it so difficult to even let me touch him, and he does not want to touch me nicely.

Tonight, I am going to try keep a really open mind, and get him to give 'us' another shot.

Here is to keeping an open mind, when it comes to Mr. Complicated

Little Ms. Twisted

I had the strangest idea: tonight, I should phone Mr. Complicated instead of text him, and so I picked up my cell-phone and dialed his number.

After six rings, it went to voicemail.

I wondered what he could be doing, and then I got a text.

Zacharie to Estelle
Zacharie- You called.
Estelle- Yes, and you didn't pick up?
Zacharie- I was in the shower!
Estelle- I called you a minute ago, and you finished your shower that quickly?
Zacharie- Did you need something?

Estelle- Yeah, I had a bad day and was really looking forward to some company; I was thinking you?

Zacharie- I am really busy tonight; I am going to help my friend put an alternator in his car.

Estelle- What about when you are finished?

Zacharie- Not tonight.

Estelle- Please, I promise I will not be a bother, I am just really lonely and want you to hold me.

Zacharie- I will not hold you Estelle, but fine, come at 10pm.

Estelle- Really? That late?

Zacharie- You don't need to come over at all!

Estelle- I will see you at 10pm, thanks.

I wondered if Mr. Complicated felt anything during sex, other than just sex. It was obvious he has fucked many women.

I can remember back to the coffee shop when we first met one another: I asked him how many women he has fucked, and he would not answer the question, what a great indicator that he must fuck a lot of random women! *And maybe right now, I was his random.*

I only wondered: if our roles were reversed, and he was trying to fuck me at my place, and I pulled out a box of opened condoms, or had a trunk of kinky sex toys, would he have felt the same way I did at his place last night, and the night before that?

I decided to go and sit in front of the computer to check my email, but I completely got side tracked, and never checked to see if I had an email from Art.

From: Art Campbelle
Subject: Eagerly Awaiting!!!

Date: September 9th, 2014 07:54 am
To: Estelle

Good morning Estelle, I enjoyed your comedy this morning, it made me laugh. But I cannot help be but a little jealous, where is this 'work' you have shown to your friends, and not to me?

Art
Managing Director at Exelby Publishing

From: Art Campbelle
Subject: Eagerly Awaiting
Date: September 9th, 2014 04:33 pm
To: Estelle

Am I being ignored?

Art
Managing Director at Exelby Publishing

From: Art Campbelle
Subject: Eagerly Awaiting
Date: September 9th, 2014 08:59 pm
To: Estelle

Estelle, as your Publisher I expect to see something in the morning.

Good-night,

Art
Managing Director at Exelby Publishing

A QUERY IDEA

I pulled up to Zacharie's place: it was dark and there was no outside light on. I was almost going to text and let him know I was outside, but I decided instead that I would just go and knock on his door, because then he would have to come upstairs and answer the door.

I did not want to text and feel stupid for coming over again, like I did the last time.

I walked up to his door, and knocked really loudly. It's a good thing no one was living in the upstairs of his house, because I am sure it's late enough that if I was sleeping in there, my knocking would even wake me up.

Hoping that tonight I would see a bit of affection from Mr. Complicated, I wondered if he would cuddle me the entire night, since I told him how sad I was, *when really it was all just a bunch of bullshit to land a spot in bed with him.*

I started knocking, and after about five minutes, a light from inside flicked on, and up the stairs I heard Zacharie come.

The door opened, I walked in, and then Zacharie immediately turned his back, and started walking down the stairs. This time, I decided to say something to him:

"Are you not going to wait for me?" I asked.

"No, why do I need to wait for you?"

"Because it's the nice thing to do," I replied, annoyed.

"I see," he replied, and then turned around where I could hear him go down the rest of the stairs into his bedroom.

I am really starting to think this prick is a waste of my fucking time, but I remembered it was for research, and I loved writing.

I walked down the dark stairs. I decided, rather than waiting to strip in front of him, I would just start stripping now, so that when I got in his room, I would be completely naked.

I quickly took my clothes off, and then took a deep breath.

I walked into his bedroom, the lights were off, and the TV was not playing either. I almost didn't know what side of the bed he was on, but I didn't care. I climbed on top of him, and then rolled onto the right hand side, closest to the wall. I was so cold at this moment because I was completely naked, and it was not exactly the warmest in his place.

I got under the blankets, and rolled myself as close to him as I could to get warm. I guess from being so cold. When I touched his skin, when he quickly jerked away;

"Are you ever going to kiss me when I come to see you?" I asked.

"Most likely not."

"Why don't you kiss me, Zacharie?"

"Because I do not like it," he replied.

"Zacharie, I kissed you two nights ago, and you never even kissed me back."

"Again, I told you Estelle, I do not like to kiss. I do not want you kissing me, and if I ever feel like it, then maybe I might kiss you."

"What are you going to do if I kiss you, Zacharie?"

"I am going to ask you to leave," he replied rudely.

And for a moment, I actually believed him, but thought I would test his reply.

"What do you even mean?" I asked, annoyed.

"Why don't you try kissing me, and see what happens," he said, in a teasing sort of tone.

"Maybe, because I am tired of being the only one who makes the first move to do something nice," I responded sourly.

"Last night I was about to fuck you, and you didn't want me to do it, but I did it anyway. So is that not considered making a first move, on my end?" He replied mockingly.

"Zacharie, that was not funny," I groaned. "I just want to kiss you, and I want you to kiss me back."

"I will never want to kiss you back, Estelle," he replied sadly.

I knew if I didn't stop his mouth from moving, that this conversation was just going to drag on, and neither one of us would be in the mood for sex, so here went nothing;

I took my right hand, drawing my fingertips to the top of his forehead, and I started to gently draw a pattern along his skin. I moved them slowly down towards his lips, rubbed his lips against my hands; they were so soft, and yet dry.

I moved my body towards his, and took the pillow from under my head, so that I was now lower than him, I then moved my lips about a half an inch away from his mouth.

Massaging his head at the same time my lips touched his, I started to see that giving affection to him, got a kissing reaction, and he started to move his lips against mine. Completely naked and helpless to his fingers, he started to massage my pussy.

I could not help but get overwhelmed by the way he kissed me; it was like he had so much to give, but didn't want to let himself go in me. I almost wanted to break the silence between us, but then my mind started to frenzy, because he was kissing me hardcore, and wouldn't let my mouth slip from his.

As he rolled himself on top of me, I started slipping his boxers off, so that he was completely naked on top of me. Slowly he started sucking my left nipple; this was my weakness; *I could not submit so easily, but Mr. Complicated was starting to drive me wild.*

I couldn't take it anymore; I wanted to move my nipple away from his mouth, and when I finally managed, he started sucking on my other one. I was in shit now, because I was so lubed, that I was praying he would have mercy on me, and just make me cum, and then kindly let me suck him off.

Zacharie stopped for a moment, and reached behind the pillows resting against the headboard. This time, he grabbed some black tape, and started taping my left hand to the bedpost and then the same with my right. *He is one kinky-complicated guy.*

Then Zacharie continued sucking my nipple, and started to extend his right hand that was propping my back up, and reached over towards the pillowcases resting against his bed. I could hear the box of condoms open, and I could hear the foil tear open.

He removed his lips from my right nipple, slipping the condom on.

"Are you ready?" He asked.

"Please be gentle," I said nicely.

"Be gentle?" He replied, confused.

"I am really tight down there, and last night you hurt me."

"I see," he replied.

He gently worked his way inside my vagina, and then slowly moved up and down a few times. At this point I thought he was going to fuck me nicely, but then, his gentle tone changed into the 'fucking Olympics'.

It was a thrust after thrust beating my pussy because he was going so fast. I just wanted him to slow down so I could cum, or even enjoy the sex with him, but he moved so quickly that before any of this could feel the least bit pleasurable, he was already finding his release; I was not even close to finding mine.

He immediately pulled out of me.

"That's it?" I asked.

"Yeah, I came."

"I didn't." I replied.

"I see," he replied, while taking the condom off his finished penis.

"Will you at least go down on me?" I begged him.

"No, I don't like it, but you can go down on me if you would like."

"Uh, no."

"Well, then I am going to bed," he replied. He then got up, went into the washroom, and then walked to his fridge for a bottle of water.

When he came back to his room, I was appalled, *can you say jerk much...?*

"Uh, were you even going to ask if I was thirsty?"

"No! Was I supposed to?"

"No, of course not. I must have forgotten, it was just you here."

"Are you mad at me?"

"Goodnight Zacharie," I said in a pissed off tone."

And he didn't even say goodnight.

I reached over to the nightstand, and grabbed my cell-phone. I wanted to type something to my Publisher while I was angry, before I forget.

From: Estelle
Subject: An Idea
Date: September 10th, 2014 11:56 pm
To: Art Campbelle

Hello Art...

I know you are expecting me to provide you with a sequel to my first book 'Loved by No Other,' but I have another project in the works.

Tell me what you think of the following:

Dear Mr. Complicated

I am appalled by your lack of disregard for the opposite sex, and my emotional attachment to the men who decide to bed me.

If you have not already noticed I am alone, looking to get fucked and pleasured.

The deal was that there was to be flowers, nights of endless dates, and lines of 'I love you.' This was to be an arranged date, and then possibly leading to 'bedtime meeting.'

I want to be cuddled and kissed passionately by a 'man' who knows how to please the opposite sex.

By the way you fuck me, sex is strictly for your gratification only, because when it comes to pleasing me, it doesn't happen. When the fuck will you be in a giving mood?

I mean the first time you ever had sex with me, was to get yourself off.

Can 'Complicated' actually love the 'Twisted?' Maybe I might just be that sort of crazy you're looking for?

How do I make this happen?
From
Yours truly
Little Ms. Twisted

A DATE COMPLICATED

September 19th, 2014

I am writing because I am so fucking angry, that I feel as though tonight I will get drunk out of my mind, and fuck Mr. Complicated retarded. If he would let me.

Who the fuck has sex with someone, and is so selfish he gets himself off, without pleasing the girl? Who the fuck does this motherfucker think he is?

I am a girl; I would like to be pleased and fucked nicely, and maybe if he is in a giving mood, even cum. But 'no', everything is about Zacharie and what he enjoys. I mean we have only fucked ten times, but I can fully see where this is leading.

I wanted a guy who would please me, not use me to please himself; just roll over and go to bed once he is done getting off.

It was so unfair; he finally kissed me, with some passion behind it, and then closed the door, once the hat was on.

I am so fucking mad.

Fuck you Mr. Complicated.

Little Ms. Twisted

Pissed off, and not satisfied.

Two weeks have now passed since Mr. Complicated and I started our 'fucking relationship,' and I must say: I am not very satisfied at all.

Every time he makes arrangements to see me, it's either late at night, or it's later at night. I am really getting irritated with this asshole. *How come I am not good enough to see during the day? Is he ashamed of me? I am a famous writer, for god sakes!*

I decided I was going to stir up the pot a little this morning, and see if Zacharie was interested in seeing me during the day. It was a Friday morning, and I wanted to be taken on a 'date.' The real kind where you wine and dine a girl, not take me for a quick bite to eat before you're planning on fucking me.

Estelle to Zacharie
Estelle- Good morning Zacharie
Zacharie- Good morning.
Estelle- Do you have any plans tonight?
Zacharie- Why do you ask?
Estelle- Well, I was wondering when you are going to take me out on a real date?
Zacharie- It will happen, you just need to be patient.
Estelle- Why don't you ever want to see me during the day?
Zacharie- It's not that I don't want to see you during the day, Estelle. I work a lot, and I don't really have the time.
Estelle- But you have time to see me at night?
Zacharie- That's different, I like to see you at night.
Estelle- Why, is it because you need someone to fuck?
Zacharie- Maybe.
Estelle- So if you are not going to take me out on a date, does that mean that you only want to have a 'fucking relationship?'
Zacharie- I would like to get to know you more.
Estelle- How do you plan on getting to know me more, when you only ever want to see me at night, to fuck me?

Zacharie- I will take you out on a date.

Estelle- When?

Zacharie- Tomorrow.

Estelle- So you are not going to see me tonight?

Zacharie- I have plans tonight to go and visit my friend who is visiting his family this weekend from Calgary.

Estelle- Do you want to see me after?

Zacharie- Not tonight.

Estelle- So you will see me tomorrow.

Zacharie- Yes

Estelle- What time are you going to see me tomorrow?

Zacharie- When I am done work.

Estelle- You are working tomorrow? It's Saturday.

Zacharie- I work weekends all the time. You have known this since you first met me.

Wow, I guess Mr. Complicated does not believe in taking a day off.

Estelle- Ok, will you at least you text me late?

A few minutes went by, and Zacharie never responded, which was typical. I only really ever got a text from him when he was in the mood for arranging a 'bedtime meeting.'

I wondered if it was possible that maybe Zacharie was not capable of having a real relationship, and for that matter, neither was I.

Initially, I planned on having a relationship with Zacharie, then writing about it, and exposing him and myself to the entire world. So I thought: why not just continue to work on customizing my plan, and see how things pan out between us.

I reviewed back to the last email Art sent me two weeks ago, when I wrote about Zacharie and how angry I was that he only pleased him-fucking-self.

From: Art Campbelle
Subject: Are you Angry?
Date: September 19th, 2014 07:01 am
To: Estelle

Estelle…

Is everything ok? Have you been drinking again? Don't take me the wrong way this is good, but really? Have you been drinking???

Concerned,

Art/Fart
Managing Director at Exelby Publishing

***

I decided to come up with a query to submit to my Publisher, and see if they decided this story idea was worth having a look at.

From: Estelle
Subject: Query Mr. Complicated
Date: September 19thth, 2014 10:22 am
To: Art Campbelle

Below is what you have been waiting for Art, let me know what you think.

QUERY: Mr. Complicated

Dear: Art

Do you know the story of how 'Little Ms. Twisted' plotted to meet 'Mr. Complicated?' When a newly Published Author decides to take the storyline of her life, and make it into a Book for the entire world, she does not exactly know what she is getting herself into.

Twenty-six year old Danielle Marie Michaud is your typical newly famous Author, but comes with a fucked-up past, and a sick twist of how she plans on creating her next piece to make her famous. After her Publisher moves her 'book tour' to next August she decides to take the advice of Melanie, her only friend in the small city of Medicine Hat, Alberta: to join an online dating site for random sexual encounters. Danielle feels alone, and decides that plotting to meet the right victim, who is supposed to be a one-night stand, is just the sadistic twist she needs right now; she plans on playing the role of the dominant sexual leader.

When Danielle first meets twenty-four year old Gaston Lapointe, a French guy from Boucherville, Quebec, who moved to Medicine Hat after finishing College, she is thrown off her plot when she finds out just how complicated he really is. His perception and arrogance really starts to frustrate her, and when it comes to pleasing her in the bedroom, it just doesn't happen; she no longer feels that she is the dominant sexual leader. A relationship established by sex, turns out to be a game of how Danielle can plot to make Mr. Complicated fall head over heels for her. During this process Danielle also decides to never lose track of how important this research truly is for exploiting Mr. Complicated to the entire world. Exploitation through the help of her Publisher, so other girls can learn from Danielle's hard research.

Does Danielle trick Mr. Complicated into falling in love with her? Can Gaston deal with Little Ms. Twisted's dirty past and closet of sexual demons? Can Mr. Complicated help Little Ms. Twisted obtain all the research she needs to exploit 'men' as the shameless assholes they are? Mr. Complicated gives Adult readers a sexy outlook on what it is that girls find attractive about the secretive, saucy, seductive side that young men have to offer older women.

Mr. Complicated is my second Erotica type of novel, and is sure to keep the reader coming back for more of Mr. Complicated, and his Little Ms. Twisted.

Thank you very much for your time.
Sincerely,
Estelle Ella Whiteside

After reading my Query, over and over, I decided it was time to send it to my Publisher and see if they thought I really had a storyline.

It would take several weeks before I would hear back from them, so in the meantime, I would not wait for Zacharie to send me a text. It was a Friday night, and by this time, I was tired.

***

Saturday morning arrived quickly, and I turned to my cell-phone, and noticed 'no texts' from Zacharie. I wondered if he was at work already, and whether or not he had fun with his friend from Calgary.

I then noticed a new message in my inbox from Art.

From: Art Campbelle
Subject: Excellent Review
Date: September 20th, 2014 07:10 am
To: Estelle

Estelle,

First of all, I must say, this storyline has had a positive review with the board, and we are pleased to offer you a lump sum for your first offer on this work.

I will have an offer letter drafted up for you by end of day, and you will have time to review.

Art/Fart
Managing Director at Exelby Publishing
Good work...

From: Estelle
Subject: Thank you?
Date: September 20th, 2014 7:26 am
To: Art Campbelle

Hello Art...

I am very interested in reviewing this offer, before I start putting my book together.

Estelle

***

I decided to text Mr. Complicated, and see what his plans were.

Estelle to Zacharie
Estelle- Hey, how is your day going?
Zacharie- It's going alright.
Estelle- Did you have a good time with your friend last night?
Zacharie- Yeah we had a few beers and went to the Casino.

Estelle- I see. So what are the plans for tonight?

Zacharie- What plans?

Estelle- Did you forget?

Zacharie- Did I forget about what?

Estelle- I am guessing you forgot that you promised to take me out on a first date?

Zacharie- Yeah, I tried to forget about that. I guess we could still go.

Estelle- You tried to forget about it?

Zacharie- I just had a lot of other things on my mind.

Estelle- Well I don't want you to feel as though you need to take pity on me, and still take me anyways, considering you did promise.

Zacharie- No, its fine. What time do you want to pick me up?

Estelle- Would it not make more sense for you to pick me up?

Zacharie- I guess, I sometimes forget you live close to all the Restaurants.

Estelle- Are you going to take me some place nice?

Zacharie- Sure, which fast food joint do you want to go to?

Estelle- Fast food?

Zacharie- No, I am kidding. Be ready around 8:00pm, I will see you tonight.

Estelle- 8:00pm?

Zacharie- Yes.

Estelle- Why so late?

Zacharie- Because I want to relax when I get home from work, and play some video games.

Estelle- I see.

Zacharie- See you at 8:00pm.

I was really starting to think that trying to get Zacharie to ever fall in love with me was going to be more difficult than I imagined; he was so Complicated.

I wondered about the other girls from his past, and how long it took him to fall in love with them?

I heard my cell-phone go off, but I didn't have time to review the offer right now; I had other things on my mind.

***

I didn't know where Zacharie was planning on taking me, so I decided I was not going to dress up tonight.

I wore a black pair of sweat-pants, and a pink sweatshirt as it was almost the end of September, and it was starting to get really cold out. *Why should I dress any different? It's not like he was probably going to dress up anyways.*

I could imagine he would probably be wearing a pair of 'blue' work pants, and some old scruffy t-shirt, with a dirty sweater. I was sure he would not wear a jacket his skin was always so hot.

My cell-phone started to vibrate; I walked over to my phone and noticed it was my Father calling me.

"Hello."

"Estelle, how are things going?" He asked.

"Lonely, and lame," I replied.

"I thought writing was keeping you company."

"It does Dad, but most of the time I am bored."

"You will get through it, kiddo."

"Dad, you do realize I am an adult right?"

"Sometimes I forget, Estelle."

"I see, well I am on my way out right now. I hate to cut this conversation short, but I will give you a call tomorrow."

"Estelle, why do you need to be like that?"

"Because Dad, I am on my way out the door. I am sorry, I will call you next week, and I love you."

I hung up the phone.

I looked in the mirror and finished putting lip-gloss on my lips, and then rubbed them gently together.

My cell-phone vibrated again.

Zacharie to Estelle

Zacharie- I am outside.

Estelle- Ok, I will be right there, I am just combing my hair.

Zacharie- Hurry up, I am hungry.

I immediately threw the phone on my bed. *What an ass! He is the one that wanted to go home and fuck around; playing his video games, and now he is rushing me because he is hungry.*

***

I walked out to Zacharie's truck, and got in the passenger side door, and I looked directly at him, and before I could even put my seatbelt on, he just started driving.

"I guess you don't care about safety too much?" I asked.

"Why would you say that?" He replied.

"Because I just got in your truck, and you pulled away as soon as I closed the door from my building, not even giving me time to put my seatbelt on."

"Oh, well I don't wear mine, so you shouldn't worry about it either."

"I do worry about it, what if you have an accident."

"I won't."

"How do you know, Zacharie?"

"Because, I just do," he replied in a smart ass tone.

I guess he must see the future, because all I can see is my grave.

"So you don't care about whether or not you have an accident, and if I have my seatbelt on?"

"I didn't say that," he replied.

"Well you might as well," I replied, rolling my eyes.

"Where do you want to go for dinner, Estelle?"

"Surprise me."

"Well there are multiple fancy Restaurants in Medicine Hat."

"Why do you want to go to a fancy Restaurant?"

"You told me you wanted to go on a date."

"So you are taking me to a really nice Restaurant on our first date together?"

"You don't want to go?"

"It's not that I don't want to go Zacharie, but I am wearing sweat pants."

"Well, next time maybe you should dress up."

I just want to tell him to turn around and take me home. What the hell is his complicated ass prob-

lem anyhow? Everything he does needs to be so diffi-cult, it's like he is purposely being mean.

"Can you turn your heat on in here, I am really cold."

"Ok," he replied, and turned it on.

There, maybe that would piss him off, I thought.

***

We pulled up to a really nice Restaurant, and Zacharie quickly got out of the truck, while I got out slowly, just to see if I could make him mad.

Zacharie walked into the Restaurant before me, and didn't even open the door, *typical complicated* I thought.

"Table for two," the waitress asked, and Zacharie quickly scanned the area.

"Yes, please," he replied.

As the waitress sat us, in a dark back corner, Zacharie was still looking around.

"Is everything ok?" I asked.

"Yes," he replied and turned his eyes to the menu.

"What are you ordering?" I asked.

"I am not sure," he replied.

"I see."

He never asked what I was going to order, and I started to get annoyed, *what the hell kind of a first date is this anyway?*

I decided to order Red Wine, and start drinking to make the night go by faster. Ultimately I knew we would end up back at his 'bungalow', if not my apart-ment to fuck.

"What do your parents do, Zacharie?" I asked.

"Why do you want to know?"

"Because, I want to know you," I replied, awkwardly sipping on my wine after the waitress brought it.

"Well, my dad works, and my mom works."

"I see, my dad is retired, and my mom works because she is bored."

"Why doesn't your father work?" He asked.

"My dad is retired, and I just never really asked him what he did before my parents had my sister Adeline and I."

"You have a sister?"

"Yes, her name is Adeline, and she is married."

"How old is your sister?" He asked curiously.

"The same age as me, why?"

"How is that even possible?" He grunted.

"We are twins," I replied in a smart ass tone.

Zacharie's eyes widened, and his mouth twitched, "identical twins?"

"Yes," I replied, sipping my wine.

"I have a brother."

"And how old is your brother?"

"He is your age."

For a moment I felt old, because I was on a date with a guy two years younger than me, who had a brother the same age. What the hell was I thinking? I started to drink more.

"So, Zacharie, tell me something, what is your longest relationship?" I said, oddly hoping he would not feel embarrassed to answer.

"Three years."

"And when did that end?"

"Six months ago."

"I see, and you have not been interested in having another relationship since?"

"No."

"Why?"

"I really don't want to talk about it, Estelle. I mean she is not with me now for a reason, so why don't we just change the subject."

"Ok, tell me how many times have you ever been in love?"

"Once."

"Wow that's a lot for someone your age," I replied mockingly.

"Why is that?"

"I was being sarcastic. Tell me something else, how many girls have you fucked, aside from me?"

"A lot."

"So I don't know my lucky number?"

"Nope, so I guess you will be left hanging," he replied, while eating his dinner.

"So you have fucked a lot of girls, and been in love once."

"Yes."

"Interesting."

Zacharie started to display a look of being annoyed at my questions. "Have you ever been on a date before, Estelle?"

I looked at him, and thought, *are you fucked?*

"Yes, Zacharie, I have been on a date before. What kind of question is that?" I replied, laughing.

"Well, when you are on a date, you are not supposed to talk about exes. You should be concentrating on getting to know me."

I was appalled by his lack of disregard for the opposite sex. He should fucking know, I am a girl, and of course I am going to have questions. And what the hell is his problem anyways, the only time he ever wants to see me is in his bed, preferably on my back, cuffed to his bedposts.

"I am really sorry, Zacharie, I guess it's been a long time since I have been on a date, I guess being good at only having a relationship with my writing is something I have gotten used to."

"I see," he replied, while taking the last bite of his steak.

"I think maybe you should just take me home after this, Zacharie."

"Whatever you want, Estelle."

"Well it's obvious, I just make you angry, and forcing you to come on a date with me was the stupidest idea ever."

"I see."

"Well, you're obviously not having a good time," I groaned, and took another sip of my wine.

"Did I say that?"

"No," I replied.

"Then just come back to my place tonight."

WINED

So after a first date 'wined and dined' experi-ence with Mr. Complicated, we decided to head back to his 'bungalow' for some after fancy Restaurant fun.

I remembered being in need to journal my ex-perience tonight down while it was occurring to me; I was about to get fucked by a drunk Mr. Complicated. Maybe he would go for a lot longer this time, and his drunken state would allow him to finally please me in away the last few weeks he has been so selfish in only pleasing himself.

My lips tried to find his, but he pulled away, and went straight for my nipples. He started sucking them, and it was such a rush for me.

I felt as though if I was sober, I would have 'cum' twice already, but I was switched off right now; I could not concentrate on climaxing and he just wouldn't give.

He started to slip my panties off with his free hand, "Zacharie please," I begged him, and I felt his erection start to get harder between my legs.

He rolled onto his side, and kept me positioned on my back. He lifted his body half over top of mine, started sucking my right nipple, and then twirling his finger around in my vagina, inside and out.

When he pushed his finger and pushed it up in-side of me, it hurt. Even being drunk I said it out loud, "ouch," I think Zacharie must have realized he was hurting me, because he pushed harder, and I could feel his erection growing. Being in the drunken state at the time, I could not remember as to why I never let a guy finger me, whenever I was sober.

Why the fuck does he like to hurt me so much?

"Kiss me," I shouted out, but he ignored my plea and kept wanting my nipples. He was sucking in a frenzy on one, and then going to the other. *I wished he would take his mouth and start licking my pussy.*

I started to feel cold, and not wanting to get turned off, I reached for his free hand to place my cold one in his.

Zacharie then positioned himself on top of me, and reached in his pillowcase for a condom. With him sitting up, and the blankets being completely off my chest, I was even colder, and starting to lose the feeling of 'almost ready to squirt for you stage,' and wither back to 'he is going to please himself now,' stage.

I felt my body start to shiver beneath his; I disliked being 'drunk,' I always got cold.

He slipped the condom on, so I took my hand, grabbed onto his dick, and shoved it inside my pussy. I was so cold, *I just wanted him to bring his body on top of mine, and quickly.*

He gently brought his body on top of mine, and pulled the blankets back over us both. I tried to kiss him, but instead he moved his head to the right side of my face, and started fucking me 'as usual.'

He was going so fast that I couldn't even enjoy it 'again.' "Can you try going a little slower?" I asked him.

Zacharie stopped, "I want to try something."

"Ok," I replied, wondering which way he was going to tie me up this time?

He pulled his penis out of me, sat up on his knees, and lifted my legs right and left over his shoulders. The blankets were completely off of me now, and I was so fucking cold; this was not fun for me anymore.

Zacharie harshly slid his dick inside of me, "ouch," I squealed.

"There, that feels better," he replied, and then started fucking me in the strangest, most painful position.

Zacharie moved in and out of me slowly, and then started thrusting harder. "You're hurting me, Zacharie," I whimpered.

"It's ok, it feels good for me."

Is he fucking serious? Of course he is! As long as it feels good for him.

"Well it does not feel good for me," I cried out.

"Stop talking, I am almost going to cum."

He started moving faster in and out of me, and now I realized that maybe he didn't give a shit about pleasing the opposite sex, and maybe sex was strictly for his gratification only. *I was right about this motherfucker all along.*

I felt my eyes starting to tear, because despite being drunk, he was hurting me, and this was not pleasurable at all.

Zacharie then penetrated as far inside me as he could, until I felt him hit my back wall. Then he pounded further, and further, until I could feel him shake. I was in utter pain, and was so happy sex with him was over.

I was so sad that he did not just tie me up and fuck me senseless the way he usually did. *This time, he really hurt me.*

Zacharie walked back to the bed, after putting the condom and foil in the garbage. He had his bottle of water with him; it was a routine every time he had sex with me.

"Can you cuddle me, Zacharie? I am cold." I said sadly.

"Estelle, we just fucked! What have I told you, beds are either for sleeping, or else fucking," he groaned.

"What if I massaged your back, then would you cuddle me?"

"Probably not," he replied, and climbed into bed.

I was starting to get angry, and I didn't give shit if I was drunk or not, I was not staying there anymore.

Book or no book, this was starting to fuck with my emotions, *but isn't this what I wanted?*

I quickly got out of bed, climbing over Zacharie, and he finally took some notice.

"Estelle, what are you doing?" He grumbled.

"I am going home," I shouted.

"What?" Zacharie said, confused.

"I am going home; it's obvious you are finished with me, so now I can go home," I sobbed.

I almost felt like I wanted to cry, because I was as hurt as when he was fucking me in that awful posi-tion, and I was not pleased at all.

"Estelle, please don't go home."

"Why? It's quite obvious you don't give a flying shit about me, so why the fuck should I stay and sub-ject myself to you treating me like a piece of shit," I cried out loudly, folding my arms.

"Why do you think like that?" He asked.

"Because Zacharie, you never kiss me when I come to see you, or when you come to see me. You never cuddle me, and for the first time in two weeks, tonight was the first time you ever took me on a date, and then got mad at me because I wanted to know more about you."

"You wanted to know about my ex-girlfriends; I didn't want to talk about it, and I still don't want to talk about it."

"Well, you could at least fucking cuddle me, I am cold and just want you to hold me."

"If you are cold, I can put another blanket on the bed."

"You just do not fucking get it, I am out of here," I shouted.

"Fine, if you want to leave, I am going to drive you," he demanded.

"No, because I do not want you to do anything for me. I can call a cab; at least 'cab drivers' give a shit about making sure their customers get home safe."

"That's because it's their job," he snorted.

"Friend, or someone you just fuck, Zacharie, everyone has feelings, and it's obvious you only think with your dick."

"Come back to bed Estelle."

"No," I replied.

"Come back to bed, your drunk," he demanded.

"No, I am not drunk."

"Do I need to restrain you for not listening?" He asked.

"Fuck your restraints Zacharie. Even cuffs and a gag will not stop me from leaving."

I was so angry; I did not give a shit what little fucking tactics he wanted to use to keep me here, I was gone!

"Come back to bed, and I will cuddle you."

"Zacharie, I don't want you to cuddle me because I fucking beg for it. A girl should not need to beg a guy that fucks her to cuddle."

"I want to cuddle you."

"You're just saying that, and now I feel so stupid."

"Estelle, please come back to bed."

Was I maybe overreacting a little bit? But even still, it would be nice if he kissed me, or pleased me one time or another. But in this case he never did.

I stripped down to my panties and t-shirt, and climbed back into bed, but this time in front of Zacharie. He was already lying on his side, so he put his arm around me, and then I fell asleep.

***

I woke up, alone in bed, and could hear Zacharie outside his bungalow talking with another guy. It sounded like he was speaking French, or at least trying to.

I thought the way he talked was funny, but maybe that's the way they speak French back in Montreal, and maybe he thinks my English accent is funny.

I got up out of his bed, and started to dress myself. Then I could hear Zacharie come in his place, and run down the stairs.

"You're up?"

"Yes," I replied, while getting dressed.

"Ok, that's good, because I am going to take you home. My friend and I are going to work on his boat; we are painting it blue. "

"Oh," I replied sadly.

"See you outside," he said, and quickly darted back up the stairs and outside.

Was he mad at me?

I decided to text Christina and see what she was doing today.

Estelle to Christina

Estelle- Hey!

Christina- Hey there girl, what are you doing up so early on a Sunday morning?

Estelle- Just at Zacharie's and getting ready to leave.

Christina- Is this the guy you have been seeing.

Estelle- Not really seeing, more or less just fuck-ing.

Christina- I don't believe that Estelle, surely you are his girlfriend.

Estelle- If I were his girlfriend, Christina, he would first have needed to ask me that question.

Christina- How long have you been fucking this guy?

Estelle- A couple of weeks. He is the same guy that I met off the dating site. Do you not remember me telling you about him?

Christina- And he has not asked you to be his girlfriend?

Estelle- Nope.

Christina- I think this guy needs me to sack him in the dick for using my best friend for sex.

Estelle- Christina, you are the one that told me to go on that fucking site, and find a guy to use me for sex.

Christina- Estelle, you have been bedding him for two weeks now. You obviously did not follow my 'random' advice.

Estelle- He only sees me at night, and then when he is finished with me in the morning, he drops me off at home. But I'm sure if I give him a few months, I will grow on him.

Christina- That's bullshit, where the fuck are you?

Estelle- I told you, I am at his place and I am getting ready to go home.

Christina- I will see you in a few hours, and I will take you out for breakfast.

Estelle- I am not hungry.

Christina- Come out for breakfast; I will drag you out of that apartment. Remember you mean a lot to me, and I like to see you during the day and night. ☺

Estelle- You always make me smile Christina. You are too good of a friend to me. From now on, I am going to be more available when you need me.

I finished getting ready, walked up stairs, and out the door. When I got outside, I stood while Zacharie's friend examined me. Then they exchanged a few sentences in French. His friend sounded funny too.

"Estelle, this is my friend Andre," Zacharie said hesitantly.

I was thinking he would have introduced me as "Andre, this is the random piece of ass I have been fucking, and get off with."

"Hello, it's nice to meet you, Andre," I replied, and started to follow Zacharie to his truck.

I was sure he was in a great hurry to dump me off at my apartment, but I was just as happy to fucking leave. I mean I was feeling a little used and needed some time to collect my thoughts, and maybe write a journal entry.

* * *

I walked into my apartment, and noticed that the dishes have really piled up. So I washed and dried them, stacking them neatly on the counter.

I grabbed my black journal and a pencil, and completely forgot about reading my offer letter from Art.

September 21st, 2014

This morning, my departure from Mr. Complicated has left me wondering: why is it so hard to get him to show any sort of emotion towards me?

Do I look like I was dropped on my face as a baby by my parents, left with just boobs and an ass, with a hole for him to get off with? I don't get it; this guy is so hard to understand.

My best friend seems to think that Zacharie is using me for sex, but that was my plan overall. Then I wanted to make him fall in love with me, but this task is proving to be harder than anything I thought possible.

Usually a guy enjoys hanging out with a girl he is seeing, and takes her to movies and out for dinner. But not Zacharie, he only takes me home to bed. If we watch a movie, it's one that he picks; he never asks me what I like.

I mean all of the times I have been to his place (he is not exactly the best host), he only ever thinks of himself, and he has never even made me dinner during the past two weeks we have been fucking. At least if he would come to my apartment, I would make him dinner and offer him a drink, before I offer him to take me to bed.

When he fucked me last night, he really hurt me. I wanted to beg him to stop having sex with me like that, but he didn't even care.

When I cried, he pushed further. I am sure he could feel my tears roll down the side of my cheeks and splatter against his hands, because I know they landed there.

Is he really that much of an asshole that he will only ever care about his own needs?

How do I get him to ever care about me?

How did his past girlfriend get him to care? Is it possible that Mr. Complicated has been hurt so badly that he does not want to care or love again?

What if I show him I can care, but then expose him to the 'world' as an incoherent asshole...? Would I be just as pathetic as the other girl from his past?

Wait a minute; am I starting to care about Mr. Complicated?

I am confused, this entry is finished.
Little Ms. Twisted

Has it really been so long since I have been exposed to the feelings of being wanted and needed by a guy?

***

Christina arrived at my place that morning with flowers, and it made me want to throw up.

"Christina, why do you continue to always bring me flowers, when you know how sick it makes me?" I asked.

"Because I like to see my best friend, and being a writer has made you so fucking gloomy. I think you should say 'fuck the writing,' and take up a normal job."

I never really thought of that, maybe Christina had a good point. The idea of my story was to get a normal job, and fit into society. I didn't need to let everyone know I was a famous author. I mean Zacharie knew, but he just was not the type of guy that needed impressing.

"Yeah I guess I should start looking for a job. I mean sitting at home and writing all day is getting really boring."

"Estelle, I can go with you tomorrow, but right now, you need to get your jacket on, because I need to take you for breakfast."

"Christina, I told you, I am really not hungry. Is it not time you got a boyfriend already? Have you been fucking any random guys? Maybe I should be bringing you flowers, girl."

"I think you need to stop worrying so much about my problems; and start concentrating on your own. Maybe you should start by cutting off ties with this Zacharie character."

I got into my truck, and drove over to one of the restaurants down the street in the strip mall.

I sat at the table waiting to order breakfast, with a blank look on my face. Christina frowned, "why are you so against being around me?"

"Because Christina, you are the one that told me to go on that stupid site. You put the idea of getting laid into my head, and now I am attached to this 'complicated' fuck."

"Estelle, you don't need to find someone to fuck; I think you need to find someone to love you."

"Well, I fuck Zacharie, and we do it every night. I plan on doing it for a really long time, so I think if you are going to be poking your nose into my fucking affairs then you need to find someone to fuck too," I shouted out loudly, causing everyone in the restaurant to turn their heads towards us.

THE OFFER

I decided to spend the afternoon reviewing the Offer Letter Art Sent me, I clicked on the attachment in the email:

September 20th, 2014

Exelby Publishing
1001 20 S E Read Street
New York, New York 12345Tel: 800-777-7777
www.exelbypublishing.com
email: admin@exelbypublishing.com
acampbelle@exelbypublishing.com

Dear Ms. Genevieve Adrienne Lapointe, (PEN NAME: Estelle Ella Whiteside)

We here at Exelby Publishing are pleased to announce that we would be interested in extending this 'first offer' on this 20th day of September, 2014 for such 'work' at present known as: 'Mr. Complicated' which you have submitted to Exelby Publishing for publication.

We at Exelby Publishing agree to produce and publish 'Mr. Complicated' on the terms and conditions specified herein:

You, Genevieve Adrienne Lapointe (LEGAL NAME), witness that for and in consideration of the mutual exchange of promises contained in this Offer, the receipt and sufficiency of which are hereby acknowledged, the Parties Exelby Publishing and yourself agree to as follows:

1.   Publication License. You, Genevieve Adrienne Lapointe, agree to grant Exelby Publishing for the period of five years the exclusive right to produce, publish, sell, and license 'Mr. Complicated' in such manner and form, and under such imprint as Exelby Publishing may deem advisable. Exelby Publishing may publish 'Mr. Complicated' in such form, as electronic e-book, paperback, and hardcover through the following territory; WORLD. You, Genevieve Adrienne Lapointe and Exelby Publishing agree that this agreement is renewable upon the date of its expiration, and will remain enforceable during an additional and successful period of five years on the same terms and conditions as herein specified, unless either the Author of 'Mr. Complicated,' or Publisher decide to decline such renewal in writing at least six months prior to the date of expiration.

2.   Royalties and Statements: An advance of Two Hundred Thousand dollars shall be paid to Genevieve Adrienne Lapointe upon acceptance of this offer from Exelby Publishing. Royalties earned by sale of printed books: During the period of five years between Genevieve Adrienne Lapointe and Publisher Exelby Publishing shall be paid at 35 % of the sales price received by Exelby Publishing on 'all' books sold until the cost of Publishing & Printing such work as 'Mr. Complicated' has been reimbursed in full to Exelby Publishing. After Exelby Publishing has been reimbursed in 'full' for all costs associated to Publish-

ing & Printing of 'Mr. Complicated' Genevieve Adrienne Lapointe shall be paid at 45% of the sales price received by Exelby Publishing on 'all' books sold.

3.   Calculations of Royalties: Royalties for Genevieve Adrienne Lapointes Published work of 'Mr. Complicated' shall be calculated no later than thirty days following the end of each calendar quarter. Exelby Publishing will provide a statement of 'Quarters' to Genevieve Adrienne Lapointe upon acceptance of this offer.

4.   Payment of Royalties: Payment of Royalties for Genevieve Adrienne Lapointes Published work of 'Mr. Complicated' shall be paid no later than forty-five days following the end of each calculated, calendar quarter. Exelby Publishing will provide a statement of 'net forecasted royalties' to Genevieve Adrienne Lapointe upon acceptance of this offer.

5.   Assignment: Exelby Publishing may at any time sell itself, one of its imprints, or the majority of itself, its holdings or licenses to another Publisher. The current offer with Genevieve Adrienne Lapointe and Exelby Publishing would transfer to the new owner(s).

6.   Future Work: Exelby Publishing shall be given the first opportunity to preview Genevieve Adrienne Lapointe's next Work, and likewise be entitled to extend first offer for new Works Publication.

This Offer represents the entire agreement between Genevieve Adrienne Lapointe and Exelby Publishing and supersedes all previous agreements re-garding the Work called 'Mr. Complicated', whether in writing or oral.

_____Date¬¬¬   _____   Art Campbelle _____

    Author's Signature Owner at Exelby Publishing

_____   Print

Author's Legal Name not Pen Name

LETHBRIDGE

It was now the middle of October, and Zacharie was away in Lethbridge for work. He officially left the first week of October, and his work extended his trip until the last week of the month.

I was still considering the offer Art sent me at the end of last month, but I would think exploiting Zacharies life to society should be much more valuable than two hundred thousand dollars. What if he sues me? It would not be Exelby Publishing paying for the costs associated to a lawsuit, it would be me.

And what the fuck was with Art using my goddamn 'legal' name anyhow? I hate my name 'Genevieve Adrienne.' Who the fuck names their daughter Genevieve?

I am so happy when I was eighteen I changed my name to Estelle Ella Whiteside. Even though it was only my 'pen name,' and at the time I was not a published Author, 'all' of my family and friends called me Estelle. I only ever used Genevieve when I was going on stage, but enough said.

Hold on, I will be right back, I need to respond to Art, I have made a decision.

From: Estelle
Subject: Regarding Offer
Date: October 14th, 2014 01:11 pm
To: Art

Art,
I still have not made a decision. I will need a few weeks to decide whether or not that amount is too low for me.

Estelle

I closed my laptop, and reverted back to my black journal.

I am really bored. I have no one to fuck me and I even miss my daily texting with Zacharie. I miss him inviting me over to his place to randomly fuck. And him not giving a shit about my needs... I sort of miss that too.

Am I even supposed to miss Mr. Complicated? Is this a part of my twisted game?

I was over the whole he 'never wants to kiss me' bullshit and have moved on to the 'used for sex only' with trunk of pain' stage. I really wish I could jump in my truck, and drive up to Lethbridge to put Zacharie in his place. But I was not ready to drive a little over an hour just to see him for sex; he might think I am desperate for abuse. I recently started working at a local bar, picking up some late night shifts whenever I could. Working was really helping to keep my mind off of Zacharie, and how I want him to fuck me the next time I am in his bedroom. Sometimes I wish he would just set foot in my 'apartment of twisted,' to see all the different 'accessories' my twisted comes with. I mean I have a 'fuck swing' hanging from my ceiling in the living-room; it reminds me of my bedroom back home. He might even be curious about my 'rub and tug' massage table; how I would love to get his sexy, naked, dominate ass on there. I would surely show Zacharie who's boss. Yet the most tainted aspect of my apartment would have to be my obsession of capturing the 'naked art.' I really wonder if Zacharie is in to posing?

The one thing I hope would not creep; Zacharie out, is the mirror I have directly overlooking my bed. I like to watch myself get fucked!

With Zacharie being away in Lethbridge meeting some new guys was also having an effect on my life. I mean it was the first time I was working at a bar, and did not want to fuck any of my clientele. Maybe it was because the name 'complicated, sexual, abusive fuck,' was not labeled on their forehead. Or maybe it was because I now had more than one friend in Medicine Hat. More than just Christina, who kept me from fucking my customers?

Today was Tuesday October the 14th, and I was looking at the clock in my living-room, hanging directly above my desk, watching the hand slowly move to four o'clock.

I closed my black journal, packed up my desk, and quickly went out to start my truck. It was really cold in Medicine Hat, but only lightly snowing I thought it was bullshit; *this did not happen back in Chicago.*

***

I sat in my truck while it was warming up, and looked to my cell-phone. It has been two days since Zacharie texted me, and I wondered if maybe he was fucking someone up in Lethbridge. I didn't want to seem too needy by sending him a message, so I tried to refrain, but my mind could not stop thinking about him. I kept wishing that he was fucking me in the back of my truck right now.

I decided to text him.

Estelle to Zacharie
Estelle- How is your day?
Zacharie- It's ok.
Estelle- Medicine Hat is lonely.
Zacharie- I see.
Estelle- I really miss fucking you.
Zacharie- I see.
Estelle- Since you cannot fuck me, have you been fucking anyone else while you are away?

Zacharie- No.

Estelle- So does that mean you only fuck me?

Zacharie- Am I supposed to be fucking someone else?

Estelle- Well, I was not sure; you never asked me to be your 'girlfriend,' so I thought we were open to being able to 'fuck' anyone.

Zacharie- Have you been fucking other guys?

Estelle- Maybe.

Zacharie- Have 'YOU' been fucking other guys?

Estelle- No, I have only been fucking you.

Zacharie- I see.

Estelle- So does this mean that I am your girl-friend?

Zacharie- I don't know if we are ready for that yet.

Estelle- Well we have been fucking since the beginning of the second week of September, so I think we are ready for it.

Zacharie- So what is it you want?

Estelle- I want to know if I am your girlfriend.

He didn't reply.

***

The next day on the 15th, I decided to send Zacharie another message.

Estelle to Zacharie

Estelle- You did not answer me yesterday, so I am going to assume your cell phone died or some-thing. Am I your girlfriend?

Zacharie- Good morning.

Estelle- Good morning.

Estelle- Am I your girlfriend?

Zacharie- How is the weather down in Medicine Hat?

Estelle- I have a feeling 'hell' might freeze over if you do not fucking tell me whether or not I am your girlfriend?

Zacharie- Did I ask you to be my girlfriend?

Estelle- No.

Zacharie- Then there is your answer.

Estelle- Ok, so you would be fine if I went out and 'fucked' other guys then?

Zacharie- If that's what you need to do, but then 'I' will not be fucking you.

Estelle- Well if I am not allowed to fuck other guys, because you will stop fucking me, does that not mean I am your girlfriend?

Zacharie- I guess in a way... you would be a girl, and a fuck friend.

Estelle- So in other words, I am not good enough to be your girlfriend?

Zacharie- I never said that.

Estelle- Do you want to continue to fuck me?

Zacharie- Yes.

Estelle- Then?

Zacharie- Will you be my girlfriend?

Estelle- Yes, now was that so hard?

Zacharie- I see.

Estelle- When will you be home?

Zacharie- Friday.

Estelle- You are coming home next Friday? ⏺

Zacharie- No thankfully I am coming home the last Friday of October.

Estelle- That is not until October 31st...

Zacharie- I know. ⏺

Estelle- Are you going to see me the night you get back to Medicine Hat?

Zacharie- We will see.

Estelle- R U GOING TO FUCKING SEE ME?

Zacharie- I WILL LET YOU KNOW.

Estelle- Ok.

As I walked into my living-room and glanced around, and my eyes caught the 'fuck swing' hanging from my ceiling. *I wondered if Zacharie liked videos?*

I was feeling a little 'twisted' this afternoon, with not fucking for almost just a little over a week, and decided maybe I would make a video of myself, naked, swinging back and forth on my 'fuck swing.' *Maybe this would get the attention of my now committed 'Complicated,' and he might want to come back to Medicine Hat early, to give my apartment a whirl. Since he has only ever been outside my building to pick me up, and take me to his complicated place to fuck.*

I took my cell-phone and located the video-record application. I walked over to where my mural for painting naked prospects stood, along with the various colored oils. I sat my cell-phone on the ledge of my mural and walked over to stand in front my phone, in full view for my Mr. Complicated.

"Good afternoon Lethbridge, this is Estelle Ella Whiteside 'cuming' to you live from Medicine Hat, in the apartment located inside my building. Zacharie you know where that is," I finished my saucy sentence and winked at the camera.

"Well, Zacharie, if you are wondering whether or not your girlfriend has some 'toys' of her own, you may have guessed I like sex as much as you do. In fact, I have my very own 'sex swing' that I am hoping that you will fuck me on, when you get back from Lethbridge."

I walked over to my sex swing, and started motioning it back and forth, while licking the tips of my fingers. I gently started to lift my shirt with my back facing my cell-phone, so only my naked back would be seen once it was removed.

I removed my shirt fully, and let it fall to the ground. I then kicked it approximately ten feet from where I was standing. "Hmm... I guess maybe I should take my panties off to. What do you think Zacharie?" I said, while turning my head towards the device recording.

"I have been such a twisted girl while you have been gone; contemplating so many different ways I would like to bend over, while you gag me, tie me up and then fuck the shit out of me. Oh my god Zacharie, I can feel myself getting a little wet for you, it's making my panties stick to my pussy. Do you mind if I take them off?"

I started to slip my panties off. As they fell to the tips of my ankles, I lifted one foot after the other, and then kicked them the opposite direction from my shirt.

I sat down on the swing, and started swinging back and forth still facing the opposite direction I was videotaping.

I then flipped backwards on the swing, motioning back and forth, and took used my right hand, to start master bating in front of the camera, so Zacharie would see my full frontal.

"Does it piss you off to see me pleasuring myself, Zacharie?"

And then, the time ran out on my recording, and I happily pushed 'send'.

***

Later that evening, while I lay in my bed, my night off, I wondered: *What did Zacharie think of my little knotty twisted side?*

Then my phone started to vibrate...

Zacharie to Estelle

Zacharie- You have got a very interesting apartment, Estelle. I am surely interested in seeing it when I return to Medicine Hat.

Estelle- I never invited you.

Zacharie- Well then, I suggest my 'girlfriend' invite me to her apartment upon my return to Medicine Hat, because if she neglects to invite me, I will unleash such a punishing that will leave her ass red for weeks.

Oh shit...

Estelle- Well in that case, Zacharie, how can I not resist to 'not' invite you, and 'invite' you to give me that red ass you threatened me with?

Zacharie-A red ass you will get. Keep in mind, the more you will beg me to stop, the harder the slapping will come.

Estelle- Bring it on.

ALL WAYS FUCKED

The last Friday of October came quicker than I anticipated. When the clock rolled to 6:00pm, I was in a hurry to get home and get washed.

I still never heard from Zacharie about whether or not he was coming home tonight, but I didn't care.

I went home, had a really hot shower, and then got dressed in a hurry.

I had a text on my cell-phone from Zacharie.

Zacharie to Estelle

Zacharie-I just got back from Lethbridge, but my friend is down from Calgary visiting his family again, and I think the two of us are going to hang out tonight. Maybe have a few beers, and catch up on our last visit.

I was fucking pissed.

He just got back after being gone for more than three weeks, and now he is going to hang out with his friend from Calgary! *Where the fuck is my invitation?*

Well there was no way I was going to sit at my apartment on a Friday night; I decided I was going out.

Christina was having problems with her current 'boy toy' off the dating site, so I decided to introduce her to my good friends, Christian and Jason, who were regular customers of mine at the bar.

The two of them rolled up to our building, and picked us up about five minutes after 11pm. Christian recently started seeing some French whore named Charlotte, and it pissed me off to see the two of them together. She was jealous of my friendship with Christian, and I was jealous that my boyfriend wanted to spend time with his friend the first Friday he returns, after being gone for almost three weeks.

"Where do you ladies want to go tonight?" Jason asked.

"I need to get fucking wasted, so any place that has an unlimited supply of alcohol is fine by me," I replied.

"Can you say alcoholic," Charlotte replied under her breath.

"Can you say slut," I looked at her and smiled.

"Would you both stop it," Christian begged.

"You're right Christian, I shouldn't fight her. That's your bitch, and I don't have a bitch, my dog died decades ago," I said harshly.

"Why do you have to be such a bitch yourself, Estelle?" Charlotte screamed.

"It takes a bitch to know one," I replied childishly.

"Estelle, what the hell is your problem?"

"My problem is that Christian comes to the bar every night during the week and tells me what a fucking bitch you really are."

"Christian, why are you talking to Estelle about our problems?"

Christian gave me a dirty look, and replied. "Charlotte I don't know what Estelle is talking about. I only go to the bar to drink with Jason."

"Keep me out of your argument," Jason said, laughing.

"What the hell is so goddam funny?" Charlotte screamed.

"Would you shut the fuck up already?" I demanded.

"Estelle if anyone should shut the fuck up, it is you," Charlotte replied.

"All you do is repeat everything I ask you to. Why the fuck did you need to come out with us anyway?"

"Because I am having a night out with my boyfriend, you fucking idiot."

"Charlotte, you are the fucking idiot. None of us even wanted you to come with us to begin with. The only reason we invited you is because we feel sorry for Christian," I laughed.

"And why would you all feel sorry for Christian?"

"Because he is dating you."

"Why did you even need to come out tonight, Estelle? Where the fuck is your boyfriend?"

"He is busy tonight, and my relationship does not concern you, cunt."

"Christian, are you going to let her talk to me like that?"

Christian sat and said nothing...

"You are ridiculous. Any bitch that needs her man to defend her is a fucking idiot. I cannot believe I have to spend the rest of my night with you," I complained.

"I refuse to go out with your friend Christian, she is such a bitch," Charlotte said.

"Well you can get the fuck out of my friend's truck anytime, hoe bag," I shouted.

"Estelle, enough," Christian said in a loud voice.

"Stop the fucking truck," Charlotte demanded, and Jason slammed on the brakes. Poor Christina was sitting on the left hand side of Christian, who was sitting in the middle. "I am getting the fuck out, and Christian, if I mean anything to you, I know you will not stay in this truck," she scolded.

"Christian I really need you. Please, Zacharie does not even want to see me tonight, so I need my best customer. I am sorry, but I tried to be nice to her, and you know she started it. I need you; please don't leave me alone to drink."

Christian kept his eyes firmly locked on my position, and then rolled his eyes to Charlotte, who got out of the truck, and stood on the sidewalk. I turned my face to her, and gave a really dirty smile, because I knew Christian would not ditch me. *I mean after all I served him at his favorite bar in all of Medicine Hat.*

"Charlotte, I am sorry, but until you can learn to be nice to Estelle, I don't want to see you," Christian said. He reached over me in the front seat and closed the door to Jason's truck.

"So that was a good round of drama for you, wasn't it, Christina?" Jason joked.

"Yeah a little more than I wanted, and now I just want to go, get drunk myself and forget about it."

"That's what happens with an uneven number of guys and girls Christian, you should know that," Jason laughed.

"Just drive to your house buddy, we can stay and drink there."

"What? We are going to drive downtown and drink at Jason's? I wanted to go out and get drunk," I said, in a pissed off tone.

"Estelle, you are going to Jason's and you can drink there," Christian said, raising his voice.

Since when the fuck did Christian become my Mr. Complicated? Why should I listen to him?

I sat back in the passenger seat in front of him, and crouched down. I knew he was really angry with me, but I didn't care. When it came to some bitch telling him what to do all the time, and using him to drive her fat ass around, there I was no way that I was going to like her.

***

The next morning, I woke up in Jason's bed. I was a little sore from drinking, and looked at my cellphone; there was no message from Zacharie.

I was so hurt that he didn't want to see me last night that I basically drank myself to the point of being tired, and then crashed on Jason's bed.

I walked into the living-room to see Jason watching TV; it was so loud that I could barely hear anything else.

"Where is Christian?" I asked.

"Downstairs sleeping. I didn't want to wake anyone up, so I decided to come and sit in the living-room when I woke up this morning, and watch TV."

"Oh! And where is Christina?"

"I laid her down on the water bed in the spare room downstairs, she was not feeling too good, and found my place really cold."

"How could she find it cold? It's boiling in here."

"I turned the heat up to 89 last night."

"Where did you sleep?"

"In the room next to mine," he smiled.

"Why didn't you wake me up, I would have gone in that room and given you yours."

"Because you didn't want to stop drinking last night, so that was the only room with a lock on it.

Christian locked you in my room until you fell asleep, and then I unlocked it this morning."

"Fuck you both," I laughed.

I was so happy that I found two guys that were now my favorite drinking buddies. Whoever said 'customers' cannot be a bartender's best friend was full of shit. I loved these guys… just not enough to replace Mr. Complicated with one of them.

"That's alright, Christian and I are going to put locks on every room, so when you get drunk, we will throw you in the closest room until you shut up."

"Well, my boyfriend won't let you do that," I replied, frowning.

"Who is your boyfriend anyways? Didn't he just get back from Lethbridge yesterday? Why didn't you see him?"

Jason had a good point, why didn't he see me? I am his girlfriend, and my own friends want to spend more time with me than he does? And I just met them!

November 1st, 2014

I never thought I would be so mentally fucked-up that I would actually write a journal entry from my friend Jason's place; whom, by the way, I just met a few weeks ago at work. But I have something I really need to get off my chest.

I promise if you just listen to me right now, I will glue this blank sheet of paper in you, upon my return home later this morning. Do we have a deal? Of course we do! You cannot talk back to me…lol.

Zacharie, the 'Mr. Complicated' I have been fucking, who finally asked me to be his girlfriend while he was out working in Lethbridge, just got back last night after being gone for a little over a three weeks.

He decided that instead of coming to see me he wanted to go and see his friend who is visiting again from Calgary. Who the hell is this guy anyway? Is he actually a 'he' and not a 'she?'

I am really confused though, because his dick has not been inside of me for over three weeks. Yes, we have gone a few days here and there without fucking, but I mean, I was going to be home, and it was a Friday night.

I had my 'fuck swing' all ready for him to fuck me in. Could Zacharie be fucking someone else?

In the middle of my confusion, my two new 'customers' I mean friends from work, took me out last night. I even made Christian have a fight with his slut last night. Then I made him choose between her or I. How is it possible that a guy I am not fucking chooses me over some bitch he is fucking? That makes no sense.

I am just as bad as Mr. Complicated, look at what I am doing to people who are at least trying to be friends to me. And I am supposed to be trying to get Zacharie to care about me, not Christian. Am I really that twisted and fucked-up, that I want to destroy everyone's life?

I wish Zacharie would hold my hands, look me in the eyes, and fuck me slowly, the way I like to be fucked. But he just can't bring himself to fuck me nicely, let alone be a good boyfriend.

Why the fuck am I wasting my time on this guy?

Why am I even playing this 'Little Ms. Twisted?'

Because I am Twisted.'

Little Ms. Twisted

***

I was so angry after Jason took me home, that I decided I was not going to text Zacharie; I would let him text me, if he wanted to see me.

I grabbed the blank, crumpled-up paper out of my pocket, and walked over to my desk. I opened the top drawer, and pulled out my black journal, flipping to a blank page. I un-crumpled the paper, gently fold-ed it four times and stuck it between two pages. I then reached back in the drawer, grabbed a black pen, and started jotting.

It is almost seven on a Saturday night, and Zacharie didn't see me last night when he got back; I was almost in tears.

I really do mean nothing to this guy, so why am I putting myself through this?

Just for a book to please my Publisher?

I decided last night was really long enough for me, so I wanted to go to bed. Around 2:00am that morning, I heard someone come into my apartment, I immediately got up, because living alone was not something I was too fond of.

I walked out into my living-room to see Christian sitting on my couch.

"Is everything alright?"

"Yeah, why?"

"Just wondering, never seen you come in so late since we started hanging out the last couple of weeks. You seem sad?" I replied softly.

"Charlotte won't talk to me, Estelle."

"Really Christian, you want to talk to her, after she couldn't be nice to me?"

"Estelle, you were never really nice to her."

"Why do you say that?"

"Because she tried to be your friend, and you just threw her to the curb because she was not your cup of tea. I have never treated anyone you liked rudely, so why are you doing it to me?"

"Christian the only friend I have that you have met, is Christina."

"You still could have been nicer to her, Estelle. After all the time I have spent at your work, drinking, and pouring my heart out to you about Charlotte."

"She is not good enough for you Christian, you deserve better."

"And a guy that fucks you and then throws you aside like trash, is good enough for you?"

Wow that was honest, but Christian didn't understand that I am doing this for research.

* * *

Thankfully, when I went to work the next afternoon Christian was gone, but I was still pissed off with my so-called boyfriend Zacharie. Yet I was not going to let him ruin my Sunday. If he wanted to be an asshole, I have decided I am going to be a bitch.

I got a text message from Mr. Complicated during my shift.

Zacharie to Estelle

Zacharie- How was your weekend?

Estelle- It was great, thanks for asking.

Zacharie-What did you do?

Estelle- Spent the weekend with Christian and Jason.

Zacharie- Who is Christian? Who is Jason?

Estelle- A couple of guys I met at the bar.

Zacharie- So now you go to bars, and meet random guys?

Estelle- NO! Since you were working in Lethbridge I got a job at a bar, and make friends with my customers. ☐

Zacharie- I see.

Estelle- And yes, for your information, I am probably going to stay over at his place again tonight.

Zacharie- YOU stayed over at his place?

Estelle- YES I did.

Zacharie- I see.

Estelle- I had nothing else to do.

Zacharie- Do you want to go and see a movie tonight?

Estelle- Are you asking me out on a date?

Zacharie- Do you want to go and see a movie tonight?

Estelle- Sure, but I get to pick the movie.

Zacharie- Well there is one that came out I want to see, so if you are going to pick the movie, maybe you should go with your friends.

Wow I am not even allowed to pick a fucking movie.

Estelle- Its ok, we can go and see whatever movie you want, I don't like picking movies any way, I just like to watch them.

***

After the movie, during which Zacharie did not hold my hand, or even touch me at all, *I started to wonder: were we really boyfriend and girlfriend?*

He decided to take me back to his place, and I knew that we were going to fuck, but for his pleasure and not mine. I was fucked all ways round.

It was late, and I was really cold, so I climbed into Zacharie's bed.

"Do you think you could put the white blanket on the bed tonight, Zacharie?"

"Why are you cold?" He asked.

"Yes," I replied, and then covered my face with his blankets.

Zacharie spread the blanket over the entire bed, and then climbed in with only his boxers on. I was completely naked, because I knew his hands would enjoy finding my tits better uncovered.

Zacharie rolled over to his side, so his face was right in front of mine. I took my nose and gently rubbed his.

"You have a big nose," I said to him.

"I see, and I also have a big dick."

"Yes, I can see that too," I replied, and used my hand to start massaging his penis.

"I want you to rub it like this," he directed, taking his hand and showing me how he liked to be rubbed.

"You didn't like the way I was rubbing you?"

"I just want you to rub it the way I like," he replied.

"Well what about what I like, Zacharie?" I asked him.

"What do you like?" He asked curiously.

"I like to cum too," I replied.

"You do cum," he groaned.

"Zacharie, you have never made me cum."

"Really...?" He replied, sounding shocked.

"Zacharie, every time you fuck me, you go so quickly that I can't cum. Or else you handcuff me to your bedposts and spank my tits for your gratification only. That surely does not make me cum."

"Well Estelle, you have never made me cum either," he replied. *I was in utter shock?*

"What are you talking about? You cum all the time."

"Yes, but I am working to make myself cum; it's different when you are working for it to make me cum."

"How the hell does that even make sense, Zacharie," I replied, really angry now.

"When I am on top of you, fucking, I am doing all the work to make myself cum."

"So if I start going on top of you, I will be doing all the work to make you cum, is that what you are trying to say?" I asked.

"Exactly."

"So if I can make you cum, will you then start making me cum?"

"Maybe, depends on what makes you cum. You have never told me."

"When someone has sex with me slowly, I cum. Or sex without a condom."

"Why is that the only way that you cum?"

"It makes me feel like the person having sex with me cares, or maybe even loves me."

"Well I will fuck you slowly, when you start working for it and making me cum."

Is he honestly for real?

I was so angry that I positioned myself on top of him. I did not give a fuck whether or not I was wearing lipstick, or what he would like; I became a mad women.

"Fine Mr. Complicated, I will fuck you the way you like."

"Who," he replied, and before he could finish the sentence, my mouth was on his, and I started kissing him.

I slipped my tongue in his mouth, and did not care whether or not he brushed his fucking teeth, fuck whatever the hell he thought was proper or even liked.

I took both my hands and placed them firmly in his, massaging his dick with the walls of my vagina. I could feel him getting erect, and this was exactly my fucking plan. I would fuck the shit out of him until the little mother-fucker blows his fucking load.

"Where are your condoms?"

"In the pillowcase."

"You better be quick putting it on, Zacharie, because I am in the mood to fuck, and hard."

"Ok," he replied, and slipped the condom I opened onto his erecting cock.

I positioned myself on him, and his dick slid right in. I was so goddamn horny and angry; I just wanted to pound his cock.

I gripped onto the headboard of his bed, and started moving up and down quickly. He took both his hands, cupped my breasts and started massaging them gently. It felt really good.

I let out a tiny moan from him rubbing my breasts, and then caught wind of the fact I was moving slower, and it was starting to feel really good for me.

"Go faster," he directed.

"No, this feels good for me," I moaned myself, and then leaned down and started kissing him.

I used the headboard to gently ride him back and forth for a few minutes, and when I was about to cum, he gripped my waste tightly, pushing his dick further into me until it hit the sore spot of my wall.

"Ouch," I replied.

"Shht..." he said.

He started moving really fast, causing my pussy to start beating from soreness.

"Please, you're hurting me, Zacharie," I cried.

"Just another minute," he groaned, and I could feel it all build in his head.

"I'm cuming," he shouted.

As soon as he said he was cuming, I started riding him, pushing his dick further into my pussy even though it was throbbing. I wanted to make him feel good, and show him that this is what I want him to do to me.

He was completely spent, sprawled out in bed, and breathing heavily.

"That's what I want you to do to me, Estelle."

"Well I would like you to do that to me," I replied.

THE CLOSET OF COMPLICATED

It was now into early November when I decided to put off my journal entries for a while, and spend some time getting to know Mr. Complicated was in order.

I recently received great feedback from Art; he was talking about offering me more money for 'Mr. Complicated.'

At this time, I never stopped to think about the effect that exposing Zacharie as 'Mr. Complicated' could have on his life, but I was too busy thinking of myself, like he likes to do in the bedroom.

However, Zacharie has come a long way in the past week since he returned home from Lethbridge. I mean, he is not fucking to please me, but he is starting to see me more often than before.

I now see him at least three to four times a week, still at night, but he must enjoy the fucking because he calls me over all the time now. Our relationship has now moved passed the texts, to him using those pleasurable fingertips and actually dialing my number on his cell.

He was 'complicated' and I was being 'fucked' like I wanted for so long, but he has still not made me cum yet.

I wondered what it would take to get his head to pleasure me the way I needed.

I decided the only way for him to ever open up to me, was for me to make him open up about his past relationship. There must be some reason as to why he does not want to pleasure me. Maybe he just does not want his penis to rope in another girl.

***

I arrived at Zacharie's place, after I stopped to pick us up dinner. I was really upset that he never wanted to make me dinner at his place, and I was always either the one cooking, or else bringing dinner, when do guys ever take a turn in this?

As we sat and had dinner, he was so quiet, and just concentrating on eating. I thought I would break the silence, and find out more about Mr. Complicated.

"What was your ex-girlfriend like?"

"Why the hell do you want to know about my ex-girlfriend," he scolded.

"I am interested to know about what your relationship was like with her, that's all," I replied.

"We were together, and then we broke up."

"Did you both live together?" I asked.

"Yes," he replied sourly.

"Did she leave you?"

"Yes... I mean no. I left her," he replied in an angry tone.

"So in other words, you broke up with her."

"Yes."

"Why did you break up?"

"I really don't want to talk about it."

"Did you love her, Zacharie?"

"Yes."

"Then why would you leave her?"

"Because she fucking cheated on me, ok," he shouted.

I looked at him in shock.

"You don't need to get mad at me, Zacharie, I am only curious."

"Well, then stop talking about her."

"I want to know about your past, because you keep yourself so distanced from getting close to me, and I only think it's fair I be allowed to understand why."

"Estelle, she cheated on me, and that's all I will say."

"Did you spend a lot of time together?"

"No, I was always working."

"Is that why she cheated on you?"

"I don't know? She cheated on me several times while we were together."

"And you stayed with her, why?"

"Because I loved her."

"You don't think you should have left her after the first time she cheated on you, Zacharie?"

"Why the hell does this matter, Estelle?"

"I would never cheat on you, Zacharie," I replied, looking him directly in the eyes.

"That's what my ex-girlfriend said to me too," he groaned, and took another bite out of his cheeseburger.

"I am not your ex-girlfriend."

Then he looked at me.

"I know that."

"Do you?" I asked.

"I know you are not my ex-girlfriend, but all girls are the same."

"No, we are not all the same."

"When she was with me, I had to support her, and drive her all over the place, because she was too lazy to walk anywhere, unless she was in a swinging mood."

"You don't need to do those things for me, Zacharie. I am capable of taking care of myself, and even if at some point in my life I got to that point, I would still not expect a guy to be there for me."

"I see, well she expected me to fucking do everything for her."

"Well, I would not ask you to do anything for me; I think you can pretty much see that."

"What do you mean?"

"Well, I bring you dinner, and drive back and forth to come and see you. I have made you dinner and fuck you the way you get off, so that should tell you I am not your ex-girlfriend."

"I know that."

"Sometimes I don't think you realize, but you keep yourself so closed off. Maybe you had a shitty past with your ex, but I am paying the price for it."

"How is that so?"

"Because you will not get over what she did to you, and that in turn prevents you from ever allowing yourself to have a normal relationship with me."

"I just don't want to get close to you, for you and I to move in together, and have you take everything from me, because my ex tried to do that with me."

"Again, I am not your ex, and I would never take anything from you. I have a place to live, my own vehicle, and my own money, so why would I need to do that to you? If I ever became broke living in Medicine Hat, I would move home with my parents, before I would ever have someone else take care of me."

"I see, well she was the complete opposite."

"Yes, because you're ex-girlfriend is not me."

"She would make me so mad, you have no idea Estelle."

"So tell me, how did she make you so mad, Zacharie?"

"I did everything for her: laundry, cooking, cleaning, busting my ass off, and she worked part-time, swinging with her friends without me. When I would come home after work, I would need to go join the fun after it already started."

"What the fuck is swinging?"

"I do not want to talk about it Estelle. Let's just change the topic, and leave this conversation to be finished another night; maybe once we know each other a little better."

What the fuck?

HAVE A CAP

Saturday, and it's party time, but I was just waking up. It was time to get myself ready for writing, and the annoying sound of Mr. Complicated with his phone was enough to wake this cookie out of his bed.

I had to be home for 7:00am and was in a dire rush to leave because he was so rude the night before with the whole pleasing himself and saying fuck my needs. I needed to go out tonight, and have a few drinks with a friend or two.

After I finished getting ready to go home, "are you going to walk me out, Zacharie?" I asked.

"No, I am too tired; just leave the door closed when you exit."

"Sure thing," I replied, a little annoyed. He had me in his bed and can't even walk me up the stairs. I don't get it.

As I left his house, I decided to text Christina, and see how her issues with her ex-boyfriend were.

Estelle to Christina
Estelle- Hey, how are you?
Christina- Could be better.
Estelle- Why, what's wrong?
Christina- Nothing, I just need a night out with my girls tonight.
Estelle- Well how about where ever you want to go?
Christina- I am not sure, maybe just Pub downtown.

Estelle- Ok good, I will text you a little later on, once I am done submitting a few chapters to my publisher.

Christina- Honestly, take a break, or else get a different job.

Estelle- I wish! And by the way, I did get a different job. Do not forget, I work at the bar down the street, but this job pays the bills.

Christina- Yeah, whatever.

Estelle- Ok, I will talk to you later.

***

I was feeling a little sexually frustrated today, and decided I would write Mr. Complicated a letter, stating exactly how I feel about our sexual relationship.

November 8th, 2014

Dear Mr. Complicated

I am appalled by your blatant disregard for the opposite sex, and my emotional attachment to all men who decide to bed me.

If you have not already noticed, I am broken-hearted and a mess; I was not looking for a fucked-up relationship to make things worse.

The deal was, there was to be no flowers, strings of broken promises, and bullshit lines of 'I love you'. This was to be an arranged bedtime greeting, with a 'see you only for sex' goodbye meeting.

I did not want to be cuddled, or kissed passionately by a 'man' who would do these things without showing any emotional attachment, or justify that he does not feel a thing for me and actually mean it.

By the way you fuck me, sex is strictly for your gratification only; when it comes to pleasing me, it just doesn't happen.
When will my cuming finally occur?
Only time will tell.
From
Yours truly
Little Ms. Twisted

***

Later during the day, I got a text from my friend, Christian, who just arrived back in town.

Christian to Estelle
Christian- Hey Estelle, how is everything?
Estelle- Everything is good.
Christian- That's great, I was wondering if you were free tonight to have dinner, it's been awhile?
Estelle- What, a whole week? I am going for a girl's night out at one of the pubs downtown, maybe we could meet there and have something to eat, with a few drinks.
Christian- I am not really into the bar scenes...lol j/k. Yeah that sounds like fun, I will see if Jason is free to come out.
Estelle- Well I look forward to seeing you, and maybe I will invite the guy I am dating.
Christian- You are dating?
Estelle- Yes, I am. Why? Did you forget?
Christian- No, must have just slipped my mind.
Estelle- Well, do not let his name slip your mind again. ☺

***

Estelle to Zacharie
Estelle- Hey Zacharie, what are your plans for tonight?

Estelle- And thanks for walking me out this morning, it was really nice of you.

Zacharie- I have no plans.

Estelle- Do you want to come out with a few girls and me tonight?

Zacharie- Where?

Estelle- Pub downtown

Zacharie- I see. Is it the one you work at?

Estelle- I work at a bar! So is that a yes?

Zacharie- I will let you know.

Oh my fucking lord this guy is complicated, it's a simple answer: yes or no.

Estelle- Ok, whatever.

***

Later in the afternoon, I decided I might hit the mall to do some shopping. However I was still unsure, and decided to see what Christina was doing.

Estelle to Christina

Estelle- Hey Christina, what are your plans this afternoon?

Christina- I was going to the liquor store to buy some booze for pre-drinking tonight.

Estelle- I guess you would not be interested in coming to the mall?

Christina- I would be interested in going to get booze.

Estelle- The liquor store is just across the street; don't be lazy because you don't drive.

Christina- I do drive, I got my license back. ⏹

Estelle- Lucky you, just do not go drinking and driving again.

Estelle- See you later tonight.

***

Estelle and Zacharie

Estelle- Have you decided whether or not you are coming?

Zacharie- Sure.

Estelle- Ok, be ready around 9pm.

Zacharie- Ok.

Estelle and Christina

Estelle- Hey, Zacharie is going to come with us to the Pub, and my friend Christian is also going to meet us there later as well. Want to be at my place around 9:30 to pre-drink with Zacharie and I?

Christina- What happened to the idea of a girl's night out?

Estelle- Christian is hot.

Christina- And if you could see my face right now, my expression would indicate 'who gives a flying fuck.' The last time I saw him, he looked like my ass with teeth.'

Estelle- Chill out, and just sleep with him. Who cares what he looks like, Christina. Just pretend you are fucking him, with a garbage bag over his head...lol.

Christina- No thanks, he is not my type.

Estelle- Then chill out and get drunk.

***

I got out of the shower, and there was a loud knocking on my door; it was Christina.

"Hey Estelle, how is your 'one-night stand,' now 'boyfriend' doing'?"

"He is more of a fuck friend than a boyfriend."

"Sure, sure."

"Whatever; I know the truth," I replied sourly.

"Honestly, stop being retarded; he is only a bedtime friend."

"He is a bedtime friend, but he is kind of my boyfriend too... I guess," I replied hesitantly.

"Estelle, you are supposed to see more than one guy; are you dumb?"

"Not the last time I checked," I replied, blow-drying my hair.

"What is wrong with you?"

"Nothing, I am doing what you told me too."

"No, I told you to see several guys, not one."

"Well, I don't do multiples."

"Have you two fucked?"

"Yes!"

"So why are you even wasting your time with this loser?"

"He is not a loser."

"Did it mean something to you when you fucked?"

"Listen, for all I know, he could be fucking all of Medicine Hat. Right now, I just want to give this a try, ok. Can you just be supportive?"

"Who cares who he is fucking, you're fucking him. Is he hot?"

"I like him, but my taste may not be what you like."

'Is he coming tonight?"

"Yes, I am going to pick him up in half an hour, after I finish getting ready. Do you not listen to anything I fucking tell you? Did you start drinking already?"

I grabbed my purse and walked out the door, leaving Christina in my apartment to wait for the drinking crew she assembled.

Walking out the door, I texted Zacharie.

Estelle to Zacharie
Estelle- Are you ready?
Zacharie- Yes.
Estelle- Ok, sounds good, be there in a few minutes, just leaving my apartment.
Zacharie- Then you will be here in ten minutes.
Estelle- Whatever!

***

I looked up as I pulled up to his driveway and then reversed out of it so I was parked on the street, he was locking his door.

Zacharie hurried to my truck, and opened the door.

"You look cute," he said nicely.

"That's great, thanks. Now let's go drinking."

"Already?"

"Yeah we are pre-drinking at my place with some of the girls."

"How many girls?"

"I don't know, my friend Christina is there. She is inviting Laura and another girl, but I have only met the one girl before. "

"There are no guys?"

"Yeah, my friend Christian will meet us at the Pub downtown."

"Who is Christian?"

"I told you this before. I met him at work, and we have hung out a couple of times."

"You hang out with your customers?"

"Yes," I replied.

"That's interesting."

He did not seem too impressed, but who gives a fuck what Mr. Complicated thinks.

***

I woke up with a surprised lapse of memory, and looked to the right of me: Mr. Complicated was sleeping in my bed. I moved and noticed that my pussy really hurt.

I felt as though someone sexually beat the shit out of me, but I could not remember a thing that happened from last night. As I looked towards Zacharie, he started opening his eyes, and then just looked at me, smiling.

"Wow, the first time you have ever smiled in the morning after waking up next to me."

"Uh-huh," he moaned.

"I take it you must have had a good time last night?"

"Yeah, it was alright."

"Well by the way my pussy feels, I am guessing you fucked the shit out of me."

"Yeah, maybe."

"I see."

"Did I hurt you?" He asked in a kinder tone.

"Kind of feels like it," I sobbed a little, looking away.

"Have you ever had sex without a condom?"

"I can't remember, I might have once with my first boyfriend," I replied. *Knowing full well, I have never fucked anyone without a condom.*

Suddenly, Zacharie was on top of me and brushing his lips softly against mine. *This was the first time Zacharie ever kissed before I kissed him; I was shocked.*

He moved his lips to my ear, "I am going to fuck you without a condom right now."

I started to squirm, but I couldn't move because his hands were firmly locked into mine. Then he moved his face between my tits.

"No, please," I moaned, but he didn't say a word.

He started to suck my left nipple so softly, and it felt remarkable. The last time we fucked, he didn't give a shit about what made me feel good, and what didn't.

His lips found mine again, and as his tongue found mine, he slipped his penis inside me so tenderly. He then slipped each one of his hands softly against mine, and then started to move slowly inside of me.

"Please Zacharie, no," I whispered, but before I could finish my sentence, his mouth was back on mine. The kissing was getting hot, and the sex was penetrating deeper.

With his every move in and out, it felt as though he was hitting the right spot. I wanted to climax so bad, and then he pushed further, and I moaned.

He drew his lips from my mouth, and started kissing my neck, finding my weak spot for arousal. My climax started to build, and I could feel his erection inside of me, ready to erupt.

"Zacharie, please, I am begging you to stop," I gripped his hands tightly, and as he pushed again into me, a sudden rush of happiness found me.

I could feel him release inside of me at the same time as I did. Within a few minutes, he was breathing heavy on top of me, and I kissed his forehead, because this sex was different.

Did he just make love to me?

BRIDGE THE GAP

November 8th, 2014

Dear Journal

It has been two days since my last sexual encounter with 'Mr. Complicated,' and he made love to me for the first time. I never imagined Zacharie making love to me would make me fall in love with him. I have never had anyone, make love to me the way he did.

I have not tried to contact Zacharie, since he dropped me off.

I placed my pencil down on my open black journal for a moment. I need to finish my letter to Zacharie, the one I started several days ago, but I just could not figure out all the right words to say.

Dear Mr. Complicated

I am no longer appalled by your blatant disregard for the opposite sex, my emotional attachment to you since, we have made love has now changed.

I understand you did not noticed, I was previously broken-hearted and a mess. I was looking for a fucked-up relationship to make my next debut novel. One that would exploit the sexual selfish side you once showed me.

The deal still is, there is to be no flowers, on-going strings of broken promises, and I love you,' during our sexual arranged time together is fine.

I do not want to be cuddled, but enjoy being kissed passionately by a 'man' who would do these things without showing any emotional attachment, but would justify that he does not feel a thing for me and actually not mean it.

By the way you make love to me; sex is no longer strictly for your gratification only; when it comes to pleasing me, it has finally happened. Was it only because you were in a giving mood?

I mean the first time you ever had sex with me nicely, was when you woke up in the morning out of the blue and didn't put your cap on. And that was just two days ago!

Maybe it was not bright enough for you that morning? You still have me wondering.

That morning really fucked me up, because it felt like we made love for the first time, and sex was such a climax for me. The further you pushed inside, the more pleasure I felt, and 'cuming' finally occurred; I was now yours. Your head really roped me in, and this is where I now must figure you out, Mr. Complicated.

Can 'Complicated' actually love the 'Twisted?' Because maybe I might just be that all sorts of fucked-up you're looking for?

Only our time together will tell.

Cheers to all the great sex we will have going forward, Mr. Complicated.

From
Yours Truly Little Ms. Twisted

***

When I first agreed to find a target to exploit to the entire world, I was looking for a man who would disregard the opposite sex, and a woman's emotional attachment to the men she beds. *Wait, I mean...* I was looking to exploit 'anyone,' I could. I had no idea at the time that I would end up falling in fucking love with him.

How do I know whether or not Zacharie loves me? Just because he slowly fucked me, and it meant something to one of us, does not mean that he feels the same way as I do.

I looked at my phone for a moment. *Maybe I should phone him...*

Ring...

"Thank you for calling 'Zacharie Gagne,' I am sorry I cannot take your call right now. I am either away from my phone, or with a client right now. So leave your name, number, and I will return your call as soon as possible."

"Hi Zacharie, its Estelle. But I am sure you know my voice by now. Can you give me a call, when you have a chance? There is no rush," I paused, trying not to sound desperate. "Talk to you soon."

I picked my pencil up, and began writing in my black journal again...

I thought because I have spent so much of my life broken-hearted, that breaking someone else's heart would make me feel better. I also thought I would enjoy a fucked-up relationship, but at the beginning when Zacharie was fucking me randomly, it hurt my feelings that he did not pleasure me.

No flowers have ever bothered me, as I am not the flower type of girl. I am the strings of broken promises type, however Zacharie seems to be changing so much more, as side from our recent love making. He is starting to see me during the earlier part of the evening, instead of just after hours before our arranged bedtime meeting.

In the beginning I also did not want to be cuddled, so I thought. I never knew how much it really hurt, to be fucked and not cuddled afterward. Especially with my emotional attachment to the men who have bed me. I never imagined there was a guy alive, who could actually portray a cold-hearted mother-fucker like 'Mr. Complicated.' But now after we made love; is he really a cold-hearted mother-fucker? Only our time together going forward will tell.

Ring...

I quickly dropped my pencil, and answered the phone: "Hello."

"Estelle, its Zacharie, you called?"

"Yes, I called."

"And..."

"What the hell do you mean and?" I replied, in an angered tone.

"I did not mean it in a bad way, babe," he replied, in a tender tone.

Babe...Since when the hell does 'Mr. Complicated' call me babe?

"Did you just call me babe?" I asked, confused.

"I did," he replied, happily.

"You seem really happy that I called all of a sudden," I replied, surprised.

"Why wouldn't I be happy that you called, Estelle?"

"I just thought since we had sex the way I wanted, that maybe you were angry with me."

"I am not angry with you at all."

"Then why have you not called me?"

"I was waiting for you to call me," he replied.

Is he fucking kidding me?

"Why would you be waiting for me to call you?"

"Because that is usually the way things go between us," he replied, sure of himself.

"Well, Zacharie, sometimes things change."

"They sure do, Estelle."

"What is that supposed to mean?"

"What do you think about the 'L' word?"

SATURDAY NIGHT OF SEX

December 6th, 2014 a cursed day I would not like to remember, for this day is to mark the second last Saturday of the year I will spend with my Zacharie Complicated, because he decided before ever having a girlfriend, he would like to take a grand trip home to Boucherville Quebec. *Or am I overreacting because I miss my family in Chicago, almost as much as I antici-pate that I will miss him?*

We have been together a little under three. I sometimes think back to the call I got at home a couple of weeks ago, and when he asked me 'what do you think of the cursed L word?' I had nothing to say other than play stupid.

I mean, I never liked the hearts, the flowers, and all the bullshit that came with loving someone, but with Mr. Complicated things were different. I mean he told me things he had not shared with other girls, and over the last month, I thought he really came a long way from being so closed, to completely open-ing up to me. But did I love him?

I was sure I could share my world of writing, but today I was feeling pulled in so many different direc-tions. I mean Zacharie has never invited me out to meet his friends, or any of his family. He pretty much keeps himself so closed off from my fucked-up life, except for when he may have time the odd night throughout the week for me.

I went from seeing him once or twice a week, to seeing him a little more often. But now because he is going to be leaving, I didn't see him very much at all practically this whole last month of November. I am almost wondering with him leaving for Boucherville in only a few weeks if he will make time to spend any with me at all?

I know he is going to his friend Justin's birthday today, but could he not invite me? I am so furious with him; I only wish he knew how much spending time with him meant to someone so broken like myself. But I guess he did have a life before I decided to come crashing in on his so called independent sexual pain parade.

I decided to grab my phone and shoot him a quick text.

Estelle to Zacharie
Estelle- Good morning.
Zacharie- Hey
Estelle- So are you excited about Justin's birthday tonight?
Zacharie- Yeah, we will probably go to Justin's, and play some Beer Pong before heading to one of the clubs.

I waited for a moment before responding to him; this situation kind of provided a good chance for me to rain on his plans, and hopefully divert his cute ass to my place for some bedtime fun.

Estelle- Why don't you come to my apartment when you are finished with your friends at the club, or where ever you all end up? I am probably going to the Club with Christina anyways. Maybe I will see you there?

Zacharie- Yeah maybe.

I decided to stop texting him, get up and do something with myself.

I made breakfast, and then had a surprise visit from Christian who brought me chocolate. He was always so mushy; it made me want to puke inside, but I held it in.

"So what are the plans for tonight?" Christian asked.

"Well, I am thinking that you, Jason, Tia, and my friend, Christina, should hit the Club."

"Why? I do that every weekend. And besides, my friend Brock is driving out tonight from Edmonton."

"Oh, that sounds great."

"Try not to sound too happy about it, Estelle; you know how much he likes you," Christian teased and pushed me into the couch.

"Fuck off, and you know how much Jason wants you to smoke his rope."

"You really have a dirty mind; too bad you could not use that brain of yours to do laundry, it would be nice to come over here, and not have to clean up after you all the time."

"Christian, it would be nice if no one came over here at all," I replied, smiling.

He moved a little closer to me, took the glass of water he was drinking, and dumped it down my back.

"What the hell, Christian!" I squealed.

"Well, now I gave you a good reason for not liking when anyone comes here," he said in a smart ass tone.

"Fuck you, Christian."

"Don't talk like that, or I will have Zacharie shove his dick in your mouth, until you learn to use better language, or at least a choice of words that are not so foul."

"Why are you bringing up Zacharie's dick to me; are you gay?"

"Because I see that look in your eyes, and how glued you are to that goddamn phone, you talk about it more than anyone else does."

"True," I replied, blushing.

"Go get ready; we are going to Jason's place."

"I don't want to go to Jason's place."

"And since when have I ever cared what you want?"

"Always."

"Shut up."

***

As I got into the passenger side of my truck, I stopped to think about just how dependent I am on Christian. *He has become one of my best friends: should I not be dependent on him, despite the fact that Zacharie is my boyfriend?*

I mean Christian is my best friend and everything, surely if it came down to him deciding whether or not he would live his life for me, I am sure he would, he would for any girl who possessed boobs and an ass. *That's just the kind of guy he is.*

Really though, I need to think clearly right now. I want him to tell me how he feels, but he just says: 'am I not showing you more affection as we go?' *What the hell does that mean anyways? Is that his way of telling me he loves me, in some strange but practical way?*

"What are you thinking about, Estelle?"

"Nothing."

"You know you cannot lie to me right? I know those eyes and that tone, what is it?"

"Nothing, really," I replied.

As we pulled up to the red lights, across from the coffee shop on main highway heading towards Jason's place, Christian turned and looked at me.

"Estelle, what is wrong?"

"I don't know, Christian. Honestly, I really don't know what is wrong with me."

"Estelle, there is nothing wrong with you."

"Then why do I feel like this?"

"What do you feel like?"

"I feel like I really like this guy I am seeing, but I don't know if he likes me."

"Does he ever tell you that he doesn't like you?"

"No, but I have never met any of his friends."

"Maybe he just isn't ready to share that part of his life with you yet."

"But why? Am I not good enough?"

"Estelle listen, you are always good enough. Your problem is that you let what your Publisher has done to you in the past, determine how things are going to work moving forward."

"How is that really fair, Christian?"

"Well, you are thinking he does not like you, based on what, him not wanting to share his life and his friends with you so quickly?"

"Christian, we have been boyfriend and girl-friend for two months, and during the first month of us dating, the only time he ever wanted to see me was at nighttime, when we were going to bed. We would fuck, and then sleep. We rarely went out; if we did, it was late at night, and when no one could see either of us. How do you think I feel?"

"Maybe he just likes to keep his relationship personal, and between the two of you. The entire world does not need to know that you are in a relationship with this Zacharie guy."

"I don't want the world to know I am in a relationship, but I just want to feel like I mean something to him, because he means so much to me."

"In what way does he mean so much to you, Estelle?"

"I think I might actually love him, Christian."

"Then you just answered your own question, Estelle; you do love him. I am happy your publisher didn't keep you from trying to find true love, because it would be sad to see you never love anything, or anyone."

***

Sitting by Jason's fireplace, I could hear him and Tia fighting upstairs. Christian was watching his favorite movie: a love story that pretty much explained his fucked-up history with Charlotte, and I was so sick of watching that. He lived too much in the past, and he needed to move forward to the future.

Estelle to Christina

Estelle- Hey Christina, are you down to go clubbing tonight?

Christina- Yeah, I could use a drink or two.

Estelle- And I could use two or three.

Christina- Alcoholic.

Estelle- Maybe, but alcoholics drink alone, at least I drink with people.

***

Estelle and Zacharie

Estelle- Hey, are you going to come over to my place after Justin's.

Zacharie- I am not sure yet, text me later.

Estelle- Ok

***

By almost 10:00pm I was feeling a little dizzy; I randomly remember getting a message from Zacharie after I slipped into a red dress:

Zacharie- I am at the Club, when are you bringing that fine ass over here?

Estelle- We are leaving shortly.

"Estelle, stop texting him and straighten your hair," Christian groaned.

"Estelle, chug that fucking beer and don't be a pussy," Christina said loudly.

Of course when it came to me and drinking, I never wanted to disappoint my fan base.

***

I stumbled into Club, alongside with my dynamic trio: Jason and Tia. Secretly I knew Tia was fucking another guy; that's why they were fighting earlier. In my mid-drunken state I remember this shit.

Christian grabbed our jackets and checked them by the bar.

"Zacharie is here, are you going to come and meet him?"

"No, I am going to stay here and drink out of the way where I can keep my eyes on you," Christian replied.

"I don't need a babysitter, Christian."

"I am not going to babysit you tonight. Zacharie is here, and you are his girlfriend, therefore you are going to be with him."

"What about you?"

"There is no what about me, Estelle; you are here to see Zacharie. Now go."

"So what the fuck, are you mad at me now, because my boyfriend is here with his friends and wants me to come dancing with him?"

"If he really wanted you to come dancing with him, should he not have escorted you here?"

"Fuck off, Christian."

But even in my drunken state, Christian had a point. He was acting like more of a boyfriend to me than Zacharie was.

"Estelle, let's go dance," Christina dragged me onto the floor, while I was holding two beers. *Could you say I like to get my drinks on or what?*

I started dancing with Christina, and glanced around for Zacharie, but I didn't see him. Suddenly there was my boyfriend, right in front of me. And boy was he drunk, and I wasn't even there yet.

"You're here," he said, but it sounded like his voice was pounding in my head with the rest of the music.

"Yeah, I am here," I replied. "Who are you here with?" I asked.

"The guys from work. I see Christian is sitting over there."

"I see," I replied, glancing over to see Christian across the bar, examining my boyfriend.

"I will be sitting over there."

"What, you're not going to dance with me?"

"Not right now?"

"And why not?" I asked, but before he could even hear what I was saying, he was back at the table with his friends; he didn't even introduce me to them yet again. *Well, I could play the same game.*

I walked to the back of the Club where Christian was sitting on a bar stool.

"Did you and the boyfriend have a fight?"

"No, he is here with his friends."

"And he didn't take you to go sit with them?'

"Of course not, now why would he do that?"

"Why don't you go and talk to Brock?"

"Why would I want to go and talk to Brock?"

"Cause Brock is your friend and would want you to sit with him. Besides, he is adjacent from where your boyfriend is sitting."

"I know what you're trying to make me do, Christian, and that's not nice."

"Let me buy you another drink, Estelle; you're done those two."

"I have one already," I replied, and noticed that I was stuttering a little.

"Well, you should have another one that's full, not empty. You always looked better with two, rather than one."

"Whatever."

I took the two beers from Christian, and walked back over towards Jason, who was sharing Tia with a random. I lost track of Christina while I was trying to pull her shirt down, since she wanted Brock's attention.

"You shouldn't do that, Estelle," Brock laughed.

"And why is that?"

"Because your girlfriend seems a little shy of me."

"Brock, every girl is shy of you because what they see the first time you meet them. You take a Viagra at a club, and have a pencil poking out of your pants; it's not exactly the greatest way to start things off with a random girl you want to fuck."

"Honestly, you're such a square."

"That's me, Estelle the squarebo, remember the nom."

"Why don't you just speak French all the time, you know I would understand."

"Really, I didn't think you have the brain capacity for two lingos."

"Smart ass."

"You know it, Brocko."

***

"Where's my beer, I need my beer," I whined.

"Estelle, your beer is not here, and hasn't been for forty minutes before we left the Club. Now shut the fuck up," Tia yelled.

"I can't leave without my beer! I was not done drinking it," I pouted.

"Estelle, that's enough," Zacharie said aggressively. I actually noticed that he was in the cab with me. Aside from focusing on what was left of my sober attention in his direction, I was worried about how mad I was that Christian and Jason got me so drunk, and then my own boyfriend knocked me off with three rounds of triples.

I need to go home and get fucked, I thought.

***

We stumbled into the building, and I couldn't remember how the hell I got the door open, but it happened.

I was hoping Zacharie was as angry as I was, but not physically angry, mentally angry. I was so mad; he never once told me he loved me, maybe tonight I would spill my drunken truths: battle of the loves.

After Tia landed on the floor and started crying about how she cheated on Jason, I decided I would come to a coma-type of sober, and help her head off to bed. Mr. Complicated and I had our fucked-up to figure out once she was out of the way.

Once she was calm, I directed her to Mr. Cab that I called to come and pick her drunken ass up, and take her home to Jason.

Mr. Complicated and Little Ms. Twisted were about to invade the bed of 'Saturday Night of Sex,' and decide whether or not love was in the cards for them. I would battle my drunken sexual demons, and he would battle his truth of feelings about Little Ms. Twisted

"Zacharie, we are going to make love tonight."

"Estelle, you are drunk."

"Well, Zacharie, wake your partner up, because I am about to saddle up."

Before he could even say a fucking word, I ripped my clothes off and undressed his sexy ass. I then threw him down on my bed of sex, and started to ride him.

I was in a drunken state, and because more often than not, I would only fuck myself when I was drunk, the name slipped out that I was so angry at. I knew which name I wanted to scream out; I wanted to scream out 'Zacharie I love you, Zacharie I love you,' but instead I screamed out 'Oh Beer Bottle,' because I didn't want to let him know just how in love with him I truly was, and always have been. He was my complicated, and so hot, which made sex such a wild ride.

I wanted to take him, in every way possible; I could feel him penetrating inside of my pussy, and it was so soft, but hard. Then I rocked his tower of pleasure.

"Zacharie, tell me you love me."

"I love you,"

"Zacharie, I want you to say it,"

I could feel the sperm wanting to blast into my pussy.

"Zacharie, tell me you fucking love me."

"I love you, I love you."

Sober 'me' cums too. *Hold up, wait a minute, he loves me? Or is he drunk?*

Who cares, he said it, and now I can.

"Zacharie, I love you."

I could feel his erection reach its' limit, and my orgasm was about to take on a new high; Zacharie Complicated in love.

BEER PONG

December 13th, 2014, it's not exactly Christmas, but I am quickly getting ready for Zacharie's Christmas Party. I mean we have only been sleeping together every night for the last seven nights, but before that, I had never seen so much of Mr. Complicated. I guess the Complicated in love was much nicer than the Complicated unsure.

I loved him so much, it was hard to believe all the awful things my heart has been exposed to during the year of being in Medicine Hat alone. This so complicated guy comes along into my life, and takes my heart for a whole new tour on love, and life.

Zacharie and I were not together at this moment, because he had to wake up this morning and go to work. Even though I was only with him less than five hours ago, I missed him so much. I wondered how I would get through the rest of the month of him being so far away, and I decided maybe I would write him a book, sending him a few chapters every day. Maybe I could also send him some of the other work I had going on in my fucked-up head. It was simply only an idea, but my vault was never open to anyone, yet this love with Zacharie was different.

I was not hanging around my friends as much as I usually did, which was different too. However, I never forgot about any of them, and how they were there for me during the last three months, when Zacharie wasn't there as often as I needed him. Right now, none of that mattered, because my heart forgave him and I loved him.

***

I decided that I would maybe have a drink or two while I was getting ready. It was such a long time since I drank before going out anywhere, especially alone, but tonight I felt like bending my outlook on Alcohol, and using it to aid me in my shyness. I never liked meeting new people; I can remember back to my ad, where I lied online that I enjoyed meeting new people when I told my fellow fishy friend.

Oddly enough, the truth is that I don't like to meet new people. Usually I am happy with the ones I already know, and I tend to keep to myself.

I feel that my boyfriend should have his group of friends, and I should have mine. You learn after passing from one relationship into the next, that you never take the same friends you entered in with, or gained, out of that relationship with you. It's always a battle against the sexes and the testosterone. With my friends, I never had to worry about it, because they all lived so far away. Although lately, I've been making a lot of new friends at the bar in Medicine Hat, thanks to my dear old friend Christina who suggested I actually get a job aside from writing.

I cracked open my bottled alcohol beverage and looked at my phone. New Zacharie would be at my place in only a short matter of time. I decided to go out and start my truck, just so it could warm up, in case he wanted to take my truck to impress his friends.

I knew Zacharie was scared of my driving, because after him came for his first ride with me (outside of the bed), his face was pale fucking white. Ever since then, he has always wanted to be the one driving. *If only he was doing it to be a gentleman.*

I bet I've had my license longer than Mr. Complicated, but if it was a choice between deciding which of us was the better driver... in bed it would be 'Zacharie' and on the road it would be 'Zacharie.' *Damn Mr. Complicated was good at so many things.* Sometimes though I wonder how good his hands are, because he has never gotten me off with though to the touch of his fingertips melting my pussy sober. *I wonder if I would shudder at the touch of his fingertips to my pussy.*

I really need to stop thinking about sex; I am going to become a mad women. I thought maybe I should just go in the bedroom and masturbate, while imaging his hands working and holding me tightly, until I am sore down there for misbehaving, but I guess I could wait until he finally takes charge and does it himself. Once I let him, I would want him to cuff me to his bedpost and finger the fuck out of my vagina; I would be in pleasure heaven.

I remember him telling me how he disliked a girl sucking his penis, and it made me think of all the books I read about sucking cock. It helped me run a successful side business, until I was exposed. *Goddamn Mrs. Hopkins.*

In my earlier years, I believed sex before marriage was a sin, and if I did it, I would become of those girls that was going to hell. A girl going for a walk outside, only to be struck by lightning, but then common sense hit me at age sixteen and I joined the rest of the sex-a-holics in the field of pleasured pastures.

***

When Zacharie arrived, I already had my vehicle started, and about four bottles down the hatch. I was hoping that Zacharie would not think my tipsiness was too obvious, because I wanted him to have the perfect night at his Christmas Party.

I never told Zacharie that I was not good at meeting new people or that I often was really shy of meeting anyone I didn't know. I am aware that by lying on my ad, he thinks that I enjoy meeting new people and socializing, but that just isn't me. I have a specific group of friends, and that's who I tend to keep close to.

My friends are aware of my likes and dislikes, and when you meet new people, or for that matter, start a new relationship, those people tend not to give a shit about you.

I walked outside since I had my vehicle running, and I remembered just how cold the air was. I wanted to run back inside and retreat from the cold, but I had worn a dress to please Zacharie, because he told me how dressed up everyone else way going to be.

"Do you want me to move the truck for you, Estelle?" He asked.

"No its fine, Zacharie. I can move my truck," I replied.

As I got in my truck, I wondered just about how my intelligence was lacking at twenty-six? *Moving a truck while I was a little tipsy.*

Zacharie moved his truck, parking in my spot, and then got out and walked towards my truck.

I got out of the passenger seat and stumbled over towards him, and asked if he wanted me to drive with an open bottle in my hand.

He kindly declined, and got in the driver's seat; so I got in the passenger seat of my own truck, because I was too drunk to drive.

"Do you mind driving me to the store to get tampons?" I asked Zacharie.

"You really need to get them now?" He asked.

"Yes I do, because I don't want to wait until after your Christmas Party, in case something happens?" I replied.

After going to two different locations on the main strip, we finally found the right place to buy Tampons and I know Zacharie must have been thrilled. Although I wish he told me whether or not he loved me when he came to pick me up. I was sort of confused.

Just last weekend he told me he loved me when we fucked, but was it because I begged him too? Or because I was on top of him, in his favorite position?

These things made me wonder.

***

When we pulled up to the Tavern, I was on bottle number five. As we walked into the establishment, my asthma started a war with my lungs, from the people smoking right outside the door. Inconsiderate mother-fuckers. You are supposed to be ten feet away from an entrance. *What the fuck is with companies that do not enforce the law anymore?*

My lungs felt as though they wanted to collapse, but I was not going to let my asthma win tonight. I was determined to stay with Zacharie and have a good night. I did not want to force him to leave because of my medical condition; he might think I am faking it because I do not want him to have a good time.

As soon as I got inside the Tavern I could feel the fluids start to retreat from my lungs, so I decided to stay inside, while Zacharie went outside with his friends. I needed to cure myself, in order to be able to handle the rest of the night.

I had two choices that night: I could either choose to become extremely intoxicated, and to the point of blackout before I went outside to associate with Zacharie's friends during his Christmas Party, or I could run home like a baby, scared to interact with his friends.

***

Later in the evening, I remember making a bet with one of Zacharie's random friends on a Fighting match, and with the amount I was drinking I was surprised I won. I found the more I was drinking, the more I could concentrate on my socializing. I loved Zacharie so much; I wanted him to have a good time.

I wanted our last weekend before he flew to Boucherville, Quebec to be special; I was just hoping that trying to control my motor skills would not make me blackout.

My friend Damian that I knew from working at the Bar showed up at the Tavern, and decided he wanted to play a game of Beer Pong. I knew that if Damian had it his way, he would surely make it so I drank myself into a comatose stage.

My friends from the Bar know me better than anyone else in my life or else knew to it would. If my

Best Friend, Christina, knew that I was at Tavern trying to purposely intoxicate myself for the purpose of socializing, *she would tell me how seriously fucked I am.*

Considering that I loved my boyfriend so much, I was willing to put myself through anything for him: hot summers, or even cold winters. I didn't care; all that mattered to me was that we were doing something together.

At the end of the day, it takes two to make a relationship work, and I will never make him suffer my anti-socialization condition. I know that it controlled by simply following the instructions I have laid out for myself: drinking lots and blacking out often.

***

After playing Beer Pong with Damian, and being flipped point to fucked-up point, I was almost ready to be fucked by Zacharie. Yet my man was not done having a good time with his friends, so I decided to sit with Damian and talk about my fucked-up issues with the lousy Bar I worked for.

Abuse. I enjoy it; meaning whether it come in the form of love, or the genre of fucked-up, I remember coming home with my Mr. Complicated. *It was a night I would never forget; I remember the both of us, on my bed.*

"I want to have sex, Zacharie."

"No, Estelle, we are going to bed," he replied in an angry tone.

I was really mad that he subjected me to such conditions. I had to completely blackout and not enjoy the rest of his Christmas Party, but Zacharie had no idea. *What was it I could have done that night to piss him off, and make him so inconsiderate of my needs?*

"Zacharie, If you don't fuck me, I am going to do something you don't like." I replied.

"And what's that?" He asked.

"I'm going to get myself wet."

"Estelle, go to bed."

And then it happened; he didn't fuck me, and I started masturbating.

"Look, Zacharie I'm playing with myself," I hollered.

At this point I think he was too angry with my actions, because he covered me in my own blanket, and decided it was time to put Little Ms. Twisted to bed.

LAST TIME

I arrived at Zacharies early in the evening, as I was hoping to spend as much time as possible together, before I drive him to the Airport. I could not believe I wasn't going to see my Mr. Complicated for four entire weeks.

Even though he made these plans long before the two of us ever started dating. I wished he would have just cancelled them.

As selfish as it was, I wish he could just stay in Medicine Hat and spend Christmas with me. However, seeing as it's been two years since he has visited back home, I did not blame him for booking such an extended vacation. Especially since he was single at the same time, I understand why he booked it. *I enjoyed spending Christmas with my family, I would do the same.*

I got out of my truck, slammed the door, and walked up to the 'bungalow' I would miss, just as much as the man I now loved.

I knocked on the door, and opened it. "Zacharie, are you here?" I called out.

"Yes, Estelle, I am downstairs."

"Coming," I replied.

I took off my shoes, and walked down his stairs, expecting he would already be packed. I expected him to just take me on the bed and make love to me, it shocked me to see him still packing, and his dishes not yet washed.

I did not want to seem useless, so I decided to give Zacharie a hand, because I could imagine how exhausted he was going to be tomorrow, after all the flying ahead of him. I mean my poor complicated had a stopover in Winnipeg, and then had to fly to Toronto, and from there he would land in Montreal, and then had to drive to Boucherville, Quebec. *I wondered how long of a drive that would be?*

I just wanted to make things as easy as possible for him.

"Zacharie, I am going to wash your dishes and clean up your kitchen, so you don't need to feel rushed."

"Thank you," he replied.

He was listening to some weird music, not the kind I would listen too. In fact, it was giving me a fucking headache, the type that made you wish you were simply on a bed being fucked.

I started washing the dishes, and asked curiously: "are you excited to go home and see your family, Zacharie?" I asked curiously.

"I think I have everything," he said under his breath.

"Did you hear me?" I asked.

"Sorry Estelle, what did you say? He asked.

"I asked if you are excited about going home to see your family," I repeated myself a little frustrated.

"Oh- right. You know I think I am going to need to step out; I left my passport in my other work truck that is at the shop getting fixed."

"What, you need to leave?" I said in a tone of despair.

"Yeah, I need to go to the shop, I will be right back."

"Zacharie, why do you even need your passport, you are only going to Boucherville?" I questioned. *It made me wonder whether or not he was going someplace else, but just did not want to tell me.*

"Because I just want my passport, ok?" he snapped.

"Ok, do you want me to take you, since I am parked behind your loaner truck?"

"Whatever," he replied, and started walking up the stairs.

I stopped washing the dishes; there was only one or two left anyhow, and since it was only three hours before I needed to drop him to the Airport, we both had time.

I walked up the stairs, got my shoes on, and went with Zacharie to get his passport.

After waiting for Zacharie to locate his passport for twenty minutes, he managed to find it. I felt as though I lost half of the rest of the night with him, because the time was drawing closer for me to drive him to the airport.

We walked into his house, went downstairs, and Zacharie started going through his stuff again; checking to make sure he has everything. I walked back over to the sink and finished washing the dishes; I did not want to bother him.

After fifteen minutes passed without either of us talking, I decided to ask him when he wanted to leave for the Airport.

"Zacharie, when do you want to leave for the Airport?"

"My flight does not leave until 9:20pm so we can leave here at 7:30pm, that way I can drop my loaner truck off at work, and then you can drive me to the airport."

"I thought I saw your itinerary: and your flight leaves at 7:20pm?"

"No, I am sure its 9:20pm."

I am really confused. I could have sworn I read his itinerary properly.

"Ok, sorry," I replied.

"What are you sorry for," he asked, and then plopped down on his bed.

"I mean I am sorry for thinking that you are leaving earlier than later; of course I am happy you are leaving later rather than earlier," I replied smiling, then I laid down beside him.

"Estelle, did you bring any condoms?" Zacharie asked.

"Sure did," I replied.

"Good," he replied, and rolled over to face me brushing his lips softly against mine.

I took my fingertips and gently started brushing them over top of his forehead.

"I love you, Zacharie," I said softly.

"I love you too, Estelle," he replied, and then moved his lips to start softly brushing mine, and then I gently kissed him back.

Zacharie lifted himself on top of me, and I lifted myself upward at the same time, and removed my shirt while we continued to kiss, and he removing his.

He then started kissing down my neck, and I started to get really wet. I knew I was not going to last long tonight; he was attacking my weak spot.

"Zacharie please, don't make me cum quick, I want to go nice and slow."

He grabbed both of my hands, and then lifted himself up a little more. He then moved down and started to suck on my nipples, going from one to the other; it made me start to cum, and I could feel my legs start to shake from the orgasm; he would not stop.

"Stop it, I can't, and ..." I breathed heavy for a moment, "please, Zacharie, you can't."

He started sucking my nipples longer and softer. Then he used his free hand to start rubbing them, he slipped himself inside of me.

"I love you," I whispered.

He grabbed both of my hands again, and started fucking me slowly. This time, there was no avoiding the build-up of emotion; everything I felt for Zacharie was there, between my legs and more.

"Zacharie," I screamed.

"Zacharie, please," I started to moan.

I tried to find his lips, but after he teased me with them for only a moment, he moved his head down more towards my breasts to suck my nipples again. Suddenly then it happened, I could feel my legs start to shudder; I was 'cuming' again for a second time.

I was not sure if he could feel my orgasm, but I wanted to feel his erection. I was ready and willing to go on top, but then he pulled out quickly, and sat up.

He was on his knees with his legs spread apart, when he grabbed my legs, and hoisted them over his shoulders; *this is going to hurt.*

Zacharie slid his penis inside me, and I winced; it really hurt, but I didn't want to say anything, especially with him leaving in such a short time. *I just wanted to do whatever would satisfy him and would make him feel good.*

I knew we never fucked like this for long anyways, so if it would please him by letting him hurt me that bad, I would let Zacharie hurt me until he finished.

With each penetration, I could feel him go deeper, and I started to tear. He didn't know I was crying; the lights in his room were off, and I tried to hold the pain in.

He started to go even harder, and this was the longest he had ever fucked me in such a menacing, painful position.

I could feel his erection building, and then finally, he released, and pushing further inside me.

It felt odd; it was the last time we would fuck for four weeks, and the only thing I would be left to remember was how good it felt at the beginning, and how much it hurt towards the end.

FOR THE RIDE

From 'Mr. Complicated's' point of view...

Boarding the plane, I got text on my cellphone from Estelle...

Estelle to Zacharie
Estelle- Do you want something to read on the plane?
Zacharie- Is it something naughty?
Estelle- Do you want something naughty?
Zacharie- Now you're talking!
Estelle- Sent you a 'FILE ATTACHMENT.'

Clicking on the file attachment, I began to read;

Non-edited version...

Preface

Running for my life, I do not take a moment to look back. Not looking back is what has kept me alive, for the last three years. Rougen's 'red eyes,' and lust for my blood drives him vampire-drunk most days sending him spiraling out of control. But today his out of control may cost us both dearly. As my heart beats faster, I pray Rougen made it out dead. The song of my love will draw him to aide in my escape from the 'Life Dealer' on my hide. You can run from me girl, but you will not escape what the gods have in store for you!"

I take a deep breath, and the memory hits me like a ton of bricks. Six months ago, when Rougen and I watched Loona and Lyle burn together on the steaks. The two of them eye and eye, and the 'Life Dealers' torch for torch. Their trial was not only unfair-but unjust.

"I can hear your thoughts, and I was there. Remember deeper Anastasia-expand your mind."

I run faster... The more I think about it-the more I will slow my pace and give in to this jerk. The faster I run, the more my heart sings aloud for Rougen... Then the cry of bloody vengeful murder. *My love is here.*

Estelle can really write well, but her grammar is lacking.

Zacharie to Estelle

Zacharie- Ok babe, you caught my attention.

Estelle- Do you want to read the rest?

Zacharie- Sure, it will keep me busy. If you promise to be a bad girl while I am gone, I will edit it for you.

Estelle- Very funny.

Estelle- Sent you a 'FILE ATTACHMENT.'

Non-edited version...

1.   Skipping Out

Thistle sits perched perfectly on the front windowsill staring out into the world blankly. I often wish my life was as simple, and relaxing as hers. I walk toward her, joining her staring outside blankly, as my left hand brushes against her fur just groomed. *I wish someone would pay to have me groomed!* I smirk mockingly.

"Ana! What is so funny?"

I turn my head back towards my mom, "how did you know I was smirking?"

"Because I could hear that childish school girl giggle of yours, and I can associate one, with the other."

"One, with the other?"

"Your smirk, smarty pants."

"I am not a smarty pants mom, I think I would be a smarty shorts!"

"Ok sure, Ana, have it your way like always. My little smarty shorts. If you do not mind me asking, did you hand in your homework yesterday to Madame Cote?"

"Yes, mom, I did," I replied angered. *Why does she only follow up on French homework?*

"Thank you! I appreciate avoiding another phone call from your French teacher this morning at work. Mr. Russell gave me shit the other day, and that's why I came down so hard on you."

"That is ok, mom, I know you are just doing your job."

"Precisely, the problem, Ana."

"And what would that be?"

"I was not doing my job."

Grabbing my school bag and fixing it over my shoulder, I waved a quick goodbye to my mom, and hurried out the door for school. Greg was already waiting outside, and I knew it was not smart to keep him waiting.

I pulled the car door open, and smiled at Greg, who looked frightfully pissed off at me. "What the hell is wrong with you Ana?"

"There is nothing wrong babe, I am perfectly fine." I got in the car, and slammed the door shut, and before I could put my seatbelt on I felt the sudden pierce of Greg's hand across my left cheek. I turned my face frontwards, and avoided eye contact with him as per usual- and any tears.

"Next time I pull up at this house, you are not ready, I am going to break something Ana."

"Ok!" I agreed, trying not to sound in pain.

"DO YOU UNDERSTAND ME," Greg, yelled.

"Yes, I understand you."

"You seem to always claim to understand me Ana, but something just does not connect inside that little tiny brain of yours. Do I need to slam your head against my car door again?"

"No."

"Then do not let it happen again," Greg, demanded and pulled out of my driveway. Placing his hand firmly on my kneecap, he started to brush my skin with care. *I did not understand Greg most days.* One moment he is a complete abusive asshole, and the next he is the loving and caring boyfriend I first met in grade eight. The one who would show his girlfriend off to his friends, open the classroom door for, take out to the little Italian Pizzeria across the street from school with my best-friend Layla, and his best-friend Brayden?

"I love you Greg." I waited for a very long time to hear the same words back, but Greg said nothing. Instead he cranked up the music on the radio station, to avoid listening to me breathe.

Ring...

And school is officially in session- as Greg and I have already parted ways in silence.

"Anastasia Franco," Mr. Scrimshaw, calls aloud.

"Present."

"Well isn't that just fantastic," Lucy wells snickers.

"Miss Smith, do you mind?"

"Sorry Mr. Scrimshaw, I was simply acknowledging Miss Franco."

"Thank you- but please keep your acknowledgement of Miss. Franco to yourself. Now if you do not mind class, please refer to our current read; *Romeo and Juliette* by *Shakespeare.*"

Reading the works of Shakespeare often made me feel sad. Especially about my love life with Greg. I mean the two of us are both tragic and just waiting for a happy ending to never come. I mean I look at Juliette- who loved Romeo so much that she pretended to poison herself- leaving those to find her with the presumption she is dead. And it pained Romeo so badly to find his beloved Juliette dead, so he swallowed poison himself because he could not stand the idea of living without her. Tragic.

But then you have Greg, and me. Tragically he is the one to poison me, and I am stupid enough to love him.

"Anastasia, can you tell me at what point did Juliette decide to kill herself?"

"I do not know, sir."

"So you are admitting that you did not read last nights assigned chapters?"

Oh wait…yes I did!

"Actually, Mr. Scrimshaw, Juliette did not poison herself, she pretended too."

"Really? And how som Anastasia- can you elaborate for us please?"

"Well, sir, you see it's like this- Juliette loved Romeo so much, she could not bear to live without him, so she drank a poison that would stop her heart from beating- so that her family would think that she is dead. Then she and Romeo could live happily ever after without the feuding of their families weighing them down."

Mr. Scrimshaw gave me a mildly dirty look, and I knew my attempt was an epic fail no matter how well I tried.

Lunch time could not come soon enough. The one only time during school I enjoyed, considering French was on the books for right after lunch. I was having a bad day, my only concern at this point is finding Layla and going outside for a smoke.

"Jessica, have you seen Layla?"

"No, Ana, I have not, she did not come to school today."

"There must be a mistake."

"No, Ana, no mistake. She was not in home-room this morning, or in Gym third period."

That was out of character for Layla. Usually if she was sick and not going to be at school I would have been the first person to know- and not her home-room. "Ok thanks Jessica."

"No worries, did you want to have lunch with us?"

"No, that's ok. I think I am going to head over to Layla's house and make sure everything is alright. "

"Ana, might I remind you that Greg is not going to be happy about you skipping off from school. From what I understand you are already on thin ice with your mother- do you really want to receive an additional grounding to the one you are already serving now?"

"I will be back before the end of lunch."

"Layla's house is more than a twenty to thirty minute walk from school, and we only have an hour for lunch. And right now its fifteen after twelve. I do not think you will make it back in time. Why don't you just wait until after school and phone her from your house? If I was sick at home, and one of my friends came poking their nose around, my mom would shit Frisbees."

"Layla's mom loves me- I am sure she would be happy I decided to pay a visit and make sure that my best friend is alright."

"I am sure you are right, Ana. But you really think she would be impressed you are cutting class to visit Layla? I think the first person who would call your mom would be Mrs. Robertson."

"Jessica- I understand you are trying to look out for my best interest- but something just doesn't feel right about Layla missing school."

"There is a lot that does not feel right- especially looking at your face. What happened to your face?"

"What do you mean?"

"There is almost what appears to be a huge hand print across your left cheek."

And then I remembered back to this morning when I got into Greg's car, and the painful slap to my face- "nothing happened... or maybe it did. I think I pissed my mom off this morning."

"See Ana, and you want to go skipping school?"

I hurried out the side doors of the school as quickly as possible- attempting to leave un-noticed.

"Ana! Where are you going?" I could hear Greg shout out from down the west hallway. I stopped dead in my tracks.

I turned around, and there was Greg right in my face again, "I am leaving school to get some fresh air."

"If you wanted fresh air- how come you did not ask me to take you for a drive?"

"Because I do not want to make you angry Greg."

Greg's face turned beat red, and as another student came out of the washroom- I could see him make an attempt to control his anger. "Ana what am I going to do with you?"

"I don't know Greg. You tell me."

"Did our little discussion this morning knock any sense into you?"

"No Greg, maybe it is because you did not hit me HARD enough!" I yelled in his face.

Greg looked around quickly to make sure no one heard what I said, "Ana what the hell are you trying to do here?"

"I told you, I am trying to go outside for some fresh air. Now would you leave me alone and let me go?"

"Ok Ana," Greg smiled wickedly. And as I turned around to exit the school, I could feel Greg pull the back of my hair, and take the door and slam my head between the edge of it- and I connected hard with the frame and fell to the floor. Taking his right leg, he kicked me in my stomach. "Greg stop it," I pleaded, but my pleading went un-noticed as he continued to give me another blow to my pelvis.

"Now Ana, lets both see if you can go outside for some fresh air now!" Greg turned around and walked away leaving me laying between the door and the frame of the west door. I closed my eyes- and the tears trickled down my face. Why me?

I managed to pick myself up and get out of the school. As I walked along Stanwix Street- I marveled at the beauty of fall. October was my favorite time of the year- but also reminded me of how I longed to be like a leaf that could fall of a tree. *How come I just cannot escape Pittsburgh Pennsylvania?*

Why did my mom and I moved here from Chicago Illinois after my parent's divorce? It was so unfair I got stuck with her- when both of my parents knew how much it meant to me to stay surrounded with my friends. Instead I ended up moving here, and finishing Elementary school- when I finally found my best friend Layla who was also dragged by her mom to move out here from Boston. Thankfully with the high school being located directly downtown - to walk to down town stretch on Stanwix took anywhere from twenty to thirty minutes at most- depending how fast you walk or ran.

I finally made it to Liberty Avenue, and walked towards the apartment buildings across from Gateway Station. This was the worst area in Pennsylvania, because of the number of drunks that frequent the area during the night- and during broad daylight.

"Do you have some spare change young lady?"

I turned around quickly to see a man who was old enough to be my grandfather slouched over with an empty beer can in hand. "I am really sorry sir, but I do not have any money."

"That's alright young lady," he smiled and went along his business.

Being polite- is key to not having yourself stabbed, or mugged.

I walked along Stanwix, to building 111. I opened the front door, and hit the buzzer for apartment 119. No one answered. I stood for at least twenty minutes or more trying to continuously buzz Layla- but there was no answer.

A very tall man entered the lobby from outside. He towered over top of me, standing about six feet or taller, tanned skin, and a very wonderful masculine structured face. His blue eyes where mesmerizing. "Did you lock yourself out?"

"Yes I did. I know it's clumsy of me sir, but I left from school sick- and my mom works out on site. So she is not going to be home for some time now. But thankfully my dad is home, but he must be sleeping because he is not answering our apartment buzzer."

"Do you think he will answer your apartment door?" The man asked curiously.

"There is no need to worry, because my dad never locks the front door," I smiled back.

"That is not very safe at all, and probably information your parents would not want you to share with a complete stranger."

"I don't think you are a stranger sir, because since we have got to talking that makes us both acquainted does it not?"

"I guess it does," the man smiled back.

"Would you mind letting me in the building so that I can get some rest?"

"Not at all."

The man unlocked the lobby door- and I hurried down the hallway, as he exited down the opposite side. Layla's apartment was the last door on the left of the hallway.

As I made my way to standing in front of her front door- I knocked gently hoping her mom would not answer, but to my surprise the front door was open because with each gentle knock the door moved a little, and then a bit further.

"Hello," I called out quietly. And there was no answer. I walked into the one bedroom apartment Layla shared with only her mom- and the entire apartment was *trashed*.

"Layla...Layla," I cried out, and hurried through her apartment. I checked the kitchen and there was no sign of her, or her mom. I checked the living and dining room area, and there was still no sign of either of them. When I walked into the bedroom I noticed all of Layla's belongings gone!

The bathroom door was shut- and my heart beat began to hurt so bad it was choking me. I turned the knob and opened the door, and the tub was full of blood- along with the mirror that read RUN...and that is exactly what I did. I ran out of Layla's apartment screaming in horror.

As I was running down the hallway in attempts to get out of the apartment building and make my way to the police station- a man came running to my aide. "Is everything alright?" The man asked worried.

"No everything is not alright," I cried.

"What is the problem?"

"The problem! The problem is that my best friend didn't show up to school. So I decided to cut the rest of the day- to come and make sure everything was alright with her. And when I went into her apartment there was a huge mess, and a blood covered washroom. That is my problem!"

"Was there anyone inside the apartment?"

"No. I just told you, I went inside her apartment- and it was completely trashed- and the washroom covered in blood."

The man looked at me bewildered- "what apartment number is your friend in?"

"She is in apartment 111."

"Ok, then let us go and check this out."

"What the heck are you thinking? Call the cops already!"

"I am not calling the cops until I see it for myself!"

I could not believe this guy. First it seemed as though he was in all fire hurry to help me- and now he thinks I am joking. "Ok fine, go ahead and see it for yourself."

I walked behind the man, back down the hallway. "Ladies first." I entered the apartment again- and to my amazement the apartment was not trashed at all- was I dreaming this? And then I felt a sharp pain in the side of my neck.

I stopped reading. *Why* is Estelle's writing so sad?

Mr. Complicated Love or Lust
Between Estelle and Publisher

Part One of One- EMAILED A DEADLINE

From: Art Campbelle
Subject: Mr. Complicated Deadline
Date: December 20th, 2014 07:28 am
To: Estelle

Estelle,
I understand that you may not realize the type of storyline you have created, but it has peaked Exelby Publishing's interest very much.

You must understand, by refusing to accept an Offer after thirty days, means that Offer will become null and void. You will subsequently be offered a substantial lower amount, if you would like to continue working with Exelby Publishing.

If you are looking to be offered more money for your 'work in progress,' I need something to show to the board.

By the end of this month, I need a well written Query, Synopsis, and First Three Sample Chapters of your work.

There are no more excuses.
Please Estelle.
Art, painfully waiting
Managing Director at Exelby Publishing

Part Two of One- THE QUERY

Query
Dear Publisher,

Do you know the story of how 'Little Ms. Twisted' plotted to meet 'Mr.Complicated?' When a newly Published Author decides to take the storyline of her life, and make it into a Book for the entire world, she does not realize what it is she is getting herself into.

Twenty-six year old Danielle Marie Michaud, is your typical, newly famous Author, but comes with a fucked-up past and a sick twist of how she plans on creating her next piece. After her Publisher moves her 'book tour' to next August. She decides to take the advice of Melanie, her only friend in the small city of Medicine Hat, Alberta, to join an on-line dating site for random sexual encounters. Danielle feels alone, and decides that plotting to meet the right victim, a supposed one-night stand, is just the sadistic twist she needs right now. Moreover she plans on playing the role of the dominant sexual leader.

When Danielle first meets twenty-four year old Gaston Lapointe, a French guy from Boucherville, Quebec, who moved to Medicine just after finishing College, she is thrown off her plot, after finding out just how complicated he really is. His perception and arrogance really starts to frustrate her, and when it comes to pleasing her in the bedroom, it just doesn't happen; she no longer feels that she is the dominant sexual leader. A relationship established by sex, turns out to be a game; how can Danielle plot to make Mr. Complicated fall head over heels for her. During this process, Danielle also decides to never lose track of how important pretending to love Gaston truly is, to exploit Mr. Complicated to the entire world. With the help of her Publisher, other girls can learn from Danielle's hard research and exploitation.

Does Danielle trick Mr. Complicated into falling in love with her? Can Gaston deal with Little Ms. Twisted's dirty past and closet of sexual demons? Can Mr. Complicated help Little Ms. Twisted obtain all the research she needs to exploit 'men' for the shameless assholes they are? Mr. Complicated gives Adult readers a sexy outlook on what it is that girls find attractive about the secretive, saucy, seductive side that young men have to offer older women.

Mr. Complicated is my second Erotica type of novel, and is sure to keep the reader coming back for more of Mr. Complicated and his Little Ms. Twisted. Thank you very much for your time.

Sincerely,

Estelle Ella Whiteside

Part Two- THE SYNOPSIS

Synopsis

Being a Famous Author living in the big city of Chicago, Illinois becomes a challenge for young Danielle Marie Michaud, when her first book, 'Loved by No Other', becomes a huge seller in both the States and Canada.

After meeting with her Publisher, Exelby Publishing out in New York, USA, all parties agree that it would be better if Danielle packed up her life in her big hometown of Chicago, Illinois, and retreat to the smaller population of Medicine Hat, Alberta. Where she could concentrate on developing her writing career, and avoid any unwanted writers block.

Danielle was also advised by her Publisher that it would be a good idea to avoid entering a long term relationship with anyone. In this way, when Danielle was to leave for her upcoming 'book tour' to launch her newly published book, 'Loved by No Other,' a fantasy Erotica that was selling like condoms to the adult world population.

When Danielle learns from her Publisher that the tour needs to be put on hold and moved to next August, because of recent cutbacks, she decides that living her normal uncomplicated life is no longer fun. She decides to take the advice of her only friend in Medicine Hat, Melanie. She tells her about the lavished life of online exploitation of one's self for sex and oral one-night stands that locals in Medicine Hat use to get off.

After putting an ad on a local Medicine Hat online dating site, Danielle decides that maybe it's time to unleash her inner character of Little Ms. Twisted, and find that Mr. Complicated she has been looking for.

When twenty-four year old Gaston Lapointe, a young French guy who moved to Medicine Hat after finishing College from Boucherville, Quebec, decides to respond to the ad Little Ms. Twisted posts online, the two arrange their first meeting at a local coffee shop. Little Ms. Twisted has hopes of getting laid that evening. However, when Mr. Complicated does not deliver, she develops an interest in Gaston, and she decides to keep a daily journal of their events, for her new and upcoming book that she hopes will make her famous all over again, while boosting the sales during her tour next August.

Danielle has a dominant character, and Mr. Complicated has a selfish need to sexually satisfy himself before ever pleasing the opposite sex; this really starts to piss Little Ms. Twisted.

One early morning, Gaston wakes up out of the blue, and makes love to Danielle. This really fucks her up both mentally and emotionally. She does not understand why he made love to her, or if it was love that he was intending to extend, but the orgasm he gives Danielle definitely makes a statement. Danielle now falls deeply in love with the egotistical and arrogant Mr. Complicated.

While Mr. Complicated learns to deal with all that Danielle has to offer, he also discovers an erotic past that she has kept under lock and key.

Can Gaston deal with her sexually battered past, and move forward? What will he do when he finds out that Danielle started this relationship all because of a book? When Mr. Complicated gets a hold of Little Ms. Twisted's daily journal of their sexual and erotic events, this dynamic love duo will take a twist, but in which direction? For the better, or for the worse?

Part Three- THE FIRST THREE SAMPLE CHAPTERS

Arranged Meeting

September 10th, 2012- The day I received the news from my amazing Publishing Company, Exelby Publishing, my Manager, Art Campbelle, decided to place my tour on hold; he thought it would be better for me to concentrate on writing a sequel to my first Published piece 'Loved by No Other.'

At twenty-six, I must say my life is everything that I imagined it would be. In less than two months from today, I was to be leaving this shit hole called 'Medicine Hat' and retreating to start my lavished 'book tour' for 'Loved By No Other.' Instead, I am now dealing with an overbearing Publisher who is up my ass every day of the week. In addition to that, I'm breaking the news to my friends and family who use me for money back home in Chicago, Illinois, that my tour has been placed on hold. *I am sure none of them could give a fucking shit!*

I decided even though my 'book tour' was being put on the backburner until next year, that maybe Art was right; this would give me the time I need to write a new book. However I was not interested in writing the sequel to 'Loved by No Other,' I wanted to start a new project.

I was battling with writing about a character who was as Twisted as my inner devil, or writing about a character that an audience would come to love.

I don't believe in the whole 'happy character bullshit writing' where you see a victim be saved by a hero. I like to write about the deeper and darker sexual types; where a guy fucks the shit out of the main character, and then leaves her helpless because guys are assholes and that's what you can expect the good 'boys' to do. Moreover, 'Men' just walk out of a woman's life just as quickly without saying goodbye.

I am sure tons of 'girls' can remember at least one relationship from the past ending because your 'boy' or 'man' wanted to go and fuck other 'girls' or 'women,' right?

This is why I made my decision to write a book; one that would be for the purpose of conducting a study about 'how' and 'why' the opposite 'sex' fall in love with 'females' and what would happen if one of 'us' bitches were as sick and twisted as these mother fucking 'men' who play us all the time. Instead of just researching it, I would write about it, and expose the fucker for what kind of sheepish asshole 'boys' and 'men' alike truly are.

My name is Danielle Marie Michaud, and I am a famous Author; one who has lived with a golden spoon up her ass during the entire expansion of her lifetime. Today I am going to reveal my research about a 'boy' named Gaston Lapointe, who by the end of this book, unveils the true 'man' he is. It takes three months and a trip back home to Boucherville, Quebec before he even starts to open up and realize that he truly does love his Little Ms. Twisted. By then it was too late, because she was going to expose the selfish fucker to the world, because loving fame and fortune was more important to her than loving him.

***

This September, I launched into my newly adopted career as an Author, and also launched a new twisted, to the already Little Ms. Twisted.

I decided to put myself out there immediately. I wanted to find someone who only wanted something physical like I did, with no strings attached. Maybe even something complicated, because uncomplicated never seemed to work for me.

***

Later that evening, Melanie, my only girlfriend who lived in the same building told me about a site that would advance my research, putting into motion immediately.

"Danielle, if you are interested in finding a pawn to fuck immediately, you should check out the new 'Medicine Hat' dating site. It's where guys advertise that they are looking for a one-night stand or some-one to get off with."

"Melanie, you are such a mind reader; I am def-initely interested in finding some dumb guy to fuck me."

Actually, I was more or less interested in finding some retard to play the role of Mr. Complicated. But I needed to find someone who would not suspect me, in order to write a book and expose his selfish side to the world, and that meant I needed to conduct interviews, or have random meetings with no sex involved; I just needed to find the right guy.

That very evening, I immediately put an ad up on the 'Medicine Hat' dating site, and went back down to my apartment.

I purposely posted a couple of old pictures of myself on my ad, because I wanted to be as scummy and bullshitting as the opposite sex. If men are stupid enough to think a girl would post a truthful picture of herself in the now, then these 'fishes' that are going to be lured in by my younger beauty, will have such a rude awakening. Okay, maybe not that rude of an awakening, considering I am a famous Author. I mean shit, if I had a penis, I would fuck myself.

***

The next morning, I decided to check my inbox. I noticed that I had an overwhelming amount of retards that decided to respond to my bullshit ad. *Perfect, let the research begin.*

I went through one message at a time, and the first one the poked my interested was a guy by the name of Doney102.

Message from: Doney102
To: Trashygirl0202
Date: September 10th, 2012 09:02pm
I saw your profile on the Medicine Hat dating site, was wondering if you are looking for a random guy to fuck, I am really interested in seeing how flexible you can be.

Message from: Trashygirl0202
To: Doney101
Date: September 11th, 2012 07:08am

I do not need to review your profile dear, because I would like to avoid any unwanted sexual transmitted disease, and your last message has that written all over. ⏥
Message from: Kelvinsagoodboy

To: Trashygirl0202
Date: September 10th, 2012 09:22pm

I just wanted to say, you have a lovely face. I was wondering if you wanted to get together for a few drinks.

Message from: Trashygirl0202
To: Kelvinsagoodboy
Date: September 11th, 2012 07:11am

Please feel free to send me a message on my cell phone at 587-000-0000 I would be interested in setting up a meeting.

Message from: SweetSexyBottoms
To: Trashygirl0202
Date: September 13th, 2012 07:02am

I just wanted to say you have really lovely eyes. I had a chance to review your profile, and it seems we are both looking for the same type of thing. I am looking to meet new friends as well; with my work schedule it has not always been easy to meet a nice girl.

Message from: Trashygirl0202
To: SweetSexyBottoms
Date: September 13th, 2012 07:14am
I would be interested in meeting, kindly send me a text. I have no plans tonight maybe we could do coffee 587-000-0000

***

I thought two dumbasses out of the lot of pigs would be enough for the time being, so I decided I would take a walk to the grocery store down the street from my apartment complex and pick up some Milk for my breakfast craving: scrambled eggs.

As I was walking across the street, I felt my cellphone vibrate.

SweetSexyBottoms to Trashygirl0202

SweetSexyBottoms- Hello, I am 'SweetSexy Bottoms' off of the Medicine Hat dating site, but you can call me Gaston.

Trashymouse- Hi there Gaston, my name is Danielle.

Gaston to Danielle

Gaston- It's really nice to meet you, Danielle.

Danielle- I had no idea we have met before... Are you stalking me, Gaston?

Gaston- Why would you say that? I simply meant to say it's nice to chat with you, please pardon my writing sometimes, my French gets the best of me at times.

Danielle- No problem, so when do you plan on cutting the text and arranging a first meeting?

Gaston- We could meet tonight if you would like.

Danielle- Where?

Gaston- Do you like coffee?

No I like fucking, but I need to conduct the interview first.

Danielle- Yes coffee sounds great.

Gaston- Which coffee shop?

Danielle - We can meet at the one by Harwood Heights.

Gaston- Would you like me to pick you up?

Danielle- I would prefer to drive myself thanks.

Gaston- Ok, no problem, just thought I would be nice and ask.

Danielle- I just thought I would be safe and decline ⍰

Gaston- What time would work for you?

Danielle- Around 7pm

Gaston- Ok, see you then.

***

I decided why the fuck should I drive to the coffee shop, it's simply a ten minute walk from my apartment, and it isn't dark out yet either.

Gaston to Danielle

Gaston- Are you here yet?

Danielle- Look around, does it look as though I am there yet?

Gaston- No.

Danielle - Then you have your answer.

Gaston- How long are you going to be, I feel awkward sitting alone, and almost as though someone is going to jump me.

Loser alert...

Danielle - Just sit tight and try not to urinate yourself, everything will be fine... lol

I walked into the coffee shop, and glanced carefully around the shop, to see Gaston sitting at the back.

He had dark hair, with dark eyes and a nice tan. He was wearing a baseball cap, and it was not even sunny outside *nerd much!*

I walked over to him.

"You must be Danielle," he said with a smile.

"I guess I could not be anyone else," I replied, taking my jacket off.

"Are you going to sit down?" He asked.

"No, I am going to order something. I would ask you if you wanted anything, but you already ordered without me," I replied with a smug tone.

"I ordered because you are ten minutes late."

"Sorry, I could not help myself; I like making an appearance later than sooner."

After ordering my tea, I returned to the table to join Gaston after I ordered my Tea (I dislike Coffee).

"So Gaston, do you often meet girls off internet dating sites?"

"No, I have not met one off there in almost four months."

"What made you want to try online dating again?"

"I got lonely."

So in other words, hand fucking himself was not working, so he would like a live partner.

"Why not just meet a girl the normal way that everyone else does?" I asked.

"What is really normal now, Danielle?"

"I guess for you, it's meeting a girl off the internet," I replied, laughing.

"You are meeting me the same way, no?"

"Yes, but for girls it's different."

"What makes online dating different for girls than guys?"

"It just gives me more of an open market."

"I see."

"So let me ask you, Gaston, was I everything you hoped I would be?"

"Well you did look younger in your pictures online."

"That's because those pictures were taken in my early twenties."

"Early twenties?"

"Yes, I am now twenty-six."

"Oh, I am twenty-four; my picture was taken this year," he smiled.

Twenty-four... BINGO, found target, now locked onto target, time to go for the desired information.

"Gaston, how many girls have you fucked?"

"I don't really think that topic is appropriate for a first meeting, do you?"

"Well I will be honest, I have fucked only one guy my entire life. Is that going to be a problem for you?"

"Why would that be a problem?"

"Well, for some guys it can be, especially if they like fucking a pale of water. I am really tight."

"I see," he replied, looking not too impressed.

"Well, it's getting late, Gaston, would you like to come over to my place and get to know each other a little better?"

"Sure, where do you live?"

Awesome, he wants to fuck too.

"Just over in the apartment buildings across down street."

"Ok, I can follow you over there."

"Would you mind driving me instead, because I walked here?"

"You are comfortable enough to get in a vehicle with me now?"

"Yeah, you seem like a really nice guy."

Maybe we could fuck in his vehicle?

Not a Good Time

So Gaston and I made it back to my apartment last night, but disappointingly enough, we never made it into my bedroom, or onto anything for that matter to fuck.

Last night in my horny state, I would have even accepted being fucked in the shower.

Who the hell did this Gaston character think he was anyway? What guy would not try and fuck a girl the first time she invites him inside? And I did not even get a fucking hug or a kiss good night. I need to brainstorm this further.

I guess arranging another meeting is definitely in order; I will give him the bait, let's see if he bites.

Danielle to Gaston
Danielle – Good morning.
Gaston- Good morning.
Danielle - Do you have any plans tonight?
Gaston- I get off work around 4pm, and then might go home and do some relaxing.
Danielle - Would you like company?
Gaston- You want to come over to my place?
Danielle - Yes.
Gaston- You could come over and watch a movie if you would like, and maybe spend the night.
Plan worked.
Danielle - Are you going to hurt me?
Gaston- I will try not to.
Danielle - Will you promise to be nice to me?

Gaston- Sure?

Danielle - Ok, well as long as you will not hurt me, then I would like to come and spend the night 'watching a movie.'

Gaston- Ok, do you want me to pick you up?

Danielle - That would be nice ☐

Gaston- Is 6pm ok?

Danielle - Sure is, see you then.

It was 5 minutes before Gaston was supposed to pick me up to stay over at his place for the night, and I decided to pack some lube for some playtime later that evening.

Gaston to Danielle

Gaston- I am outside.

Danielle - I will be right there.

I ran out of my apartment so quickly that I forgot to grab my jacket, and it was so cold outside. I quickly got into his truck, and then he started to drive.

"I guess you don't wait until your passenger has a seatbelt on?"

"Why, what's the point? It's not like I am planning on having an accident."

Was this the same Gaston I had coffee with last night?

"Oh, so I guess you can see the future," I replied rudely.

"Maybe," he said with a grin.

"Ok."

"Are you cold, Danielle?"

"A little," I replied

Gaston turned the heat on in his truck, and I felt a lot warmer.

Why would he care if I am cold, but not if I am going to die? That's kind of strange.

***

We pulled up to a bungalow, which looked a lot like the summer home my parents had back in Ontario, California.

"Do you like it?"

"Yeah it's nice," I replied.

"I designed this myself, with the help of a couple of my builders."

"You have friends in Medicine Hat?"

"Yes, quite a few, what about you?"

"All my family and friends are back in Chicago."

"What brought you to Medicine Hat?"

"My publisher."

"Your publisher?"

"Yes, I am a writer."

"Really?"

"Yes."

"What books have you written?" He asked.

"Loved by No Other."

"What kind of book is that?"

"I am guessing you do not read much?"

"I work too much to have time to read."

Major loser alert!

"I see, well if you must know; it's an erotica."

"What does that mean?" He asked, confused.

I loved his French accent. It was cute, and I wanted him to just take me inside and start the fucking.

"It means I write novels that are about sex."

"About sex?"

"Yes, and it is very detailed," I replied, getting out of his truck.

***

Well, the good news is we both made it into his place safely; the bad news is we made it to the bed before the movie.

I started teasing him while he pretended to want and cuddle me. We were on his bed, rolling around, having a power hungry kissing episode, but even thought I was doing most of the kissing, he was getting very erect.

I stripped my clothing off, he assisted with my bra, and then started to assault my nipples. He was gentle, much more than what I expected he would be.

Wait, this is not how it happened, let me start again.

Gaston, first off, did not even live in a bungalow; he rented it out to the ghosts who occupied it. He lived in a 'garbage can' or so I thought. It felt like I was in a fucking compactor, or dump truck.

And the fact is, he never did anything nice to me the first evening we fucked. This is exactly what happened:

I took my clothing off in the bathroom, because I never got undressed in front of a guy before, and Gaston was not exactly welcoming the first time he brought me to the basement of his bungalow.

He went in the bedroom, he picked out the movie, and then he picked to sit on the bed, closest to the TV, so I could not see a goddamn thing.

Then when he fucked me for the first time, he got himself off, and did not give a shit about pleasing me.

***

Chapter three is in Fucking Progress I need some time to think about all of this, I am sorry.

Mr. Complicated Part One of Two;
Love or Lust

DEAR ZACHARIE

December 25th, 2014

Dear Zacharie,

There are so many things I wish I could say to you in person right now, but since you are so far away, I thought of writing you a letter, because I feel dazed and confused.

I am sad on so many levels. First, I miss our fucking. Second I miss our love making. Third, and most important, I miss seeing you every day.

Before you left, we were spending every moment of every day we had together, in one another's arms. I knew our relationship was based on more than just a physical connection.

I have come to know you on so many more levels than I did three months ago, and I really feel what we have is special, and I want you to know how much you mean to me.

Today is Christmas, and the one gift I would like to give to you is my heart; it's yours, forever and always.

I promise to think of you every day in the morning when I wake up, and in the evening before I go to bed. I will never go to bed angry, because I love you so much, and sometimes I wish you would tell just how you feel.

I know you are not good at expressing your emotions, but since you have made love to me, I feel like I cannot get enough of you expressing yourself sexually, but mentally as well.

We have talked on the phone every day you have been in Boucherville visiting your family, and I feel I know more about you now, than I did before you left.

love you so much Zacharie, and I cannot wait until you get home in a few weeks.

Love Estelle

Using my cell-phone, I took a photo of the handwritten letter that I wrote especially for Zacharie in my black journal, attached it, and hit the send button.

DEAR ESTELLE

My cell-phone beeped with a text and attachment from Zacharie; I clicked on it curiously.

> December 25th, 2014
> Dear Estelle
> I wanted to 'thank you,' for the letter, I got it this morning express post (thanks to your cell-phone). I decided to write you back today, so this letter could reach you tonight. Through your writing, I can feel how eager you are to have me back in Medicine Hat.
> Over the past two weeks, I have been in Boucherville visiting with my family, and I have started to realize just how special to my heart you truly are. That is why I decided, instead of coming home on January 12th, 2015, I am flying back to be with you for New Years on the 29th of this month. Will you pick me up from the Airport, babe?
> I know you are quite excited right now, and I am sure I wouldn't even need to ask you to pick me up at the Airport Estelle, but please do not wait there all

day for me. The parking bill will be outrageous.

I don't think I ever told you about my past two relationships and why I was so scared to open myself up to you.

What you will find in this letter will give you a better understanding of who 'I' am as a person, and what has happened to me in my past relationships.

I want you to know the truth, and the real 'Zacharie Gagne.'

Four years ago, just before my twentieth birthday, I met young women named Charlene, from North Bay, Ontario. She was a nice French girl, with a not-so-wise head on her shoulders.

I was working in Calgary when Charlene and I met. We hit things off instantly, and decided to get our own place here in Medicine Hat.

We dated for six months, and I started noticing a regular pattern with Charlene: she would leave an hour early before I started class every morning, and return a half an hour after she was off work from.

On a continued basis, every Thursday and Sunday of the week, she would arrive a few hours after her shift ended; she claimed to be spending time with Amanda and Nathan, a couple that she knew from work at the bookstore.

I did not think anything was going on until I found something in the laundry a pair of lipstick marks stained on her thong. When I questioned Charlene about the lipstick marks smudged on her panties, she claimed that her and Amanda where kissing their own underwear, to see who had the hottest lips.

I of course did not believe her, so I extended a call to Nathan, who's number I retrieved off of Charlene's cellphone.

When I talked to Nathan, he explained that him and Amanda were both 'swingers.' At the time, I did not understand exactly what a 'swinger' was. He extended an invite for myself to join the three of them on Sunday; of course

Charlene was not aware of my extended invitation.

When I arrived to Amanda and Nathans apartment in the downtown of Medicine Hat, I was shocked, and disturbed by the interactions that took place that night.

Charlene was thrilled that I showed up, and had no idea I was into 'swinging.' My first three-some happened that night with Amanda and Charlene, while Nathan got off watching the three of us, and then fucked Charlene and Amanda after I got off.

It was quite the interesting bonding experience.

After almost three years of fucking around on several occasions, with different swinging couples, I decided I was no longer interested in sharing my girlfriend with other men, or women.

When I told Charlene that I wanted to have a normal relationship, she told me it was over between the two of us. I then moved out of my Apartment, decided to buy a bungalow, and focus my mind on forgetting her. . .

Prior to being with Charlene, when I was eighteen, I was in College, and spent most of my time with Nicole; a girl in one of my study classes that I fucked on occasion.

Nicole ended up falling in love with me over a period of four weeks, and when I told her I was not interested in having a serious relationship with her, because I was planning on taking my career out West, she stalked me for the rest of my school year.

Maybe now you can understand why I could not open up to you at the beginning of our 'fucking' relationship.

But now, I am ready to give myself to you in every way you deserve Estelle.

I love you,

Zacharie Gagne

Ps. I cannot wait to see you when I get back, and spend 'New Years' with my favorite girl.

RETURN

In order to get my mind off the fact that Mr. Complicated would be back in my arms in only a few short hours, I decided to get myself off on my fuck swing. In the midst of my orgasm, all I could think was how excited I was to see him since I read his heartfelt letter, telling of his impending early arrival in Medicine Hat.

I felt terrible for ever wanting to exploit his selfish ass to the entire globe! But right now, I was only focused on one thing, aside from us surely fucking in the parking lot of the Airport Terminal, and that was: seeing Zacharie, telling him how much I love him, and that I don't give a shit about his fucked-up past relationships.

Since he has been gone, my heart has missed him, as much as his heart claims to miss me.

I could not even concentrate on writing anything new since he has been gone, and my inbox has remained closed, not wanting or caring to know what Art thinks about my 'first three sample chapters,' I could not complete.

All I could think of was our late night conversations over the phone, when we talked to one another every couple of hours after my shift at the bar.

Ping...

Zacharie to Estelle
Zacharie - In only a few short hours babe, I will be all yours.

Estelle- I take it you landed in Winnipeg alright?

Zacharie - Yes ⏸

Estelle- When does your plane leave?

Zacharie - In almost forty minutes. I wish you were here to keep me company, Estelle.

Estelle- What would you do, if you had me there, all to yourself?

Zacharie - I would take you for a washroom break, and 'flushingly fuck you.' ☺

Estelle- Flushingly?

Zacharie - Yes, I would fuck you over the toilet seat, for being such a bad girl.

Estelle- But I have not been a bad girl, Zacharie.

⏸

Zacharie - I would think back to a time you have been a bad girl, and re-punish you for being bad.

Estelle- Zacharie, can you answer a question?

Zacharie - Anything for you babe.

Estelle- When have I ever been a bad girl?

Zacharie - I can think of several times, Estelle.

Estelle- Ok, when?

Zacharie - Does 'not wearing a bra' ring a bell?

Smart ass...

Estelle- Sure does.

Zacharie - You were a really bad girl that night.

Estelle- Well, was I supposed to be nice?

Zacharie- I can think of many other things you have done, that would have caused me to spank you for being a naughty girl. That would very much please me.

Estelle- Well, I can think back to a number of times you never gave a shit about pleasing me so I really don't think you have any right to punish me for that little stunt I pulled that day.

Zacharie - Is that so?

Estelle- Yes, I think so.

Zacharie - Oh, Estelle, when my hands find your hips, you are going to get fucked.

Estelle- What if I want you to make love to me?

Zacharie - I think making love is only for when I am fucking you in a bed.

Estelle- Why is that?

Zacharie - Because anywhere other than a bed, I consider it fucking, because I don't want to be gentle with you.

Estelle- When you left to go to Boucherville a few weeks ago, did you not fuck me nicely in your bed?

Zacharie - If I remember correctly Estelle, I made love to you, and then had my way with you.

Estelle- I really want you to make love to me Zacharie ... ⍰

Zacharie - Well if your pout is cuter than the one on my phone, I might consider making love to you, but it will not happen at the Airport, and you will need to blow me home.

Estelle- And how do you suppose I blow you home, Zacharie?

Zacharie - Be creative; you don't have to drive.

Estelle- I am driving to come and get you?

Zacharie - Yes, but we both have a license babe. Anyways, I am turning my cellphone off now; I will see you in a few hours. I love you.

Estelle- I love you too. Have a safe flight. XoXo

***

As I was driving to the Airport, my cell-phone started to ring, and I did not have time to check to see who was calling me.

"Hello."

"Hi Estelle, how are you doing honey?"

"Mom, long time, no talk. I am doing well thanks," I replied.

"I am glad to hear dear, I just wanted to call and see how things are coming along with your sequel?"

"My sequel?"

"Yes Estelle, your sequel."

"What sequel?" I replied, confused.

"I thought you were working on a sequel to 'Loved by No Other?'"

"Oh, that sequel, uh- right now I have had to put things on hold."

"Why, is something wrong?"

"No."

"Then why would you need to put your sequel on hold?"

"Because I am not quite ready to start working on it yet, I have had my mind on other things Mom."

"What have you had your mind on darling? Do you want to talk about it?"

"It's no big deal, trust me."

"Estelle, you obviously want to talk about it, or you would not admit to me that you have your mind on other things right now."

My Mom was definitely onto my bullshit cover-up.

"Well, if I tell you, do you promise not to say anything to Dad?"

"Estelle, anything you tell me will stay between the two of us."

"I have been working on a new book."

"That's exciting, dear."

"Yes, it has been, up until a few weeks ago that is," I replied, sobbing a little, while still keeping my concentration on the road ahead of me.

"Why is it not exiting for you anymore, Estelle, did something happen?"

"Something did not happen, Mom, someone did."

"Oh- really!"

"Yes," I replied.

"You have met someone?" She asked.

"Yes," I replied, skeptical of divulging too much information.

"What is his name, Estelle?"

"Zacharie."

"Is he a nice boy?"

"He is interesting, you could say."

"Does he treat you nice, darling?"

"When he wants to, I guess."

"Well, Estelle, it's either he treats you nice; or he does not," my Mom replied.

"He treats me normal, I guess."

"Did the two of you have a nice Christmas together?"

"We did not spend Christmas together."

"Why not?"

"Because he went to visit his family back in Boucherville, Quebec," I replied again, sadly.

"Why did you not go with him?"

"Because I was not invited, Mom. And what the hell is with all the fucking questions?" I asked, starting to get angry.

"Well, I am just trying to figure this out, Estelle, you said you met someone."

"Yes, and I told you about him, now can we change the subject?"

"What did Zacharie get you for Christmas?"

Nothing...

"Something really nice," I lied.

"Oh, that is wonderful, Estelle, and what did you get for him?"

I wrote a book about how complicated he is, and now I am going to exploit him to the entire world...

"Something really expensive," I lied.

"That sounds nice, and did he like it?"

"He sure did."

"Well it sounds like you have met someone that is going to treat you good, and what does Art think about all of this?"

And I knew she would fucking poke her nose into my 'Writing' business.

"Art is very happy for me; in fact, he really wants me to concentrate on our relationship to the fullest."

"And why is that, dear?"

Because I am writing a biography about my fucked-up twisted idea to exploit asshole men, because they are stupid.

"I guess after cancelling my tour, he just wants to see me happy."

"That is great, Estelle, would you like to talk to your Dad?"

"I am really sorry Mom, I do not have the time, I just pulled up to the airport."

"Why are you at the airport?"

"Because I am picking up Zacharie, he's just getting back tonight."

"It's awful late, Estelle, are you going to call me when you get home?"

"Mom, you do realize I am a grown adult, living on my own, right?"

"Sometimes Mom forgets, darling."

"I love you, Mom, have a good night, and try not to hit your head too hard when you hit the bed."

"Don't get smart with me, Estelle."

"Good night Mom," I replied, and then hung up the phone before she could talk anymore.

I sat in the truck for a few minutes, thinking that my Mom brought up a very good point: *why the heck did Zacharie not get me anything for Christmas? Could it be because I trashed the holiday to him, being sad that he was going away and leaving me here in this god forsaken city to be enslaved by my publisher...*

I walked into the terminal, and saw the luggage swirling around on the conveyer. I guess Zacharie landed early.

I looked around the entire airport and did not see him, so I decided to pull my cell-phone out and send Zacharie a quick text.

Estelle to Zacharie

Estelle- Zacharie, where are you?

Zacharie - I am where I told you I would be waiting before I got on the plane, to fuck you when I landed at the airport, and you are not even in here yet.

What the fuck, was he seriously joking with me?

Estelle- Zacharie, I am standing by the luggage, waiting for you.

Zacharie - I am standing in the stall, by the toilet, waiting for you.

Estelle- You're fucking complicated.

Zacharie - I would like to show you how 'complicated' I can be, babe.

Estelle- Which bathroom are you in?

Zacharie- The 'boys' bathroom by the sandwich shop.

Estelle- So let me get this straight: you expect me to walk past an audience of strangers, and walk into a washroom that is clearly labeled 'boys' and not 'girls?'

Zacharie - Exactly.

Estelle- And how do you suppose I do that?

Zacharie - Oh babe, you think that I did not have a plan already?

Estelle- Well if you did, what the fuck is your so-called plan?

Zacharie - Look over by the lady sitting down in the chair, with an erotica book, to her right you will see a blue hoodie.

Estelle- Ok, hold on.

I glanced around the Airport, and saw the lady sitting down, reading some type of an erotica. I started to walk towards her, and as I got closer, I noticed she was reading my book, 'Loved by No Other.'

Estelle- Ok, I got the hoodie.

Zacharie - Now put it on.

I did as I was told, and put the hoodie on.

Estelle- Ok, it's done.

Zacharie - Did you put the hood over top of your head?

Estelle- Yes.

Zacharie - Now I want you to come into the washroom.

Is he honestly for real?

Covering myself in a blue hoodie was not going to save me from being fucked by Mr. Complicated, ready to 'Flush and Fuck.'

How the hell was he even going to fuck me over a toilet, anyhow? And what if there are other guys in the washroom at the same time?

I walked towards the washroom, keeping my head facing downwards, and then slipped into the washroom, I hoped unnoticed.

Once I was inside, I lifted my head, and there was no one in there.

I glanced softly, and saw 'beware of wet floor' sign.

"Zacharie, are you in here?" I whispered.

"I am in the last stall. Come, I have been waiting for you, babe."

"Honestly Zacharie, what the fuck are you thinking?" I replied in an angry tone.

"Aw, is my babe angry? I find your tone hot."

"You find my tone hot, well I am sure you will not find the look on my face hot, Zacharie. This look reads 'flaming fucking pissed,'" I hissed.

I walked into the last stall, and there he was, standing beside the toilet. It had been almost three weeks since the last time I saw him, and then the first time I see him is standing beside a toilet at an Airport.

"So might I ask what the hell you plan on doing to me in a washroom?"

"Flush fucking you, babe."

"Zacharie, I have not fucked you in almost half a month. I want to go back to your place or my own, and make love."

"Estelle, I have not had you in almost a month, and my penis is erecting at the sight of you, we are flush fucking."

"What the hell is flush fucking, Zacharie?" And before I could say anything else, his mouth was on mine.

He harshly leaned me into the washroom stall wall, and stripped his hoodie off of me.

Slipping both his hands up my sweater, I could feel his moan rage against my ear: "what did I tell you about wearing a bra to come and get me from the airport, Estelle?" He moaned.

"I cannot remember," I whispered.

He grabbed my tits really hard, "tell me," he demanded.

"You told me not to wear one," I yelped.

He started to loosen the grip on my breasts, removed my bra, and started to cup them nicely.

"Estelle, you are going to get fucked so hard, and then maybe tomorrow, if you wake up in the morning without a bra on, I will make love to you."

"I want you to make love to me now," I begged.

"Not right now babe, I need this," he replied, with a sense of getting off on what he knew was only his.

"Ok Zacharie, flush fuck me," I moaned.

He ripped my pants off, then my panties, and unzipped his jeans.

He bent me down, so my face was almost in the toilet.

"I am going to fuck you really hard Estelle, and when you cannot take anymore, I want you to flush the toilet. If you can take the entire thing, I will shove my face in the toilet after we are done fucking, and you can say I got flushed."

"Oh my fucking god Zacharie, that is the sickest thing I have ever heard. Where did you learn this, from your fucked-up friends back home?"

Suddenly, I could feel him thrust inside of me, and it was not nice at all; it was a harsh, ripping feeling.

It pained me, and it was the meanest way Zacharie has ever fucked me. *I thought he said he loved me, what the hell is this?*

As I was bending over, with my head almost in the toilet, he lifted my hands until they were touching the walls and my arms were straight, and then he started to penetrate further inside me.

As my pussy was begging his erection to find a release point, he lifted my arms further up along the wall, and fucked me deeper.

"Ouch, Zacharie please," I moaned.

"Take it Estelle."

"I am taking it."

"Take it like a good girl," Zacharie demanded.

"I will take it," I screamed.

"Are you going to take it, babe?"

"Yes, Zacharie, I will take it for you."

"Scream it louder, babe."

"I will fucking take it for you," and with the last word that ripped out of my mouth, Zacharie released inside of me, taking his hands from gripping mine and massaging my breasts.

Slowly, he nicely pulled my pants back up.

"Estelle, you have no idea how much that meant to me," Zacharie gasped, while zipping up his pants.

"And you have no idea how amusing it will be when you stick your head in the fucking toilet, and I flush it, because you flush fucked me, and now it's your turn."

***

The next morning, I woke up with Zacharie's arm wrapped around me; he never used to like cuddling me, because he would complain about now a bed was only for fucking or sleeping.

I was not going to complain though. It was nice being back in the arms of my Mr. Complicated, and I never wanted to be out of his reach again.

He was still snoring in my ear, but I did not want to move. I started to think about all the ways he has fucked me during the last three months. Then I thought back to last night, and how it also hurt so much the time before then.

Maybe it was his way of dealing with the pain of being away from me, *but then again how was I supposed to know?*

"What's wrong, babe?" Zacharie asked.

"Nothing, I was just thinking," I replied.

Zacharie lifted his elbow, and propped his head up so he was looking directly at me in my eyes, "what were you thinking about, Estelle?"

"Well I don't want you to get mad, Zacharie," I pleaded.

"Why would I get mad?"

"Well I was thinking about the way you fucked me last night, and the time before, when I dropped you off at the airport."

"Oh- why? Is something wrong?"

Slightly I rolled my eyes to avoid looking at him, but then my eyes found his again, and the truth came out: "The way you fucked me the last two times, it really hurt."

"Yeah, I know."

"You do?"

"Yes, of course," he replied.

"Well, why did you want to hurt me so badly," I sobbed.

"Aw, babe, it's not that I ever meant to hurt you; I just wanted to fuck you hard."

"Well, it hurts when you fuck me hard like that, Zacharie."

"Ok, then you need to be more open about what it is you like, Estelle."

"I told you that I like to make love."

"So you would prefer me to only make love to you?"

"I want you to want to make love to me, not because I tell you too."

"I do want to make love to you, Estelle, but I also want to fuck you."

"So, then what could we do to compromise, so we both get what we want?" I asked.

"How about in the mornings when you stay over, I will make love to you, but then when we are fucking any other time, in my bed or yours, 'we' can both decide whether or not we are going to make love or fuck. But when we are not in bed, then it's an automatic no brainer; 'we' fuck."

"That sounds fair," I replied.

Zacharie brushed his lips against mine, and started biting playfully on my lower lip; it was the first time that he had ever been playful like that, so I decided to bite his lip back.

"You really shouldn't bite on my lower lip, babe, it gives me such a hard on."

I started to tug at his upper lip, and then Zacharie slipped his tongue into my mouth.

We started battling to see who would be the first to submit to the drive that sex was giving us both.

Zacharie placed his right hand under my head, drew my face closer to his, and then removed his lips from mine. He gently started to kiss my earlobe, and nipped at it playfully. "Now I will make love to you, Estelle," he whispered, and I let out a tiny moan.

I could feel his penis against my side, as he slowly and ever so gently rolled himself on top of me.

He continued to kiss me, lifting my head further towards his. He kissed softly down my chest, as he lifted himself up off my body a little.

"Zacharie, kiss my lips," I begged.

He moved his lips from my chest, to my left nipple, and started to gently tug at it. I let out a tiny moan from the arousal that his generous mouth was causing me.

"Please Zacharie, no," I moaned.

Zacharie then moved his lips to my right nipple, started sucking, nibbling, and then kissing. He pressed both his hands softly into mine, and moved slowly inside of me.

I could hear him groan and then whisper against my ear: "I am not going to fuck you babe, I am going to make love to you."

Before I could respond back to Zacharie, his lips were on mine, and he was moving in and out of my pussy so softly, so tenderly.

I could feel his erection building against my explosive orgasm, which was about to blow. He pushed harder, and then released at the same time; my legs started to shake.

He remained lying on top of me, his body pressing gently against mine, while I tried to find a normal breathing pattern.

ENGAGED A TWISTED NEW YEAR'S SCANDAL

So it's New Years, and my boyfriend is here to spend it with me. It was nice to have him back in Medicine Hat with me for one of the end of year holidays.

I peeked my head out of the covers, and saw the light shining in through the half-window in Zacharie's basement apartment. There was still no one occupying the apartment upstairs and I wondered when he was going to show me his finished accomplishment?

"Good morning Estelle," Zacharie whispered, while pressing his lips softly against my ear.

"Good morning to you too babe," I replied, and playfully kissed his nose, climbing out of bed.

"Where do you think you are going, missy?" He scolded, grabbing my shoulder gently and pulling me back in his direction.

I moved myself slightly forward, trying to use all my weight, but I was helpless to his grip, and decided that giving in would be my best option at this point.

I looked Zacharie directly in his dark eyes, "I was going to get up and make my lover breakfast," I replied smugly.

"You know, having you here with me all the time makes me think of us as an old married couple," he laughed.

"Now, Zacharie, you are younger than me; would you not at least need to be the same age as me to be considered the least bit old," I teased, while brushing my lips against his.

"Estelle, you really are the best thing that has ever happened to me. Have I ever told you that?" Zacharie asked.

"Today would most definitely be the first time for those words," I replied, and then crawled back out of bed.

***

Tonight, Zacharie's friends have decided we are going out; I will rock out the 'New Year' with a bang, with my 'Complicated.' First on our list of places to party up: The Casino, and then we were going to hit one of the many bars in Medicine Hat.

"How is everyone else dressing tonight, Zacharie?" I asked out of curiousness. *What if we were not going out with the same friends that were at his work Christmas Party?*

"Estelle, I would really like it if you would wear a black dress, but I cannot force you to do anything you do not want to do," Zacharie replied, while slipping on a pair of black dress pants.

"Well I would feel bad if I did not dress up, because you are already putting on black dress pants. If I were to wear jeans, and a hoodie, would I be underdressed?" I asked.

"I would say so," he laughed.

"Are we driving any of your friends tonight?"

"No, I am thinking they are adult-enough that they can drive themselves. And not to mention, I really do not want to take a chance of not having you able to suck me off before we get to the Casino," he replied with a wink.

"Zacharie, if I am going to wear a dress, you can forget about me sucking your dick on the way to the Casino."

"Is that so?"

"Yes," I replied, irritated.

"Why is that babe?"

"Because why would any girl want to get dressed up for a 'New Years' outing just to suck her boyfriend off before going. My make-up will run all over my outfit, and I will have 'just fucked' hair," I replied sourly, while slipping into a black silk dress.

Zacharie's eyes widened when I turned around to face him, buttoning up his blue shirt. "I am going to have the hottest girlfriend tonight," he said, while pressing his lips together.

Has he been drinking already?

"Zacharie, you really flatter me too much," I replied, and then slipped into a pair of black dress shoes.

"Wait here Estelle, I am going to go out and switch my truck on."

"Why?"

"Because I do not want to have my babe getting cold," he replied, while walking towards me. He then softly kissed my forehead.

"Zacharie, you really do have a soft side; it is really fucked-up how anyone could have hurt you in the past."

And then I paused for a moment, and remembered: I still never responded back to Art's last email. The thought of looking at his review never crossed my mind until now.

I started sweating.

"Is everything alright Estelle?" Zacharie, asked concerned.

"Yes, everything is fine," I replied.

***

Zacharie and I pulled up outside of the Casino, he dropped me out front, and then went to park his truck.

"Wow Estelle, you are looking mighty hot tonight," a random guy said to me. I did not even recognize him.

"I am really sorry to seem rude, but do I know you?" I asked.

"I am Mike, a friend of Zacharie's," he replied, smiling.

Oh shit, he must remember me from the Beer Pong night...

"Oh Mike, I am so sorry, it's been a few weeks since I last saw you," I replied, a little embarrassed.

"I was surprised you remembered me at all Estelle, but no worries."

In the distance I could see Zacharie walking towards where Mike and I were standing and conversing about the Beer Pong night.

"Hey buddy," Zacharie said, while putting his arm around me.

"How was your trip back home?" Mike asked.

"It was good, but I missed my girlfriend," he replied, while giving my hip a squeeze.

"And I missed you very much too, Zacharie," I smiled.

The three of us walked into the Casino to join the rest of Zacharies friends. I wished that Christina would have accepted my invite to come out and try a few dollars on the slot machines, but she was too busy hanging out with Christian now, who she just recently started dating a few weeks ago.

Whatever happened to Jason and Tia, I wondered?

"What machines are you going to play, babe?" Zacharie asked.

I glanced around, "gambling is really not my thing, Zacharie, so maybe I will go to the lounge and have a couple of drinks," I replied.

"Estelle, if gambling is not your thing, why did you not say something in the first place?" He asked.

"Because Zacharie, I really did not want to place a damper on your 'New Year's" plans," I replied.

"Estelle, you would not have put a damper on anything, but it would have made planning what I am about to do next a little more difficult."

"And why is that?" I grinned.

Mr. Complicated got down on one knee, and looked directly into my eyes, "Estelle Ella Whiteside, I have never loved anyone in this entire world the one I kneel before this this evening. And before we ring in the year of 2015 together, I want you to know, I flew back to Medicine Hat because I wanted to show you just how much you really do mean to me. I want to wake up to your lovely face tomorrow and every day after. Would you do me the honor of being my wife?"

Standing before Zacharie Complicated, I was speechless. *Was this some sort of a fucking joke?*

"Well?" Zacharie looked at me with his darkened eyes, wide and waiting for my response.

"Please, Estelle say something... Anything," he begged.

"Yes Zacharie, I will marry you," I replied. Within seconds of my response, there was applauding, clapping. Within several hours, my engagement with 'Mr.Complicated' was broadcasted all over the world.

I wondered how the fuck Art was going to take this? And for that matter how would my parents react?

A CLOSET OF TWISTED

I was sitting in a dark room, hands bound behind my back, my mouth gagged, and my nostrils wide open. *I feel him behind me, as he takes a piece of duct tape over my nose, and closes off my ability to breathe.*

I feel the tears trickle down from my eyes, one drop at a time. I try to breathe, but my air supply is blocked, and he is trying to make me pass out again.

"Stupid fucking bitch," he yells, and takes his fist, ramming it into my rib cage. I feel the insides of my mouth, and want to spit the metallic tasting contents from within; I try to swallow without choking.

My eyes start to flicker back and forth, "oh no you don't Estelle, not so fucking easy, you are going to be awake for it all," he roars, ripping the tape from my mouth.

The light starts to find my eyes, and I can slowly make out the image of Derek, while he walked back towards the dining room table in his parent's house.

He grabs my bottle of 'anti-depressants' from the table, and walks angrily towards where I am sitting prisoner, at his mercy like always.

"Estelle, what the fuck have I told you?" he screams.

"Derek, I don't understand what I did to make you so angry," I cry out.

"I fucking told you, stop dressing like a little slut, and making the other guys at the bar want you. Do you know how distracting it is for me, to see other

guys looking at you? Fuck Estelle," he yells again, and hits me across the face with his fist.

I feel my jaw break, and I cannot move my mouth.

He sets the bottle of 'anti-Depressants' down between my legs, takes both his free hands and spreads my legs further apart. "You want to be a little slut, Estelle, and you wonder why I won't fuck you! Maybe it's time I fuck you like a little slut too," he yells furiously.

Taking his foot, he digs the tip of his steel-toed boot between my legs, and starts moving it up and down slowly, while my chair rests against the wall.

I start to cry because I cannot even move my mouth; he hit me so hard this time. Derek leans in, taking his free hand and making a fist that it connects with my throat. I spat out the blood that I swallowed only moments ago.

He puts his right foot back down on the ceramic tile, and then rips my pants off, and removes my panties by ripping them from my body; I wince from the pain once again.

"Open your fucking mouth, Estelle," he demands. I try, but I can't because he broke my jaw.

"Open your fucking mouth," Derek screamed again, giving me a backhand to the face, and this time, connecting with my left eye.

"Ok bitch, if you won't open your fucking mouth, I will open it for you."

He took both his hands and opened my mouth: I wanted to scream, but only my vocal cords could cry out, and they couldn't make any sense.

"Fuck you, Estelle," Derek picked up the bottle of pills, tilted my head back, dumped the bottle down *my throat, and closed off my mouth. I tried not to swallow, but he placed his right hand over my mouth, cutting my air supply again. "Swallow, like you want to swallow my cum, you dirty mother-fucking slut."*

I tried to fight Derek's grip on my mouth, just so I could open it to get a bit of air in my lungs, but sadly I knew this was a fight I was sadly going to lose again. Again and again with all the physical and mental abuse he put me through.

I finally swallowed...

Seconds after swallowing, he reduced his grip from my mouth and waited a minute until I was almost ready to pass out, "now what goes down, must come back up," he said twistedly.

He lifted me off the chair, and slammed my body to the dining room floor. As he was standing over top of me, he took his right foot and started kicking my ribs, one thrust at a time. "Come on Estelle, spit them back up," he demanded.

One spit at a time, with blood spurting from my insides, I counted twenty-one blows to my stomach...

I wake up in the Hospital, an IV in my left arm, and I notice that my throat feels as though a tube was shoved in it. *I look to my left, and can barely make out the image of Derek talking to one of the nurses at the station outside my room.*

His eyes lock on mine, and he turns back to the nurse: "if you would excuse me, I am going to attend to my girlfriend, would you call Mr. and Mrs. Lapointe and let them know Estelle is awake."

"Yes of course," the nurse replied in a soothing tone.

Derek walked towards my hospital bed; eyes locked on me, and shut the door to the room behind him.

"You really had me worried, Estelle, I thought you were not going to make it this time."

I tried to open my mouth, then the joints in my face were too sore, I could only tear.

"Yes Estelle, your mouth is going to be sore, because you had your jaw re-located. And if you are smart, you will say exactly what I tell you to, when the police come to question you."

I looked away from Derek, how could he fucking do this to me? What did I do to him?

"Estelle, you are going to tell the Police that you were beaten by a random guy you met at the bar last weekend. Do you remember the onlooker who was staring down that low cut top you were wearing at the bar?"

I shook my head.

"Estelle, if you don't do as your fucking told, I am going to beat you worse next time."

***

I woke up, sweating in the arms of my now fiancé, Mr. Complicated. I quickly moved away from him, I thought he was Derek for a moment...

"Estelle, are you alright?" Zacharie asked, while reaching over me to turn on the lamp beside the bed.

I didn't answer him.

"Estelle, what the hell is going on?"

I rolled over towards Zacharie and cuddled into him, "just a bad dream," I replied.

"A bad dream?"

"Yes Zacharie, a bad dream, it does happen," I replied, trying to avoid him asking any further questions.

"Well I know what would make my babe feel better after having a bad dream," he teased, and started kissing my neck softly.

He took his right hand, and started rubbing the outside of my vagina, and then inserted his middle finger up my vagina, I shuttered, "no, please Zacharie," I begged and hesitantly moved away from him.

"Estelle, would you please tell me what the hell is going on?"

"Zacharie, I can't," I replied, turning my head from him.

"Why don't you like me to finger you? Every girl I have ever been with has loved that."

"Zacharie, I am not like other girls you have been with."

"I know, and that is why I love you babe."

"No, I really don't think you get it, I am different. There is a reason why I am a writer."

"Why are you a good writer, Estelle?"

"Because a lot of my writing I do, the characters are an expression of my inner self."

"I see," he replied, kissing at my neck again.

"Zacharie, do you really want to know the reason why I move away when you touch me below?"

"Yes, I want to know what pleases you, Estelle. I want to make you feel good, because I love you."

"Well, there is a reason why I have been single for a long time."

"Why is that?" He asked.

"Because my ex-boyfriend was really abusive," I replied.

"Your ex-boyfriend abused you?"

"Yes, in ways that you have no idea."

"Ok, then can you tell me."

"I have never talked to anyone about it."

"Well, maybe if you talk about it, you would feel better, and I would not wake up to you having a nightmare during the middle of the night."

"Well my ex-boyfriend before you, his name was Derek, and he was older than me, much older than me actually. He is one of the reasons I did not have a problem with my publisher wanting to move me so far away from home after I became a Published Author."

"Ok, I thought your publisher moved you out here because he wanted you to live in a smaller city."

"Yes, Zacharie, my publisher moved me out here because he wanted me to live in a smaller city, but my Publisher also wanted me to concentrate on my writing. I developed writers block because of all the memories I relived in my everyday life in the big city."

"Well, can you tell me something he did to you?"

"What do you want to know?" I asked.

"Tell me what he did to you that makes you not want me to insert my finger inside your vagina to pleasure you."

"Well one day after Derek had a few beers with his friends, he came over to my parents' house in Chicago. Both my parents were away on Vacation in California at their summer home, so there was no one at the house except for him and I. Derek wanted to finger me, and I told him I did not want anything to do with him when he had been drinking, because he usually got really abusive. Well, to make a long story short, he took the burning end of a hot candle, stripped me of my pants and panties, and then blew the candle out, shoving the end of the candle between my legs while the wax was still hot. Needless to say, I could not have anything inserted up my downstairs for several months until I was fully healed," I explained, while looking away from Zacharie.

"You really had someone do something that awful to you, babe?"

"Zacharie, you have no idea what the fuck I have had done to me. You think a girl swinging on you is bad, try having someone abuse the shit out of you for several years, and see how twisted you are."

"Estelle, I am sorry that happened to you."

"Don't be," I replied.

Zacharie hugged me tightly, "I would never do anything like that to you Estelle, ever."

"That's what Derek said to me too," I replied, while the tears rolled down my cheeks.

BATTLE OF SEXUAL DEMONS

This morning was really confusing, especially after waking up sweating in the middle of the night sweating, and finally opening up to someone my past. About the abuse Derek inflicted on me for several years, while my parents stood by, and were completely oblivious to the whole ordeal. *Zacharie was going to be my future husband, so why shouldn't I share the dark parts of my past with him?*

The entire media was still rewinding to last week's proposal Zacharie made, without asking my Father's permission. I left my phone off for the entire week.

After getting up this morning, Zacharie made us breakfast, and we sat across the table in his kitchen anymore barely speaking to one another. I wondered if he thought I was too fucked-up for him to want as a future wife, so I sat and looked at my reflection in my own half emptied plate.

"Estelle, do you trust me?"

I looked at Zacharie, *did he really just ask me that?*

"Yes, why wouldn't I? I said yes to marrying you did, I not?"

"Well, how would you feel if we did something today?"

"What did you have in mind?"

"I was thinking, maybe you could let me finger you," he replied.

"Zacharie, I thought this morning when I woke up after that horrible dream, you said you understood," I replied looking away from him.

Zacharie grabbed my hand, "look at me Estelle, please," he begged.

I looked at him...

"Could you not let me show you that fingering you can be as pleasurable as when I make love to you," he asked.

"Zacharie, I want you to finger me, but sometimes, I just get so scared that you are going to hurt me. I'm scared that you will not stop, because my ex didn't."

"Estelle, I promise, I will never hurt you, and if I do, I want you to tell me because I love you babe, and I would never do anything to hurt someone I love."

"Do you swear?"

"Babe, I promise, I would not hurt you."

"If you wouldn't hurt me, then why do you fuck me in that harsh position," I replied, pouting.

"Estelle, that is completely different."

"How do you figure, Zacharie? It still hurts me."

"If you don't like me to fuck you in that position, then from now on, I will never again have sex with you in that position."

"You would really do that, Zacharie?"

"Estelle, I do not think you realize just how much you mean to me."

I started to think back to my book, and the time when Zacharie was away, and just how much the two of us really connected.

"I love you so much, Zacharie."

"I love you too, babe," he replied, pressing his lips to my forehead.

"Ok, I will let you try, but please don't hurt me."

I sat down on Zacharie's bed, and then began to lay back gently, while he slid his hand behind my back, and started kissing my lips gently.

I felt comfortable enough to let him try and help me get over my sexual demons. Thanks to a twisted ex I once loved, who fucked me mentally and physically. I was constantly plagued by those demons.

Zacharie took his free hand and started slipping my pants off, then released his lips from my mouth, and drew them towards my ear. "I am never going to hurt you, Estelle. This is going to make you feel good," he whispered.

He took his fingers and started gently arousing the outside of my vagina; I could feel myself getting wet, and my breathing starting to get heavy. Had to try and avoid having an orgasm before he even stuck his finger inside of me.

"Come on baby, orgasm for me," he demanded.

"Zacharie, please, I don't want to cum so quickly," I moaned.

He lifted my shirt with his teeth, exposing my nipples as I was not wearing a bra, as my shirt was high enough. I tried to move away from his mouth, but it was too late, he was sucking on my nipple. He was going from one to the other, and I started to get overwhelmed.

He concentrated on sucking my left nipple, and did not stop until he felt I was wet enough. He took his middle finger and inserted it up inside of me, slowly starting to move in and out of me.

"Zacharie, please, I am going to cum," I moaned.

"I know babe, I want you to cum," he said in a husky tone.

I felt myself ready to release to the torment of his hand, but then he stopped.

"Zacharie, please I want to cum," I moaned.

"You are going to cum babe, but I am going to make love to you."

Zacharie gently stood at the end of the bed and took his clothes off, while I lay on his bed, panting like a woman needing to get fucked.

He slowly got onto the bed, "come get under the blankets so you don't get cold," he said.

I lifted my body, and slowly jerked myself until I was under the sheets, then he was on top of me.

He lifted his body a little, slipping his penis inside of me.

I noticed the lights were on in the bedroom; this would be the first time he was leaving them on while we were going to have sex.

"Zacharie, are you not going to turn out the lights?" I asked.

"No, I want to look at the women I am going to marry, while I make love to her," he replied, and then pressed his lips to my forehead and stared into my eyes.

Oh shit, what the fuck have I done?

I cannot have sex and look at him, knowing that I am in the middle of a huge Publishing deal, about a book, that I wrote to exploit Zacharie, aka Mr. Complicated, who I am now engaged to. *He really is in love with me.*

"Look at me Estelle, please I want to see your beautiful eyes," he begged.

I tried to avoid looking at him, but my eyes wanted to find his just as bad. We both locked eyes and his mouth found mine. The kissing was so passionate, and he slipped his hands in mine.

He was going so slow and deep; this time was so much different than all the other times we have fucked before. Mr. Complicated was deeply and passionately in love, with me, his Little Ms. Twisted.

He released his lips from my mouth, and looked me directly in the eye, "Estelle, I love you."

My eyes started to roll back, because I was about to explode, as his mouth found my tits again, tormenting one, and then moving to seize the other.

"Zacharie, please," I moaned, and started to tear.

He was making me feel so good, *could I really continue this any further?*

"Don't cum Estelle, not yet, I want to look at you while you cum, babe," he growled.

"Zacharie, I don't think I can hold on anymore."

He started thrusting deeper, and this time I let go, with my heart and my orgasm, climaxing to a point so fucking high, that my legs and entire body were shaking.

"I love you, Zacharie," I said under my breath, as I could feel him releasing inside of me too.

"I will love you always, and forever Estelle Ella Whiteside."

OFFER REJECTED

From: Art Campbelle
Subject: Regarding Offer
Date: January 7th, 2015 04:22 pm
To: Estelle

Estelle,

I understand you are busy, with your project and all, but to ignore my Offer for almost two months now is absolutely ridiculous. I demand that you get in contact with me today, or else you can consider getting yourself another Publisher.

Art
Managing Director at Exelby Publishing

From: Estelle
Subject: Regarding Offer
Date: January 7th, 2015 04:24 pm
To: Art Campbelle

Art,

Please do not send me such rude emails, this only makes me further delay giving you an answer.

Estelle

From: Art Campbelle

Subject: Regarding Offer
Date: January 7th, 2015 04:26 pm
To: Estelle

Estelle,

I am starting to lose my patience with you Estelle, and my last email was not a joke.

Art
Managing Director at Exelby Publishing

From: Estelle
Subject: Regarding Offer
Date: January 7th, 2015 04:28 pm
To: Art Campbelle

Art,

Please tell me something:
How the hell can you resign from being my Publisher, since we have a five year Publishing Contract, that is in writing for my first book, 'Loved by No Other', which I am also contracted to write the sequel to?

Estelle

From: Art Campbelle
Subject: Regarding Offer
Date: January 7th, 2015 04:34 pm
To: Estelle

Estelle,

A Contract is only as valuable as a Writer to Publisher, Estelle. It has been six months, and I have not seen anything from you, except another story line, that Exelby Publishing has extended an Offer to you for Publishing, and you have been dicking 'us' around.

I have also not seen or heard from you regarding the sequel to 'Loved by No Other', in which you are Contracted to provide such details to me within a timely manner of being asked.

I need to see something by the time I go home today, or else, as I have explained, and will explain again in this email, IF I HAVE NOTHING BY DAY'S END, CONSIDER YOURSELF PUBLISHLERLESS.

Art
Managing Director at Exelby Publishing

From: Estelle
Subject: Regarding Offer
Date: January 7th, 2015 04:41 pm
To: Art Campbelle

Art,

Can I please ask one question?

Estelle

From: Art Campbelle
Subject: Regarding Offer
Date: January 18th, 2013 04:42 pm
To: Estelle

Estelle,
What is the question?
Art
Managing Director at Exelby Publishing

From: Estelle
Subject: Regarding Offer
Date: January 7th, 2015 04:45 pm
To: Art Campbelle

Art,

Is Publishlerless even a word? Because according to my spell check, the word does not exist?

Estelle

From: Art Campbelle
Subject: Regarding Offer
Date: January 7th, 2015 04:52 pm
To; Estelle

Estelle,
I am not playing games, and my patience is getting thin.

Art
Managing Director at Exelby Publishing

Zacharie walked towards me, and I placed my cell-phone face down on his bed, he gently kissed my lips.
"What are you doing, babe?" He asked.

"Nothing, was just checking my email," I replied.

"Did you get anything interesting, babe?"

"No," I replied, hesitantly.

"Are you ok, Estelle?"

"Yes, everything is fine. I am going for a shower, Zacharie, and maybe when I get out maybe we could go for dinner, my treat."

"You are going to take me out for dinner after you get out of the shower?"

"Yes, to any were you would like, Zacharie."

"Well, first of all, I do not want anyone else seeing the woman that I love naked, so I would like it if you would at least dress yourself before taking me to dinner," he replied with a smirk.

"Zacharie fuck off, you obviously know that I am not going to dinner naked."

I grabbed my phone as I was in the washroom, stripped down to my naked self, and looked in the mirror. I sat down on the toilet, and decided it was time to face the music.

From: Estelle
Subject: Rejecting Offer
Date: January 7th, 2015 04:59 pm
To: Art Campbelle

Art,

I would like to take the time to 'Thank' you for initially offering me, such a wonderful Publishing Contract, but I must decline. After careful consideration of the effects this would not only have on my life, but also the life of the 'man,' my Mr. Complicated, whom I have grown to love over the last several months of getting to know him.

I did not realize, at the beginning of my plot, how self-centered I was really being. After simply reading through my journal entries and through several of the emails you and I have exchanged over the last several months, I am sad to definitely decline.

However I will continue my work on the sequel to 'Loved by No Other,' and I will send this to you no later than one week from today's date.

I hope you understand Art, but I love him too much.

Estelle

I got up off the toilet, and walked out of the washroom with my cell-phone because I forgot my body-wash in my overnight fuck bag I take with me to Zacharie's.

"Is everything ok Estelle?" Zacharie asked.

"Yes Zacharie, everything is fine, I just forgot my body-wash," I replied, placing my cell-phone down on his nightstand, beside the bed.

"I want you to wash yourself really good, because when we get back from having dinner, I want to be able to have you for dessert."

"Zacharie, honestly you are so disgusting," I replied.

From: Art Campbelle
Subject: Regarding Offer
Date: January 7th, 2015 05:07 pm
To: Estelle

Estelle,

You are rejecting the offer???

Do you realize how much money you could make by exploiting this stupid Mother-fucker who you have been bedding and pretending to love.

Estelle, you do not love this guy, really I know you. Think about your writing career and what this research you have been doing over the last four months could do for you, career-wise.

Two or three years down the line from now, is this guy really going to matter to you? Will he even be in your life?

Think about what this type of money could do for you, independently. This book will sell like condoms to the adult population; you even said that yourself in your Query to me.

What the hell are you thinking?

Art
Managing Director at Exelby Publishing

PLOT EXPLAINED

I finished my shower and walked into the bedroom, to see Zacharie holding my cellphone in his hand.

Zacharie had a blank expression across his face.

"Zacharie, is everything ok?" I asked, walking over to him, while drying my body off with a towel.

Zacharie got up off his bed and moved away from me. He then threw my cell-phone on his bed, and crossed his arms.

"Zacharie, what the hell is going on?" I asked, suddenly alarmed to the tone of anger that his body language was expressing.

Zacharie said nothing...

Then I thought for a moment back to the emails that Art and I were exchanging before I went in the shower, and then to Zacharie holding my cellphone. Shit, he must have read an email I sent to Art, or maybe got the reply Art sent back to me with my rejecting of his offer.

"Zacharie, it's not what you think," I sobbed, starting to tear up.

"Then what the fuck is it, Estelle?"

"Zacharie, let me explain."

"Estelle, I think you should get dressed and get the fuck out of my house."

"Zacharie, please let me explain."

"I trusted you Estelle, and I thought you were different."

"I am different Zacharie; you need to let me explain."

"Estelle, you are just like all the other bitches I have fucked; you fucked me in the end, now get the fuck out," Zacharie screamed.

"Zacharie, seriously, you are over fucking reacting."

"How the hell am I overreacting Estelle? You wanted to fuck me, make me fall in love with you, and then exploit me to the fucking world as some asshole called Mr. Complicated. Who the fuck is Mr. Complicated, anyways?"

"Zacharie, Mr. Complicated is you," I replied.

"Why Estelle?"

"Zacharie, if you would let me explain it to you, then you would understand."

"Fine Estelle, I will give you five minutes of my time, because it will be the last and only time you will ever see or talk to me, and it starts now."

I wanted to cry so bad, but if I was going to have any chance of Zacharie not leaving me for what I was planning on doing to him (but did not do because I loved him so much), I needed to pull myself together, and just come clean with him.

"Zacharie, what you read in that Email from my Publisher to me, well it was true. I do not want to tell you otherwise, because doing so would be lying to you further. The truth is; when I first met you, I only wanted to fuck you, and I am sure you were looking for the same thing. I told my Publisher that I had a great idea, and it was to exploit men for the inconsiderate sexual assholes that they are. Art, my Publisher, told me he thought I was onto something. I told him that I was going to put myself out there in the tiny city of Medicine Hat and find some guy who was stupid enough to fall in love with me."

"And that stupid guy you found was obviously me," Zacharie shouted.

"You are not stupid, Zacharie. Yes, at the moment in time when I met you, I thought you were that guy to exploit, but then after I started to get to know you, I fell in love with you."

"I don't believe you."

"I can prove it to you, Zacharie."

"How?"

"I kept a journal."

"You kept a fucking journal about me?"

"Yes, I did."

"Where is it?"

"I have it in my night bag, I will show it to you, but it will take more than five minutes. I guarantee by the time you finish reading my journal entries, you will see that I fell in love with you. Also at the end of today, even when my Publisher offered me two hundred thousand dollars to exploit you to the world, I couldn't do it."

"Let me see the journal entries, Estelle."

BLACK JOURNAL
OF ESTELLE ELLA WHITESIDE

From Zacharies point of view,

September 3rd, 2014

Project Complicated; By Estelle Ella Whiteside

The life of an Author is never an easy career choice, I must say moving so far away from my family for the love of pen to paper, or fingertips to keyboard, is not something I imagined leaving home for. My career has dragged me to a small town called Medicine Hat, in the Canadian province of Alberta, when I have lived in the big city of Chicago for the last twenty-five years of my life.

At twenty-six, I must say my life is not everything I imagined it would be. In less than two months from today, I was supposed to go to New York, and start my first Book tour out of Jersey City, heading west towards Washington. Instead, I am now trying to deal with an overbearing workload that my Publisher has assigned. I also had to break the news to my Father back home in Chicago, Illinois, that the tour will need to be placed on hold, until next August.

It's rather embarrassing, especially from a newly Published Author's perception, when you tell everyone back home that your Publisher & Agent think you really have a 'golden' piece of work, yet they halt all the plans that took months to coordinate, and re-route your professional career path.

An entire year of my life not wasted, but lived in Medicine Hat, Alberta with no one to love me, and my life so not together.

My life before moving to Medicine Hat was simple and uncomplicated, until my fabulous Publisher launched my first book, 'Loved by No Other.'

The book was launched one month too early, and it really took off in the United States of America. Almost two months later my book saw the same chain of events take place within Canada. Everyone wanted to know: who is 'Estelle Ella Whiteside?'

My Publisher decided to fly me out to New York last Christmas, and tell me it would be best-suited if I would relocate to a much smaller town, with little-to-no population. It would give me the chance to expand my writing talent, instead of leading me down the road map to writer's block, which is where I was headed if I stayed in Chicago. Especially after a recent nympho breakdown I had at my previous place of employment.

Taking my Publisher only one week to decide the next year of my life would be spent in Medicine Hat, Alberta, I was shortly packing whatever belongings I could fit into my suitcases, and saying goodbye to my friends, and preparing for a goodbye to my family.

My parents and I talked, but never argued about the move I would make, which I ultimately knew would end the life we shared so close together and for so long. Associated with my little scandal, but after everything that happened, they thought it would be best for the time being.

I never kept any secrets from my Father or Mother growing up, and with my twin Sister just getting married a couple of years prior to me launching my career as an Author, what was there really to keep me in Chicago anyway?

I had no one who loved me in Chicago, except family and friends. Fans claimed to love me, but I knew they only loved my talent of storytelling, not the 'girl' I was inside.

No one ever thought I was a decent enough girl to date, because my past was too twisted for them. I mean my track record for sexual ways to exploit myself was all over the internet; it might as well be broadcasted on a billboard for the entire 'World' to see my shame. Since I decided to publish my first book, the amount of criticism surrounding my sexual intellect can sometimes become overbearing.

I can remember back to most of my childhood, which I spent rebelling against my parents by doing drugs, or partaking in any illegal event where I could get a free ride home in the back of a cop cruiser.

I wanted to be everything the opposite of my twin sister Adeline, who was so perfect her entire life.

On days I was not over-dosing on Alcohol, I was drowning myself in writing my daily diaries; something I have done ever since I could first remember being able to hold a pen.

Some of my best works of writing are derived from such truth, or jarred memory of an abusive past, or fucked-up scenario I was role-playing with a random oral sex partner that I found on the internet. I have continued to advertise my body over the years, since I found that trying to hold a steady relationship with an un-abusive guy, just wasn't in the cards for me.

I have always wondered, if I had never decided to take my shirt off that night, would the two of us still be together; but being that I am so fucking twisted, I wished I would have done that at a concert. Honestly in the state of mind I was in, I would have sexually exploited myself for attention any way at that time.

Not much has changed from the girl I once was, to the woman I am not today.

My Publisher and Agent suggested I not get involved with anyone in Medicine Hat, because I would not be staying long; after one year of living here, I would be leaving for my tour, re-united with my Father who would join me, as my Mother would still working full-time.

During the first year I spent living in Medicine Hat, away from my family, I worked vicariously on my writing. I wrote several books that I could not finish because my mind was going in so many different, uncertain directions.

I attempted to concentrate on other matters, like my fan-blogging site, or else answering fan e-mail, but it was not enough to keep my mind from lingering to other areas ready to become a disaster.

I felt so alone and so scared to fall in love. When my Publisher broke the news to me that I would not be going on tour until next August, creating some free time for myself, I decided to fill the void.

I started to plot a sadistic storyline, and thought how sick and twisted it would actually be if I made my characters come to life in the real world. I mean most of the stories I wrote were about fantasy, erotica, and romantic suspense. But what if I created a female character; a character just as 'Twisted' as I am?

Could I actually find a random guy to fall in love with me? Why not put this 'Twisted' character out in Medicine Hat, for the sole purpose of fucking different guys, and twisting the nice one which could fall in love with her? Would it be possible, could I actually find a true love this way, since I can never find it normally because I lived so uncomplicated, and in a manner everyone expected?

Surely I would be the first writer to develop my own self into a role-playing character, but living in the realistic world of reality. The one where you pay bills, actually have a job aside from a writing career, and deal with all the hardships life has to offer. I could mold myself into a normal girl, but mentally still be that all sorts of 'Twisted' everyone knows back home.

Until my character is sought out and planned.

Yours truly,
Little Ms. Twisted.

***

September 7th, 2014

I am so angry right now with Art, my Publisher, with Exelby Publishing. I was trying to tell him about a new book I have in the works, but he is too focused on continuing my last big seller: 'Loved by No Other.' When do I get to call the shots? It seems as though everyone else makes my life decisions for me.

One year ago, I was happy living in Chicago. I had my family, and could go out with my friends whenever I wanted. Everyone knew who 'Estelle Ella White side' was.

Since I have moved to Medicine Hat, Alberta, no one recognizes me out in public, or points a finger and say's 'look there she is.' Instead, I walk down the street on a sidewalk, because the red carpet has been pulled out from under my feet by my goddamn publisher.

I have millions, but feel so poor at heart, because I have no one to share my fame and fortune with.

The only thing I can spend my time doing is writing stories for other people to turn pages, and fall in love with. Or else I spend my time plotting to meet a guy, to trick him into falling in love with me.

Why would anyone ever want to love Estelle Ella Whiteside? Would they want to love me for money? Fame? How about my Fortune that will continue to have roll in from all the future works I publish going forward?

Is there no one real in this screwed up World anymore that 'we' all need to just pretend, and read about how great life could or should be?

I guess after my movie night later, I might have something to write about.

At least my journal will always love me, because I can keep writing, and there will always be pages to turn until I am finished.

Love Estelle Ella Whiteside

Xoxo

***

September 8th, 2014

What makes a good writer a successful Author? For me it was never really about writing about what happened in my life, but writing about fantasy and erotic behavior that I wanted my characters to role-play.

I only dreamed of becoming a famous 'anything' and now here I sit, ten years post that daydream, configuring my career path into a real life scenario. One where I am playing the main character, and I held only one audition. Now here I have a young man, so complicated, yet so appealing to try and understand his complicated sexual methods.

I have never attempted to put an ad on a dating site. Well ok, maybe that's an utter line of spilt bullshit, but so is a lot of things I say.

I find it sexy that Zacharie drove his work truck to the coffee shop to meet me, and does not feel he needs to impress me with expensive accessories, because really, that's all money is to someone like myself who already has everything.

Love and passion; it does not seem like Zacharie is really made for these things, so the two of us might hit it off very well. I am planning on staying with him for a minimum of four months so that my research can be conducted properly. I will make sure to note every detail, from the time we fuck for the first time, to the time I suck his penis and finally get him off.

This morning was the angriest morning I have had in a long time, and also the most degrading.

He didn't say anything rude to me, but the fact that I cannot make him cum, this is a problem for me.

I am the queen of sucking cock; ok, maybe at one point in my life I use to be, but just because I am getting older does not mean I can't suck cock the way I use to.

I almost feel like taking a pole and stripping myself off in front of Zacharie, and see how complicated his penis feels when I give it a lap dance, and take my panties off.

But being allowed to take charge in the bedroom might be a problem with Zacharie. He did some kinky shit last night that I have never been exposed to.

He asked if I wanted to play a game, and then tied my hands and legs, not to mention gagging me with a dildo. What the fuck is up with that?

I hope he did not have a video camera taping the two of us? That would be some fucked-up shit.

Sorry, maybe I am just full of it. Most guys do this to get off or something; I really need to get a grip. I mean why the hell is Zacharie having such an effect on me? We just met for fuck sakes.

Could it be that I have spent too long away from the real world, and fabricated my life plot with science fiction, rather than reality?

If he would have just lifted me up this morning for being naughty, and held me against his bedroom door, and let me fucking have it, I would have been so happy. I want him to make me cum, but how the hell do I get him to bed me? Should I take control? Does he want me to take control?

I am really good at wanting to fuck, but I have never played the lead role. Maybe I should have a few drinks tonight and indulge in my submissive side?

Only tonight will tell....

Until such times

Little Miss Twisted

My pussy would like to be assaulted by Mr. Complicated.

***

September 9th, 2014

Mr. Complicated is 'fucked.'

I am really confused? I do not understand why Mr. Complicated needed to keep both my left and right hands cuffed to his bedpost last night?

I mean the fact that he spanked my tits, and then fucked me harshly, until he got off on causing me pain was fucked-up enough. Is it even legal to have sex with someone of the opposite sex in such a manner?

His ad on the dating site never said 'Mr. Complicated seeks submissive,' and this is certainly not what I signed up for.

Yet, my ad did not say 'Little Ms. Twisted seeks Complicated for exploitation,' so as long as both our needs are being satisfied, I guess there really is no harm.

But I do want to highlight the first thing that initially turned me off from wanting Zacharie to fuck me, was the fact that he didn't even kiss me back two nights ago. Not to mention, he had a box of open condoms under his pillowcase, and told me he was going to fuck me. Who tells a girl he is going to fuck her? Just do it, don't talk about it.

Is it normal for a guy to be this fucking difficult? I mean I don't think I have been unreasonable. I mean I let him use his trunk of sexual pain on me, and I will continue to, but when do I get pleasured?

Maybe I am being the difficult one; I mean it was my idea to be the Author who decides she is going to start writing a random book about how to find a guy, and make him fall in love with her, based off sex. But Zacharie makes it so difficult to even let me touch him, and he does not want to touch me nicely.

Tonight, I am going to try keep a really open mind, and get him to give 'us' another shot.

Here is to keeping an open mind, when it comes to Mr. Complicated

Little Ms. Twisted

***

September 19th, 2014

I am writing because I am so fucking angry, that I feel as though tonight I will get drunk out of my mind, and fuck Mr. Complicated retarded. If he would let me.

Who the fuck has sex with someone, and is so selfish he gets himself off, without pleasing the girl? Who the fuck does this motherfucker think he is?

I am a girl; I would like to be pleased and fucked nicely, and maybe if he is in a giving mood, even cum. But 'no', everything is about Zacharie and what he enjoys. I mean we have only fucked ten times, but I can fully see where this is leading.

I wanted a guy who would please me, not use me to please himself; just roll over and go to bed once he is done getting off.

It was so unfair; he finally kissed me, with some passion behind it, and then closed the door, once the hat was on.

I am so fucking mad.
Fuck you Mr. Complicated.
Little Ms. Twisted
Pissed off, and not satisfied.

***

September 21st, 2014

This morning, my departure from Mr. Complicated has left me wondering: why is it so hard to get him to show any sort of emotion towards me?

Do I look like I was dropped on my face as a baby by my parents, left with just boobs and an ass, with a hole for him to get off with? I don't get it; this guy is so hard to understand.

My best friend seems to think that Zacharie is using me for sex, but that was my plan overall. Then I wanted to make him fall in love with me, but this task is proving to be harder than anything I thought possible.

Usually a guy enjoys hanging out with a girl he is seeing, and takes her to movies and out for dinner. But not Zacharie, he only takes me home to bed. If we watch a movie, it's one that he picks; he never asks me what I like.

I mean all of the times I have been to his place (he is not exactly the best host), he only ever thinks of himself, and he has never even made me dinner during the past two weeks we have been fucking. At least if he would come to my apartment, I would make him dinner, and offer him a drink, before I offer him to take me to bed.

When he fucked me last night, he really hurt me. I wanted to beg him to stop having sex with me like that, but he didn't even care. When I cried, he pushed further. I am sure he could feel my tears roll down the side of my cheeks and splatter against his hands, because I know they landed there.

Is he really that much of an asshole that he will only ever care about his own needs?

How do I get him to ever care about me?

How did his past girlfriend get him to care? Is it possible that Mr. Complicated has been hurt so badly that he does not want to care or love again?

What if I show him I can care, but then expose him to the 'world' as an incoherent asshole...? Would I be just as pathetic as the other girl from his past?

Wait a minute; am I starting to care about Mr. Complicated?

I am confused, this entry is finished.
Little Ms. Twisted

***

November 1st, 2014

`I never thought I would be so mentally fucked-up that I would actually write a journal entry from my friend Jason's place; whom, by the way, I just met a few weeks ago at work. But I have something I really need to get off my chest.

I promise if you just listen to me right now, I will glue this blank sheet of paper in you, upon my return home later this morning. Do we have a deal? Of course we do! You cannot talk back to me...lol.

Zacharie, the 'Mr. Complicated' I have been fucking, who finally asked me to be his girlfriend while he was out working in Lethbridge, just got back last night after being gone for a little over a three weeks.

He decided that instead of coming to see me he wanted to go and see his friend who is visiting again from Calgary. Who the hell is this guy anyway? Is he actually a 'he' and not a 'she?'

I am really confused though, because his dick has not been inside of me for over three weeks. Yes, we have gone a few days here and there without fucking, but I mean, I was going to be home, and it was a Friday night.

I had my 'fuck swing' all ready for him to fuck me in. Could Zacharie be fucking someone else?

In the middle of my confusion, my two new 'customers' I mean friends from work, took me out last night. I even made Christian have a fight with his slut last night. Then I made him choose between her or I. How is it possible that a guy I am not fucking chooses me over some bitch he is fucking? That makes no sense.

I am just as bad as Mr. Complicated, look at what I am doing to people who are at least trying to be friends to me. And I am supposed to be trying to get Zacharie to care about me, not Christian. Am I really that twisted and fucked-up, that I want to destroy everyone's life?

I wish Zacharie would hold my hands, look me in the eyes, and fuck me slowly, the way I like to be fucked. But he just can't bring himself to fuck me nicely, let alone be a good boyfriend.

Why the fuck am I wasting my time on this guy?
Why am I even playing this 'Little Ms. Twisted?'
Because I am 'Twisted.'
Little Ms. Twisted

***

Random Entry,

It is almost seven on a Saturday night, and Zacharie didn't see me last night when he got back; I was almost in tears.
I really do mean nothing to this guy, so why am I putting myself through this?
Just for a book to please my Publisher?

***

November 8th, 2014

Dear Mr. Complicated
I am appalled by your blatant disregard for the opposite sex, and my emotional attachment to all men who decide to bed me.
If you have not already noticed, I am broken-hearted and a mess; I was not looking for a fucked-up relationship to make things worse.
The deal was, there was to be no flowers, strings of broken promises, and bullshit lines of 'I love you'. This was to be an arranged bedtime greeting, with a 'see you only for sex' goodbye meeting.
I did not want to be cuddled, or kissed passionately by a 'man' who would do these things without showing any emotional attachment, or justify that he does not feel a thing for me and actually mean it.
By the way you fuck me, sex is strictly for your gratification only; when it comes to pleasing me, it just doesn't happen.

When will my cuming finally occur?
Only time will tell.
From
Yours truly Little Ms. Twisted

***

November 8th, 2014

Dear Journal

It has been two days since my last sexual encounter with 'Mr. Complicated,' and he made love to me for the first time. I never imagined Zacharie making love to me, would make me fall in love with him. I have never had anyone, make love to me the way he did.

I have not tried to contact Zacharie, since he dropped me off.

Dear Mr. Complicated

I am no longer appalled by your blatant disregard for the opposite sex, my emotional attachment to you since, we have made love has now changed.

I understand you did not noticed, I was previously broken-hearted and a mess. I was looking for a fucked-up relationship to make my next debut novel. One that would exploit the sexual selfish side you once showed me.

The deal still is, there is to be no flowers, on-going strings of broken promises, and I love you,' during our sexual arranged time together is fine.

I do not want to be cuddled, but enjoy being kissed passionately by a 'man' who would do these things without showing any emotional attachment, but would justify that he does not feel a thing for me and actually not mean it.

By the way you make love to me; sex is no longer strictly for your gratification only; when it comes to pleasing me, it has finally happened. Was it only because you were in a giving mood?

I mean the first time you ever had sex with me nicely, was when you woke up in the morning out of the blue and didn't put your cap on. And that was just two days ago!

Maybe it was not bright enough for you that morning? You still have me wondering.

That morning really fucked me up, because it felt like we made love for the first time, and sex was such a climax for me. The further you pushed inside, the more pleasure I felt, and 'cuming' finally occurred; I was now yours. Your head really roped me in, and this is where I now must figure you out, Mr. Complicated.

Can 'Complicated' actually love the 'Twisted?' Because maybe I might just be that all sorts of fucked-up you're looking for?

Only our time together will tell.

Cheers to all the great sex we will have going forward, Mr. Complicated.

From
Yours Truly Little Ms. Twisted

***

I thought because I have spent so much of my life broken-hearted, that breaking someone else's heart would make me feel better. I also thought I would enjoy a fucked-up relationship, but at the beginning when Zacharie was fucking me randomly, it hurt my feelings that he did not pleasure me.

No flowers have ever bothered me, as I am not the flower type of girl. I am the strings of broken promises type, however Zacharie seems to be changing so much more, as side from our recent love making. He is starting to see me during the earlier part of the evening, instead of just after hours before our arranged bedtime meeting.

In the beginning I also did not want to be cuddled, so I thought. I never knew how much it really hurt, to be fucked and not cuddled afterward. Especially with my emotional attachment to the men who have bed me. I never imagined there was a guy alive, who could actually portray a cold-hearted mother-fucker like 'Mr. Complicated.' But now after we made love; is he really a cold-hearted mother-fucker? Only our time together going forward will tell.

***

December 25th, 2014

Dear Zacharie,

There are so many things I wish I could say to you in person right now, but since you are so far away, I thought of writing you a letter, because I feel dazed and confused.

I am sad on so many levels. First, I miss our fucking. Second I miss our love making. Third, and most important, I miss seeing you every day.

Before you left, we were spending every moment of every day we had together, in one another's arms. I knew our relationship was based on more than just a physical connection.

I have come to know you on so many more levels than I did three months ago, and I really feel what we have is special, and I want you to know how much you mean to me.

Today is Christmas, and the one gift I would like to give to you is my heart; it's yours, forever and always.

I promise to think of you every day in the morning when I wake up, and in the evening before I go to bed. I will never go to bed angry, because I love you so much, and sometimes I wish you would tell, just how you feel.

I know you are not good at expressing your emotions, but since you have made love to me, I feel like I cannot get enough of you expressing yourself, sexually, but mentally as well.

We have talked on the phone every day you have been in Boucherville visiting your family, and I feel I know more about you now, than I did before you left.

I love you so much Zacharie, and I cannot wait until you get home in a few weeks.

Love Estelle

"I really am, Mr. Complicated."

TRAILER OF SEX MOVING FORWARD

We got to the Chinese Restaurant just around the corner from Zacharie's bungalow and we were seated by one of the nice waitresses.

"Estelle, I am so sorry that I yelled at you," Zacharie said, while looking at me with the menu facing down.

I looked at him, "it's ok Zacharie, I deserved it."

"No Estelle," Zacharie reached across the table for my hands, "I never should have yelled at you like that."

"It is ok, really Zacharie," I replied, while looking at him.

"Estelle, do you realize how much I love you?"

"Yes, you tell me all the time," I replied.

"Remember, when we were on the phone when I was away in Boucherville, and you thought I was joking about you moving in with me?"

"Yes, I remember," I replied, slipping one of my hands away from Zacharie's to open up the menu and have a glance.

"Well, how would you feel about moving in with me, babe?"

I looked at Zacharie, in shock...

"You want me to move into your apartment?"

"Yes, we are getting married," he replied.

"Zacharie, are you sure you could even live with me, after me almost exploiting you to the world?"

"Almost Estelle, but you did not, and that's why I love you and want to spend the rest of my life loving you everyday, like I do now."

"Zacharie, I love you so much," I replied, looking at him.

He reached over the table and brushed his lips against mine.

"Do you know what you are going to order, babe?" He asked.

"I know what I would like to order, but they do not serve you here," I replied in a teasing tone.

"Estelle, what do you say, when we get out of here, we head back to our place and have some fun."

"That sounds really sexy," I replied, licking my lips.

"Good, because I am going to take you upstairs, and fuck you in the top part of my bungalow."

"That sounds perfect. How long have you wanted to ask me to move in with you?" I asked.

"I was thinking about having you move in with me for awhile, but I did not know whether or not you would consider it. So that's why I asked you to marry me first."

"Zacharie, of course I would move in with you, I love you."

***

Zacharie and I arrived back at his place, and I was unsure if he was kidding or not about actually finishing off the night in his vacant apartment upstairs, but I was game to play.

Zacharie got out of the truck, and waved me up the front steps of the main entrance.

"Are you seriously going to take me in there, Zacharie?" I asked.

"Babe, there are three beds to fuck on in here."

"Really?"

"Yes, and if you fuck me on the one of my choosing, I will let you conduct an 'Interview' with your Mr. Complicated, tomorrow. And then I will take you back to the apartment tomorrow, to start packing it up, so you can move into Complicated territory."

The way Zacharie made that sound was so erotic...

"Ok, Zacharie, I will let you choose the bed, but I want to conduct the interview after we are finished. It will be a way for us to have closure."

"Agreed."

Zacharie and I walked into the upstairs apartment. He stopped in the living-room, turned on the Television above the couch he rolled out.

I noticed a video-camera above the television, and when he turned the Television, on I could see him and I standing in the living-room.

"Estelle, this is where I want us to fuck," he said.

"Zacharie, you cannot be serious, there is no way I am fucking while you record us."

Zacharie did not even respond, he picked me up over his shoulder, and spanked my ass so hard that I could feel my right ass cheek beating. "Ouch," I pouted.

"You have been a really bad girl, Estelle, or should I call you Genevieve?"

"Please do not ever say that name," I groaned.

"It's time for Mr. Complicated to punish Little Ms. Twisted."

He slapped my ass again in the same spot, and I 'yelped.'

Zacharie placed me down on the couch, and I watched on the screen as he stripped my clothes off, and then stripped his own off.

"What have I told you about wearing a bra, Estelle?"

"Zacharie, I am sorry," before I could finish my sentence, he rolled me on my stomach, and smacked my ass again. "I want you to look at the screen Estelle, this is what is going to happen when you are Little Ms. Twisted."

"Zacharie please, I do not want you to spank me anymore; I learned my lesson," I pleaded.

"Have you really, Estelle?"

"Yes," I replied.

Zacharie took his penis and started gently spanking my ass over the spot that was beating from his slaps.

I started to feel myself get wet.

He was getting hard.

"I am going to fuck you like this, Estelle. I want you to take both your hands, and hold the edge of the fold out."

"Zacharie, it's going to hurt."

"I want to punish you, babe, for being a bad girl."

"Can't you make love to me?" I begged.

"Making love is for a good girl, and you have been really naughty. I am going to fuck you like you wanted me to in your Journal."

Oh shit…

Zacharie gripped my hips tightly, and shoved his dick inside of my vagina while I was on my stomach. Then he started moving slowly in and out of me.

"Oh my fucking god, Zacharie," I moaned.

He started fucking me slower, and then deeper, and I could feel him hit my wall. The way he fucked me felt incredible, he was going to make me orgasm.

"Grab the edge of the fold out babe, this one is going to hurt."

He slammed into me hard, and I 'yelped' again. "Zacharie, oh my god," I moaned.

His erection started to get harder, and as it got harder, I started to get wetter.

"Zacharie, I am going to cum, please." I begged.

He slammed into me harder, I was holding onto the edge of the fold out to prevent my head from hitting the wall in front of me, because he was fucking me so hard.

Before I could cum, he pulled out of me, rolled me onto my back, and stuck his penis back into me.

"Hold the edge of the fold out, babe," he demanded, and I did as I was told.

I looked in his eyes, as he started assaulting my tits with his mouth, and it was over for me; I began to cum.

I could feel his erection building up inside of me, "Oh fuck Zacharie, I am cuming," I cried out as he released inside of me, and I was spent.

"Did you enjoy the trailer, babe?" He whispered in my ear.

"Yes, the trailer of sex," I laughed.

INTERVIEW WITH MR. COMPLICATED

Have you ever been on the quest to meet a one-night stand, or maybe that guy you could randomly fuck on every other occasion after the one-night stand, but have no emotional attachment? Well if you answered yes to the following question, you are not alone.

Four Months from Now
Interviewer Estelle Ella Whiteside (Little Ms. Twisted)
Interviewee Zacharie Gagne (Mr. Complicated)

It's January 8th, 2015 and I hand him the letter I wrote two months ago. "Zachary, I want you to read this before our interview." I smile and hand him the crumpled up letter, address to 'Mr. Complicated.'

Dear Mr. Complicated

I am no longer appalled by your blatant disregard for the opposite sex and my emotional attachment to you, since we have made love and that has now changed.

I understand you did not notice, I was previously broken-hearted and a mess. I was looking for a fucked-up relationship to make my next debut novel. One that would exploit the sexual selfish side you once showed me.

The deal still is, there is to be no flowers, on-going strings of broken promises, and I love you,' during our sexual arranged time together is fine.

I do not want to be cuddled, but enjoy being kissed passionately by a 'man' who would do these things without showing any emotional attachment, but would justify that he does not feel a thing for me and actually not mean it.

By the way you make love to me, sex is no longer strictly for your gratification only; when it comes to pleasing me, it has finally happened. Was it only because you were in a giving mood?

I mean the first time you ever had sex with me nicely, was when you woke up in the morning out of the blue and didn't put your cap on. And that was just two days ago!

Maybe it was not bright enough for you that morning? You still have me wondering.

That morning really fucked me up, because it felt like we made love for the first time, and sex was such a climax for me. The further you pushed inside, the more pleasure I felt, and 'cuming' finally occurred; I was now yours. Your head really roped me in, and this is where I now must figure you out, Mr. Complicated.

Can 'Complicated' actually love the 'Twisted?' Because maybe I might just be that all sorts of fucked-up you're looking for?

Only our time together will tell.

Cheers to all the great sex we will have going forward, Mr. Complicated.

Zacharie finishes reading the crumpled-up letter, and licks his lips slightly, and then directs a dark glare of excitement towards my direction.

I bite down on my upperlip gently, and look towards his direction cautiously "Mr. Complicated, were you aware the entire time we have been seeing each other, that you were simply a plot for me to end up Fucking?" I asked whisking my head back, so that my long dirty dark hair would fall evenly down my back.

"Ms. Twisted, I am aware of your blatant disrespect for the opposite sex," Zacharie replied, keeping his dark brown eyes focused on my posture while he pressed his soft lips into a straight line. *I could not help but notice, and my throat suddenly became desperate to produce saliva so my tongue could wet my dry lips that I was dying for him to brush his against.*

"Mr. Complicated, you are aware that this entire scenario occurred because of your lack of disrespect for the women you bed, correct?" I asked, while I gently bit down on my lip, and then opened my mouth slightly to run my wet tongue across the dry cracks. *I was hoping he wanted to fuck me in the front closet after we finished making a 'trailer of sex': a saucy epilogue for my book Mr. Complicated.'*

"Ms. Twisted, if the women I bed should develop an emotional attachment simply after I have only fucked them, how can I be to blame for this?" He said in a smart ass tone, while taking his left hand and brushing it against my naked kneecap.

I could feel myself start getting a little excited by his touch, and we had only finished fucking moments before starting the interview: *I needed to contain myself.*

"Well Mr. Complicated, if you don't mind me pointing out; you did not advertise you were looking for a one-night stand," I replied, pressing my lips into a firm line, and then taking my tongue I licked my wet lips again, and again, hoping he would notice I was being a little naughty.

"Please Ms. Twisted, call me Zacharie. And by the way you did not publicize you were not looking for a one-night stand. If I do recall your journal entries were very forthcoming; and you were looking for a 'see you only for sex bedtime greeting," he teased, lingering his exquisite fingertips up my skirt. I immediately closed my legs, and bit down on my bottom lip. *He was making it extremely difficult for me to concentrate on the interview.*

"Actually if I can remember my choice of writing correctly, this was a meeting," I whispered as I was trying to catch my breath.

"Ms. Twisted, I was exactly everything you asked me to be," Zacharie said while looking me in the eye with his serious look. I could only defensively bat my eyelashes at him, hoping he would receive my invite to fuck on the edge of the fold out just aside from where we fucked (taping the whole thing, for his pleasure and my twisted).

"Please Zacharie, I would like you to elaborate." I begged.

I never gave you my heart, and did not come with flowers, and when push came to shove, I was the selfish mother-fucker you were looking for." He replied, firmly squeezing the inside of my leg towards my pussy, making me flinch.

"So why did you finally open up to me, Zacharie?" I asked hesitantly.

"Because after reading your journal entries I realized just how bad I really did treat you," Zacharie replied, un-gripping his hold on my leg and starting to pat my vagina gently.

"So because you read my journal, this suddenly gave you a change of heart about Little Ms. Twisted?" I asked.

"Yes Ms. Twisted it did," he said again looking me directly in the eyes, and I couldn't take mine away from his. *The dirty on-set look he gave me was direct, and to the fucking point.*

"Please call me Estelle," I said softly.

"Ok then, Estelle," he replied, taking his nose and sniffing my hair.

"I love the way that sounds coming from you," I replied, tilting my head towards his nose further. *I was hoping he would take his tongue and start running it down my neck, the way he did in bed when we made love.*

"I love the way my name sounds when you scream it out loud while I fuck you," Zacharie moaned, pressing his lips to my forehead.

"How did you feel the first time you fucked me?" I asked, pressing my lips to the bottom of his chin, while I looked him deep in his dark eyes.

"Well Estelle, I felt like I just fucked you," Zacharie said, moving his head a little more than half an inch from my lips.

"So it did not mean anything to you?" I whispered slowly.

"No," he said painfully.

"When did sex with me start to feel like 'something' to you?" I asked.

"The first time I fucked you without a cap," Zacharie answered softly.

"Why?" I asked, taking the tips of my fingers, and twirling them through his medium length, dark brown hair.

"Because I fucked you that morning out of the blue, and it was strange for me to ever want to make the opposite sex feel good." Zacharie answered, and I knew he was being honest.

"Did you love me that morning, Zacharie?"

"Yes."

"Then why couldn't you show it?" I asked, trailing my fingertip up and down his strong jaw, while we stared directly at one another.

"I did not want to get close to you, because I was so afraid of getting hurt again."

"And then when you found my journal, this did not prove your theory?" I said, changing the tone of my voice to mock him.

"I knew you would not publish the book, Estelle," he said in a lowered tone.

"How could you be so sure?"

"Because you would not have the guys to exploit your own sexual life and let others read about you, for the sake of making money."

"But what would make you think anyone would know this book is about me, Zacharie?"

"When your friends from back home would walk into their local bookstore in Chicago and buy a copy of Mr. Complicated, they would all know who the book refers to."

"I think you are sadly mistaken. My friends do not know me as well as you think," I replied in a manipulative tone.

"The ones who know about your fucked past do. People in big cities talk; all it takes is one person to open his or her mouth, and then the truth is out about Estelle Ella Whiteside."

"You do not think I have already aired my dirty laundry for the entire world to see and cast their judgment on," I accused.

"Estelle, this is our sexual life you are talking about here. I do not think you would have the guts to do such a thing," he replied with a jerked smile.

"You would be more afraid about me exploiting myself, than the world finding out about Mr. Complicated," I replied, surprised.

"Mr. Complicated is just a character," Zacharie snorted.

"No Zacharie, Mr. Complicated is you," I laughed.

"Yes Estelle, even utterly so, the world would still know the story is referring to you, and would have no idea who the hell I am. So are you not happy with the decision you made to be in love with me, and say "fuck you" to your publisher?"

"Well, now that I have fucked my Publisher over, you do realize you now have to take care of me, right?"

"I do not need to take care of you, because I know that you can take care of us."

"You're the man, you are supposed to take care of me."

"Is that not being sexist?"

"No."

"Let me ask you again: is that not being sexist?"

"I don't think it is, but if you do, I think you are the biggest sexist there is out in Medicine Hat."

"Is that so?"

"Yes."

"This is an interview with Mr. Complicated, right?"

"Yes."

"Then I hope you don't mind, but I am going to make the interview complicated."

"How is that?"

He slipped his hand up my shirt, and started cupping my breasts with both his hands, "I want you to continue the interview while I am massaging your breasts Estelle, and at any point I will start pleasuring you any other way I see fit."

"Ok," I gulped.

He started massaging and pulling at my nipples, as I tried to resist moaning from the pleasure.

"Are you a boob or an ass man, Mr. Complicated? With the last word I spoke he started grabbing my breasts firmer, and then started to lift up my shirt; my nipples started to get really hard.

"A little cold, Estelle," he asked, while grabbing my breasts harder.

"Please leave my shirt on, Mr. Complicated; it makes it very difficult for me to conduct my interview."

"That's the point," he replied, lifting my shirt off completely.

"No," I begged.

"What are you begging for, Estelle? Do you want me to suck those nipples?"

"You are not supposed to be asking the questions, Mr. Complicated."

Zacharie removed his hands and then moved to bend down on his knees in front of me. "This is how I would like you to kneel down for me, Estelle, but we have forever, so I don't mind being the first one."

He moved his lips towards my left nipple, and as I tried to jerk myself away from him, he grabbed my hips firmly, and moved my breast towards his face, and started to suck.

"Oh my god."

"You called," he teased.

"Mr. Complicated, you are really getting out of line."

"Am I making it complicated for you to conduct your interview? What if I take those pants off?"

"Then I would get really cold, and I thought you didn't like to make girls cold."

"No, just you," he replied, peeling off my pants.

"Zacharie, it's really cold, and you are making it so hard to finish this interview."

"Fuck the interview, Estelle; it's time for Mr. Complicated to fuck you Twisted."

He immediately pulled me to the cold hardwood floor of the bedroom, and started sucking my nipples, going from one to the other. Every time I tried to say a word, he would take his free hand and cover my mouth; I could only defenselessly rub my lips against his palm, and pray he showed me mercy.

"This is how I want us to fuck everyday, twice a day, for the rest of our lives."

"Zacharie, I..."

"Oh Estelle, what I am going to do to you," he said feverishly.

He placed his hands in mine, as his penis penetrated my pussy, and he started making love to me slow. I was so wet, that I couldn't defend myself enough to get dry for even a moment; he would not give and let me go.

"I love you, Zacharie," I gasped, as he was tenderly making love to me, and my insides started to tingle.

"I can't feel my legs, Zacharie," I whispered.

"I know," he moaned.

"Why?"

"Because I love you," he whispered in my ear, and then started kissing my neck.

"I am so cold; I cannot concentrate on cuming for you."

"I know, I want to fuck you for awhile."

"No, I can't."

"You will Estelle; this is all a part of the interview."

"Zacharie, why did the last time we have sex hurt so much?"

"Because sometimes you need to take pain, in order to receive the other side of pleasure, my love."

"So you promise to never again hurt me sexually," I moaned.

"Estelle I cannot promise you that Estelle, but I do promise not to stop loving you."

I felt his erection building. He moved his lips to my left nipple, and this was another weak spot for me, and he pushed deeper inside.

"I am going to cum."

"Scream for me, babe."

"I am going to fucking cum."

"Is the interview over Little Ms. Twisted?"

"Yes, yes..." I screamed.

"Are you ready to get Complicated?"

"I am ready," I shouted louder.

"Then here cums complicated."

EPILOGUE

As I stood across the way from Ms. Covered Up Perfect, I looked over to the critical eyes or Mr. Sanity, passing his judgment on my mental perception.

Since when the fuck have I ever gave a shit about pleasing anyone? Why the hell shouldn't I move in with Zacharie? Or get married to him? Five months is long enough to start our forever, isn't it?

If I need to ask myself any of the above then am I really ready for the next stage of our relationship; the stage called 'commitment?'

I mean I have been committed to my Publisher for the last year and a half, living in this shit hole of a small city, but I mean 'me' the city girl moving in with the 'country complicated,' *what the fuck was I thinking?*

He had a hard enough time exposing his closet of complicated so I could better understand his complicatedness, but actually living the complicated, *am I really ready to give up the life of uncomplicated for Zacharie?*

The answer is: *yes I am.* I am ready to fully commit myself to him fully for the rest of my life, and no longer feel the pressure of having to live a certain way.

When it comes to sexually pleasing my complicated, he could write me a 'fucking script' and I will play his sexy little partner for the rest of our complicated and twisted lives.

"Estelle, what are you thinking about right now?" Zacharie asked, while kissing my forehead, as I was packing up the last container of my clothes.

"Nothing," I replied, pressing my lips together.

"Are you having second thoughts about the moving in together, babe?" Zacharie asked looking me directly in the eyes.

I could melt when he looked me in the eyes with, his dark, sexy, brown, complicated eyes.

"Not at all, Zacharie," I replied, closing the container. I then stood up.

Zacharie looked at me again, and this time, he began to stride over towards where I was standing.

"Are you going to carry this for me?" I asked, while batting my eyelashes at him, and biting down on my bottom lip.

"Sure am, I would not make you do it," he replied, taking his free hand and patting my ass.

"Really," I replied, shocked at his sense of sweetness. Then I brushed my lips against his.

"Yeah, I don't want you to become crippled before we go home to 'our' place and fuck," Zacharie smiled.

"Zacharie, you're so sick," I teased, smiling back.

"Why am I sick? I am talking about fucking my fiancé," Zacharie snapped.

"Can't you talk about us making love in our bed?" I whispered gently.

"Babe, you know every time we have sex, I make love to you, whether or not I call it fucking," he smirked.

"I know, I just like to hear you say it," I whispered, to his forehead, before I ran my lips in tiny kisses from one side of his cheek to the other.

"You know, I love when you kiss my forehead and taunt me with that kissing trail."

"Which forehead do you preference me to kiss?" I chuckled.

"I like it when you kiss both," he replied, locking his lips on mine.

***

As we walked outside to Zacharie's truck, he threw the last of my belongings inside, and got in.

I stood quietly for a moment, looking at the apartment I had lived in for the last year, and said goodbye. Then I looked at Zacharie, for instead of living the simple life, I would be now living the 'Mr. Complicated.'

COMING SOON

Mr. Complicated
A Touch of Past Unwanted

NOVEMBER 2015

****

PROLOGUE

Dear Mr. Complicated,

I want to be frank with you in sharing my concern over a past fling you once 'fucked,' who is now interested in 'fucking' both of 'us' together.

If you have not already noticed, I am not the 'type' of 'twisted' who enjoys sharing the man who stole my heart; we are now in a forever relationship, and there is only room for 'two,' and no more.

The deal was: there was to be many nights of sexual encounters, no strings of drama, and faithful relations on both an emotional and personal level. This was not to be an arranged living condition, followed by a deranged ex raining on my 'sexual orgasmic parade.'

The bottom line is, Mr. Complicated, you will need to make a choice, and make a choice fast, or else I will take matters into my own hands.

By the way your 'basket-case' ex-girlfriend describes your 'bedtime' meetings in her emails, and (on my fan blog), you must have been one 'complicated fuck' that she could not get enough of. That's why I am giving you a chance to redeem yourself in bed with me, after this is all said and done.

I want you to bend me over, handcuff me to a fucking goal post, and fuck me until I scream "touch down." I want you to give me the crazy erotic side that this bitch is claiming you have, because I simply have not seen this side of Mr. Complicated.

So now the time comes, Complicated, to make a choice, because there will be no 'threesomes.' Nor any 'ménage-à-trois,' as you would have it said in French. There will only and ever will be a 'gruesome sexual twosome.'

Can 'My Complicated' actually live with fucking 'One Twisted,' because he is ready to actually have a commitment?

Saying goodbye to an unwanted past will only tell my heart that you are sincere.

Still sexually inclined, and hoping for a forever 'dual relationship.'

Unsure,
Yours truly Little Ms. Twisted

AN OVERVIEW ON COMPLICATED SWINGING WITH THE EX

In Calgary, years before Little Ms. Twisted.

Two weeks before Zacharie's Twentieth Birthday...

Zacharie was walking with a group of friends from his work, going to the local café shop in downtown Calgary, when suddenly he bumped into a young girl, carrying a pink traveling case.

"Excusez-moi mademoiselle, je suis désolé de tomber sur vous," Zacharie said, as he made the strange girl drop her pink travelling case.

"Oh, please do not apologize, it was clearly an accident," the girl, replied batting her eyelashes at him.

"Pardon me, I thought you spoke French. I am very sorry miss, please let me help you," he pleaded, while kneeling down to pick up the contents that had fallen out of her pink traveling case. As his eyes scattered the contents that covered the sidewalk, his gaze met her green eyes.

"Have you never seen a condom before?" The girl asked, while smiling at Zacharie with a playful smirk.

"I have seen a condom mademoiselle, but carrying around enough to cover a sidewalk is a bit strange, don't you think?"

The girl blushed crimson from embarrassment, "please let me introduce myself, I am Charlene, and you are?"

"My name is Zacharie."

Charlene took her hand and extended it out to Zacharie, "very nice to bump into you, Zacharie," she replied, smiling.

"Same to you, Charlene," he smiled back.

Zacharie's friend Donald left Zacharie's side with the rest of his friends heading to the café and saying, "nous allons au café, nous y rencontrons une fois que tu obtiennes le numéro de la demoiselle."

Zacharie looked at Donald and waved, and then locked his eyes back on Charlene.

"Are you a student?" Charlene asked.

"Yes," Zacharie replied, while trying to make sense of how lucky he was to bump into such a pretty young girl.

"What are you studying?" She asked, while jarring her head.

"Many things," Zacharie replied.

"Many things," Charlene replied in disappointment, and then pursed her lips, "well you seem to know a lot about different colored condoms, and recognizing the difference between how many should cover a sidewalk slab, and how many one should have on them," she blushed again.

"May I ask you a question, Charlene?" Zacharie asked, while biting his top lip from being nervous.

"Sure."

"Why do you need so many condoms?"

"Well, what if I am out randomly meet someone, and want to have sex? You are never safe with just one, because if the 'girl' wants to fuck more than one time, guys always have the typical excuse: 'I don't have enough condoms.' Usually they cannot get it up again, so they lie; I carry so many so I can test if the guy is lying," she replied back, with a wicked smile.

"So I am assuming that you really like sex," Zacharie smirked back in amusement.

"Who doesn't like sex?"

"Some people are really not as open as yourself to discussing sex with someone they randomly bump into on the street,"

"Well some people who you randomly bump in- to on the street, sometimes randomly bump into you at night too," she smiled

"I see," Zacharie replied, confused.

"Do you currently bump anyone in the night, Zacharie?"

"That's getting a little personal don't you think," he replied in shock.

"Zacharie, you got personal, when you bumped into me just now," Charlene replied, batting her eye- lashes again.

Zacharie started to feel himself getting a little turned on.

"So Zacharie, you did not answer my question: do you currently bump anyone in the night?" Charlene asked again, while biting down on her bottom lip.

"No," he replied.

"I do not bump anyone either, and I can see the way you are looking at me. Would you be interested in bumping me sometime?"

And this was the start of a swinging relation- ship.

***

One year later...

Charlene grabs her pink travelling case, the one she never leaves home without, "Ok, Zacharie, I will see you later tonight."

"I thought you were done work early today?" Zacharie asked, confused.

"No, my boss asked me to stay and work late tonight," Charlene replies hesitantly.

"Is everything alright, babe?"

"Yes, why wouldn't it be?"

"Well, it's just in the past year we have been together, whenever worked has asked you to stay and work overtime, you have always declined."

"Well Amanda is staying tonight as well, so I want to pitch in too. I do not want Mr. Bruin giving her the promotion when I have been with the company longer."

Zacharie walks over to Charlene, to give her a kiss goodbye, but she turns her back and walks out the front door, forgetting her phone.

Zacharie was walking over to the kitchen counter, when he heard a buzzing sound coming from the dining room table. He walked in the dining room to see what the buzzing was all about.

Nathan to Charlene

Nathan- Hey, Charlene, cannot wait to see you tonight for the swinging. Amanda and I are so excited, and we have some new ideas for the three of us.

Zacharie was confused, *what was swinging*?

Zacharie *using* Charlene's phone to Nathan

Zacharie /Charlene- I cannot wait to see you tonight either, what did you have in mind?

Nathan- Well Amanda and I were thinking the regular, but wanted to change positions up.

Zacharie /Charlene- What positions?

Nathan- Charlene don't be scared, I know this is new for you, but soon you will realize just what a climax swinging really is.

Zacharie /Charlene- Would you mind if Zacharie comes?

Nathan- No actually four is better than three.

Zacharie /Charlene- Better how?

Nathan- More satisfaction.

Zacharie /Charlene- How do I tell Zacharie to get some of this satisfaction?

Nathan- Tell Zacharie to come to 111 24th Transcona Hwy Apt 405.

Zacharie /Charlene- What time.

Nathan- We are planning on getting things started around 6pm.

Zacharie /Charlene- He looks forward to meeting you and Amanda.

Nathan- We look forward to a couple.

Zacharie wonders why they are looking forward to a couple.

***

Later that evening, Zacharie shows up at 111 24th Transcona Hwy Apt 405, and knocks on the door.

A guy answers the door, he is young but looks a little older than Zacharie, "Hi, you must be Zacharie, my name is Nathan, please come on in, Charlene is not here yet."

"Thanks, it's very nice to meet you too," Zacharie replies, while walking in the front door of Nathan's apartment. He vicariously scans the surroundings, and noticed a blonde girl in a sexy leather outfit, sitting on the living-room couch. She has long, straight hair and a slim build; almost the build of a model. Then he notices that she has a naughty little whip,

"This is my girlfriend, Amanda. Please go and have a seat," he directed Zacharie to the couch where Amanda was sitting.

Zacharie walked towards her, but sat on the adjacent love-seat.

There was another loud knock on the door. Nathan went to the door, and there was Charlene, dressed much differently than what she left the apartment in the morning.

"Glad you could join us, Zacharie is already here," Nathan said in a pleasant tone.

"What the fuck is he doing here?" She hollered, locking eyes on Nathan, and then looked to see Zacharie sitting on the love-seat.

Welcome to the world of swinging complicated.

INTERVIEW WITH MR. COMPLICATED

Have you ever met a guy with a swinging past of Complicated? One shared with a 'fucked' ex, looking to 'rain on your sexual orgasmic parade?' Well if you answered yes to either of these questions you are not alone.

Interviewer Estelle Ella Whiteside (Little Ms. Twisted)
Interviewee Zacharie Gagne (Mr. Complicated)

"So, here we are again, Mr. Gagne," I mocked, biting my lower lip and teasing his dick; I knew it wanted to assault my vagina.

"Oh my Little Ms. Twisted, I have told you, do not call me Mr. Gagne, either address me as Zacharie, or else by the given name that you chose: Mr. Complicated. Although it turns me on more when you scream either of them," he replied, pressing his lips together.

Why the fuck does he make me so goddamn tense? I immediately closed my legs, "Mr. Complicated, the purpose of me conducting this interview is because I have questions about your swinging," I said, while taking my hands and running them up and down my bare legs, for my pleasure, and his torture.

"If you do not stop rubbing your legs, I am going to spank you twisted, and make you cry complicated, missy," he teased.

"Mr. Complicated, might I add, the reason all this started in the first place was because of your 'fucked' passion for swinging with three, as well as your long awaited decision: if two was good enough for you."

"Estelle, you surely have always known that I have been complicated from the beginning; what would ever give you the idea I was not continually complicated?" He replied, leaning in to inhale my scent.

I backed away and parted my legs, giving a wicked smile, "Mr. Complicated, I told you, before we entered the house there would be no fucking, touching, sniffing, or any other weird behavior related to anything sexual on your behalf towards me, until I was finished."

"Oh, you will be finished alright, Little Ms. Twisted," he laughed.

"Listen Mr. Complicated, the strings of drama do not work with me, did you not learn that when I said 'no' to your 'insane to moi puss-ay' ex 'swinging fuck tart' of a girlfriend."

"Do I still detect jealousy?" He replied, taking his right hand and grabbing a string of my hair.

"No, why the fuck would I be jealous?" I snorted, and before I could even finish ranting, Mr. Complicated was 'swinging me' into his arms, and walking towards the back bedroom of his dirty upstairs apartment.

"Little Ms. Twisted, you are about to get fucked for your jealousy," he whispered, while brushing his lips against mine.

He was still my Mr. Complicated, and I was still his Little Ms. Twisted.

But how did it get to this point?

My thoughts were blacking out, because I knew he was going to make it up to me in the bedroom.

He sat me down on the edge of the bed and leaned me back gently, while I unbuttoned his checkered shirt.

"Oh Zacharie, how could I doubt you!" I moaned, while taking my lips and gently kissed the nape of his neck.

"Estelle, you are my only twisted, there is no one else," he gasped, while running his mouth down my bare stomach. I began to shake, and tried to move back from his lips, but he took both his hands and grabbed onto my hips.

I started to undo the zipper on his jeans, trying to slip them down as far as I could, but by the time I had them just riding under his ass, he had his tongue riding up inside of my pussy, and his fingertips tormenting the outside.

"Shit, Zacharie," I moaned.

He took his tongue and started swirling it on the outside of my pussy, and as I took my legs, and as I tried to close my legs, he spread them further apart; I was helpless.

"Zacharie, fuck," I screamed, and I could see his erection rising to my tone.

He removed his lips from my pussy for a moment, and lightly started blowing on my wet skin, "I want you to scream for me, Estelle. When you scream your loudest, I will know you want it," Zacharie tormented.

"No, please no!" I screamed, begging him not to slip his tongue back; it was going to be my undoing.

He slowly took his face and buried it between my legs, and then spread my legs apart again, "if you move your legs, I am going to squeeze your tits really hard, Estelle. Do you understand me?" He said assertively.

"Uh-huh," I moaned.

With his tongue, and the tips of his fingers he started rubbing the my clit, and I could not take it, I started to scream...

"Fuck, oh Fuck," I screamed, his tongue was torture.

He then reached up under my shirt, and since I was not wearing a bra, my breasts were defenseless.

"Shit, no, please," he started rubbing, and I started *cuming* in Zacharie's mouth.

"That's a good Little Ms. Twisted, give me all you got, babe," he moaned, and started swirling his tongue faster.

"Fuck, Zacharie, ok, ok I am complicated..."I screamed.

"Not complicated enough," he replied and started swirling his tongue until my legs were shaking.

He moved on top of me, and started sucking on my nipples, "Zacharie, fuck please, I cannot take anymore," I pleaded with him moaning.

"You are going to take it, Estelle, because I am not done with you yet," he whispered, and then slipped his tongue in my mouth.

I ripped his pants down below his ass, so that his erection could rub against my pussy. I then I pulled his boxers down, he slowly slid his penis into me, and then gently gripped both of my hands, as started motioning tenderly inside of me.

"Oh my Mr. Complicated, you are really twisting me," I moaned.

"Scream my name babe," he demanded.

"Fuck me, Mr. Complicated," I screamed.

"Scream it again," he begged.

"Fuck me, Mr. Complicated, "I moaned.

"Scream it for me, baby, louder," he screamed.

"Fuck me, Mr. Complicated, I am cuming," and as I started cuming again, I could feel him releasing in my pussy.

He stared into my eyes, "fuck the way you twist me, Little Ms. Complicated, whatever the fuck am I going to do with you?"

~*~*~

Meet The Author; of Mr. Complicated Book One Love or Lust- A Twist of Complicated Events Trilogy-

ISABELLA MICHELLE

Born and bred in Toronto, Canada- loving the sexually open city and pushing my writing limits. Toronto offers a diverse outlook on all that sex has to offer, from swinging couples, to same sex couples exploring the open mind- while the opposite sex still awakens the love and lust in one another. Growing up in an over-populated big city allowed me to create many diverse characters, expanding as an author into different genres of creativity. I am best known for my love of Mainstream Erotica, BDSM, Ménage, Gay, Lesbian, Bi-sexual, Romantic Suspense. I am not only an Author- I am a lover, great friend, and vivid dreamer with an expandable imagination.